Advance Praise for
Baby Shark's BEAUMONT BLUES

"Robert Fate writes lean, powerful prose. His first book, Baby Shark, was hard to put down; with Beaumont Blues I didn't even try, I just inhaled it."
—Dianne Day, *The Strange Files of Fremont Jones*

"I'd sell my soul to have this heroine on my side when the shooting starts."
—Shane Gericke, *Blown Away*

"Once again, the body count is high, the action non-stop, and the story makes your pulse race."
—Lesa's Book Critiques

"Everything Fate writes holds your interest to the very end with a style that is unequivocally readable."
—BookPleasures

"Baby Shark's Beaumont Blues is a fascinating and twisted tale of too much money and a lot of people who want it."
—Sarah Bewley, Award-winning playwright

"Again, Robert Fate gets to it quick, stays on the point, and delivers that continuous punch."
—Grant McCune, Academy Award winner, *Star Wars*

"Kristin has grown as a young woman, grown into her strength, yet retains an aura of vulnerability."
—Bill Cameron, *lost dog*

"The fast pace, action packed sequences, and ultimately likeable characters come together to form a well told and enjoyable tale."
—Mystery Book Spot

"Robert Fate has done an excellent job. A good story, well told with characters that seem alive."
—Gumshoe Reviews

Praise for BABY SHARK

There are very few books that I read these days that take my breath away. But Robert Fate's Baby Shark is one of them. It's certainly the best book I've read this year, and possibly one of the best I've ever read. That may sound like overblown hype, but believe me, this is an amazing debut.

This is a story of love and revenge, of acceptance and deceit. The setting of this story is Texas in the 50s, a time when young women who run into 'trouble' are outcast or shamed into silence. As Baby Shark so eloquently and painfully puts it, "Not so many years ago I would have been called Soiled Dove instead of Baby Shark." Instead, Baby Shark finds herself, buried in the rubble of her soul.

The desolate beauty of Texas is a character unto itself. The people who populate Fate's book are so finely drawn they leap off the page. Add to that Fate's command of spare, devastating language—all combine to make Baby Shark a must read. To say much more would ruin this amazing title.
—Reviewing the Evidence

Baby Shark's
Beaumont Blues

Robert Fate

Capital Crime Press
Fort Collins, Colorado

First edition published in the United States by Capital Crime Press. Printed in Canada. Cover design by Nick Zelinger.

Capital Crime Press is a registered trademark.

Library of Congress Catalog Card Number: 2006934248
ISBN-13: 978-0-9776276-2-2
ISBN-10: 0-9776276-2-4

www.capitalcrimepress.com

For Jennifer

ACKNOWLEDGMENTS

First, I must acknowledge my continuing debt to my friends Bruce, Sheila, and Gwen for their wise advice and selfless support.

Thanks to Dr. Kurt Neubauer for being there with learned answers.

Mil gracias to Juan Manuel Gonzalez for his advice concerning all things Mexican.

And special thanks to Grant McCune, for his cold eye and cryptic reasoning.

"After a few run-ins with somebody, you start thinking you know them. But it turns out all you ever really know about them is what they're willing to let you see."

Otis Millett, PI, Fort Worth, Texas

1

September 1956

LEON DROOLED WHEN he smiled at me.

I smiled back, and he yelled, "D'you sayer name's Christian?"

"Kristin," I corrected him. "Kristin Van Dijk."

I could've told him Marilyn Monroe. He wouldn't have known the difference.

"Crishin," he slurred as the long string of sparkling saliva reached his chest, and his head eased back to rest against the dark brown Naugahyde.

With his eyes still open, Leon began snoring. The live country music was so loud, no one could hear the racket he made. The way his lips fluttered, he just looked like any other drunk in there that night, staring at the ceiling and singing.

I finished my Dr Pepper and caught Virginia's attention. She nodded that she'd be right there. She was one of the two dozen or so pretty young waitresses that the cowboys kept hopping at Spurs, one of the biggest and most popular honky-tonks in South Dallas. With her thick, unruly red hair, light sprinkling of freckles, long legs, and outsized bosom, she was a perfect specimen for the cut-off Levi's, boots, and halter-tops the girls were required to wear.

"What happened to him?" Virginia stared at Leon sawing logs.

"He must've been drinking on an empty stomach."

"Two beers?" She didn't buy it. She leaned across the table and gazed into his unseeing eyes.

"Maybe he was tired," I said.

I coughed up the five bucks that I'd promised her and moved her out of the way. I went around, grabbed him by his shirt, and dragged him to the edge of the booth. I got him by one of his arms, and indicated that she should take the other.

"What're we doing?" she asked. But she knew, because she picked his hat up and put it on.

I pulled, and when he fell off the seat and onto the floor, some guys across from us clapped and whistled like I wanted the publicity.

Virginia and I dragged Leon by his arms back through some swinging doors into a short hallway. The music behind us was suddenly muted. Before we got to the next set of swinging doors, a waitress came through them with a tray full of food hiked up on the palm of her hand, and we were briefly assaulted by the boisterous voices of the kitchen staff and the banging of pots and pans. The jaded waitress passed us without a word.

Without changing our pace, we cut behind her and off to the side through an open door that led outside. Virginia pushed open the screen door.

My God, the humidity on that late summer evening mixed with the odors from the fly-crusted collection of garbage cans near the exit made it feel like stepping into a rancid stew. Ah, the glamorous life of a PI. I made a face and began sweating.

"He's heavy, huh?" she commented, imitating my face while misreading its meaning.

We crunched down into the gravel parking lot. When Leon's feet cleared the doorway, the screen door slammed shut behind us.

"Heavy for a scrawny little guy, I mean. I had to haul him up off the floor once by myself."

The heels of Leon's boots opened trenches in the gravel as we dragged him over to a beat up old Studebaker convertible with its top down. With the door wide open, the seat thrown forward, and both of us working at it, we got him into the back seat. He grunted some during the last part, but he didn't wake up. The Mickey Finn I'd put in his beer would keep him in the arms of Morpheus for an hour, maybe longer.

I shut the car door and turned around sensing that Virginia would still be there. She had something on her mind besides Leon's cowboy hat.

"The last time you was in, you had a camera with you," she said.

"Did I?"

"You know you did. I saw it in your bag. I know cameras... a Leica. Am I right? And a couple of good lenses, too."

"Where're you going with this, Virginia?"

"So, you take pictures, right?"

"Not really."

"Long lenses. High-priced camera. I say you do."

"Okay, say I do. So what?"

"I need some pictures taken, that's what."

My immediate lack of interest must've shown on my face because she bristled.

"What's your problem? I just did you a favor."

"And I paid you for it."

"That don't mean you can't be civil."

I paused and looked at her. I saw ambition, which might have been okay if it hadn't been so raw. Maybe I felt sorry for her. I got the look off my face and paid attention.

She said, "Besides that, you don't even know what the job is."

"You want to be a model or an actress or a singer like every other waitress I ever met."

"Wrong. A guy I know needs something special. The pay's good, but here's the hard part, sweetie. You have to shoot good. Do you shoot good?"

Before I could respond, a nearby car door slammed. We looked over to see the driver of a late model Cadillac sauntering toward us.

Timing's everything.

He was tall and slim and looked sharp in his ivory-colored western suit with brown piping, shiny brown boots, embroidered snap-button shirt, and string tie. He held a hand in front of him and spun his key ring around his finger as he walked. The keys made a little ching-ching sound. As he got closer, I could see he was pushing fifty. His tailored suit did an okay job of concealing the holster under his arm.

He dismissed Virginia with a curt, "Ain't you supposed to be waiting tables?"

After she tossed Leon's ratty old hat into his ragtop and walked away, the cowboy in the new, fifty-dollar Stetson spoke to me.

"I come here to pick up Leon. I'm a friend of his. Name's Chuck."

He spun his key ring and waited for me to speak. He could wait. I kept quiet.

"I think that was Leon you stuck in the car there."

We looked at each other and waited.

"I told you, didn't I? I'm a friend of his."

"You told me," I said, figuring I'd made him wait enough.

Chuck looked over at Leon snoring away. "He was supposed to work for me tonight."

I shrugged.

"Now, he's kind of put me behind the eight ball."

"Oh yeah? That's something I can understand."

"How's that?" he said.

"I shoot pool."

"You don't say. Pool. Not many gals can say that."

He spun his keys. Ching-ching.

I let a moment pass before I started my pitch. "You don't suppose I could help you out."

"How d'you mean?"

"You know, do whatever you wanted Leon to do."

He stared at me with squinty eyes. My guess was he squinted when he thought hard.

He finally asked, "You interested in something quick, are you?"

"Quick, you say."

"Won't take long at all. You think you're up for a little job?"

"Maybe I would be. What's the pay like?"

"I'm paying good money." He gave me the once over. "You look like you could use a couple of bucks."

Good.

That was why I had on worn-out boots, faded and torn Levi's, and a washed-thin work shirt. Even my scuffed-up soft leather purse that I carried by a thin strap over my shoulder cried better times. My hair hadn't been washed for a day or so. However, that very morning I had cleaned and oiled the snub-nosed .32 that was ready in my ankle holster.

"It seems like you know how to keep your face shut," he said.

I remained silent.

He squinted at me again. "Well, seeing as how you're a friend of Leon's, let's say a sawbuck for a couple of hours."

"Doing what, Chuck?"

"That's a fair question. Driving. You know how to drive, right?"

"I drive," I said.

"Okay, then. We're going outta town a spell, me and

Cecil." The guy he called Cecil sat on the passenger side of their car. He was giving me a hard stare through the glass. "We're going out to get a feller, bring him back to town. Just need a driver." He spun his keys. Ching-ching. "That's the size of it."

I made him wait like I was thinking it over before I said, "Half in advance."

Chuck pulled out an impressive roll, peeled off a five, and handed it over. I stuffed it in my pocket and followed him, stopping a few yards from the big four-door. I heard Johnny Cash when the window rolled down.

"Leon's drunk," Chuck told Cecil. "This is a friend of his."

"Who gives a fuck?" I heard Cecil snarl. "I don't know her and I don't like her."

Chuck leaned in for a quiet *tête-à-tête*, and all the time they were jawing, Cecil glowered at me. He moved Chuck back, threw open his door, and began struggling out, slow and stiff. Bad knees. He was large and seemed even larger in his boots and Stetson and a western suit that could've fit an elephant. He didn't look happy about me watching as he struggled to pull himself from the car. I kept watching anyway.

"I'm gonna kick your ass," he assured me.

"Maybe you will and maybe you won't," I told him.

"Come on, Cecil," Chuck wheedled. "We're running outta time, we need some help, and she's right here."

Cecil limped over and stared down at me. The guy was seriously big, and I wasn't sure where it might come from if he decided to hit me.

"You're a sassy little bitch, ain't cha?"

I didn't feel little at five-seven and one-thirty, but he was so big. The good part was he appeared to be just a talker. So, I held my ground, showed him neither fear nor malice, and reasoned that Chuck would take care of things.

"I use to clothesline running backs twice your size," he told me.

Football got his knees.

Chuck wasn't going to give up. "Who's gonna drive us back, Cecil? It's surely gonna take us both to do this. You wanna be in the back alone with him?"

That did it.

The ex-lineman turned away and limped back to the car, grumbling, "This humidity makes me peevish."

2

NO ONE SPOKE.

We listened to country music and the hum of the air conditioner as we drove southwest out of Dallas. There was an enormous full moon that illuminated the ranch land—flat, open range with dark bumps of sleeping cattle, and here and there tall trees. It was bright enough out for a car to drive without headlights.

Chuck left the highway and took us on a narrow gravel road for a while, then moved beneath a tall wooden archway onto a hard-packed dirt road.

We were miles from any neighbors. It was just us putting up dust until we arrived at an ancient ranch house. A soft light from a table lamp burned in the curtained front window. The effect was charming and old fashioned. I could see as the car lights swung across the little place that it had had a whole other house built onto it. The original modesty was little more than a façade for the sprawl of new construction.

Chuck parked the Cadillac under a stand of huge, white-barked sycamores near a new Chevy pickup, one of those big three-quarter ton trucks with some impressive Texas Longhorns sticking up from the hood.

Chuck got out and told me to come with him. I smelled cattle on the heavy night air as I followed him to the middle of the spacious yard.

He stopped there and glanced back. We were waiting for Cecil, who was still struggling out of the car.

"This guy we're here to pick up don't like strangers," Chuck said to me, keeping his voice down. "He's a little peculiar, see, and he may get rowdy. So, stay out of the way. Don't get involved. Don't look him in the face. Don't talk to him even if he talks to you. Just open and close doors, you know, help out like that until we can get him in the car. Then, you'll do the driving. Me and Cecil'll handle the rest of it. You understand?"

I nodded, and Chuck spun his keys for a moment. Ching-ching. "You ain't gonna have no trouble driving a new Caddy, are you?"

"Can't imagine why I would."

Chuck nodded his approval. "What kind of work do you usually do?"

"Rodeo," I lied, probably because of those Longhorns on the truck.

"Rodeo?"

"Yeah," I confirmed, punching my ticket to hell, so to speak.

Chuck squinted. "How old're you?"

"If it's any of your business, twenty-one."

"I doubt that," he said, which taught me a lesson about telling the truth. He spun his keys, and squinted at me some more. "What's your event?"

"Calf roping."

Chuck made a face indicating his disbelief, and shook his head. "First pool, now rodeo." He looked over at Cecil who had caught up with us. "Did you hear that?"

"What?"

"Our driver gal here ropes calves in the rodeo."

"She does, huh?" Cecil chuckled.

In fact, they both had a good chuckle as they continued on to the house. I thought it was kind of funny, too, but I kept that to myself.

Chuck was across the big porch and to the front door before his partner could pull himself up the two steps.

"I can't remember a September this fucking humid," Cecil reminded us, as if we might have forgotten.

"We're due for a rainy spell, I reckon," Chuck told him.

As I waited in the yard for the football player to take the high ground, I had a chance to look around.

There was a sky full of stars, though with the moon so bright they weren't too showy. About the only sounds that far out in the country came from the insects. Although, I did hear some coyotes yipping off in the distance when we first got out of the car.

I followed the lumbering lineman across the porch. Chuck already had the front door open.

"You wait here, Rodeo," Chuck said, relinquishing the squeaky screen door to Cecil before stepping into the quiet house. "Bobby Jack. It's Chuck, Bobby Jack. Chuck and Cecil," he called out as he started up the dark hall, his boot steps resounding on the hardwood floor.

Cecil, short of breath from conquering the porch stairs, gathered himself before giving me a hard look and issuing orders. "I'm giving you a piece of advice. Don't say another fucking word till we're back in the city."

He clumped away after Chuck up the dark echoing hall.

I closed the screen door and stepped into the entryway where I was determined to be quiet. I glanced around. The limited light came from the dim, bug-covered porch bulb and the soft glow of the lamp in the front window.

So far, things were going as planned. Using these guys to locate Bobby Jack had been the first challenge.

Now, if the rest would go as smoothly.

I waited where I'd been told for a few minutes, listening to the silence, before moving into the parlor.

The table lamp provided passable light for the small space. There was a door to an adjacent room. It was closed. The wallpaper and furniture was Montgomery Ward, circa 1930. Someone's grandma had done the crocheted doilies displayed on the backs and arms of the prim sofa and traditional wingback chairs.

There was a group of framed photographs arranged on top of the old upright piano, and I had just looked at them when I heard voices. Arguing voices. I heard glass break, and the voices growing louder.

I stepped back into the hall, and made sure I could get to my .32.

Heavy footsteps. I listened.

They were coming up the hall.

No, they left the hall. A door slammed somewhere.

I heard something scrape across the floor—maybe furniture being pushed around.

The door on the other side of the parlor slammed open. I hadn't expected that. My narrow view of the room through the hall door didn't allow me to see much.

I pushed farther back out of the light, which constricted my view into the little parlor even more. So I was surprised when Cecil limped backward into view. He was terrified of something that I couldn't see from my angle.

The big man scuttled back until he knocked over the table and lamp.

A shotgun blast rang out, hitting Cecil in the chest, and startling me out of my wits.

I pulled up my pant leg and grabbed my pistol as Cecil tumbled back, crashed through the front window, and fell out onto the porch with a sickening thump. He was dead before the thin cotton curtains that he pulled with him through the demolished sash had time to float down and settle around him.

It grew quiet. The smell of burnt gunpowder was thick in the air.

It was even darker where I was with the only light that

remained coming in from the porch. Sweat dripped from my face. I held as still as I could, but adrenaline had my knees trembling. I couldn't hear a sound.

Given my partial hearing loss from a beating I'd suffered a few years back, I was never certain that I was aware of everything there was to hear. I was more concerned that the killer would hear the pounding of my heart.

I forced myself not to react to the metallic clack-clack of the shotgun's pump action and the hit, bounce, and roll of the spent casing.

From the depths of the house, I heard Chuck approaching—ching-ching. He arrived in the room adjacent to the parlor, the room in which I assumed the killer still stood with a loaded shotgun in his hands.

"What've you done, Bobby Jack?" Chuck asked the killer in a conversational tone of voice. He crossed the parlor, moved around the upset furniture, and looked out the broken window at Cecil's body. I saw his shoulders sag. "Aw, Christ, BJ. This weren't our idea, you know. Vahaska sent us out here."

Chuck turned back, his boots squeaking in the broken glass, and faced the maniac that had just murdered his friend.

"He's coming up. He's driving up from Beaumont and he wants you to lock your guest in the basement and meet him in Dallas. He said you'd know what to bring. His words. I'm telling you, BJ, he's coming out here hisself if you don't getcher ass back with me. Come on now. No more nonsense. Let's get on some clothes and get going."

No more nonsense? Unbelievable. I was in a mad house. I was already in up to my neck, and there were still things to get done.

I listened hard as they returned to wherever they'd come from, Chuck continuing to chat with Bobby Jack as if he were a rational human being instead of a bloodthirsty murderer.

"Maybe Cecil didn't come atcha just right," Chuck said. "But ask yourself, was shootin' him the right thing to do?"

I remembered that the screen door squeaked, so I tiptoed into the parlor to look out the window at Cecil. I didn't know the ex-ballplayer. Still, I was sorry that every day had been painful for him because of his knees. And who was he to Bobby Jack that he should be gunned down in cold blood?

A second shotgun blast—from the interior of the house.

It was an unwelcome sound. Not a shock, though. Something had told me that Bobby Jack wasn't finished. And moments later another shotgun blast. Two violent sounds bracketed by a period of utter silence—eerie. I had to believe that he'd shot Chuck.

A faint sound coming my way. I turned my head, used my best ear.

Footsteps. A floor squeak. The hall.

I moved across the parlor, into the darkness of the adjacent room, into the original dining room. From there, I watched by the almost non-existent light from the porch as Bobby Jack entered the parlor from the hall. He was in more darkness than light.

I could just make out that he was slim, muscular, naked—late twenties, maybe. He carried a short-barreled, pistol grip 12-gauge.

The sick animal went to the window and stared out toward the road for a few moments before raising the gun to shoot Cecil again. He pulled the trigger, but nothing happened. He'd used the three-shell capacity of the weapon.

I had earlier eased the hammer back on my revolver. I wanted single-action if I had to put that killer down. I was back in the dark room and hunkered down below the level of the dining room table, so I didn't think he could see me even if he looked in my direction.

He showed no emotion as he turned away from the

window, stopped in the middle of the parlor, and just stood there. I could see the slight motion of his jaw. It was like he was grinding his teeth.

Hell, if I'd been Bobby Jack, I'd have been grinding my teeth, too.

Graceful as a panther, he moved through the archway and disappeared into the hallway. I stayed where I was without moving for several minutes and considered my situation.

I didn't think he knew I was there, but I couldn't be sure. And—he was moving on bare feet in his own house.

As Otis, my partner, would say, I had to double-watch my ass.

I wiped the sweat from my face. I took my purse off my shoulder, put it on the floor, and removed my boots and socks.

I had a job to finish.

3

I EASED DOWN the dark hallway with a cocked .32 in my hand. It was a small caliber, I knew. But up close and put in the right spot, it would do the job.

Light came from around the corner that I approached. No sound—dead quiet. I noticed small spots of blood on the hall floor. I glanced back and saw the trail. Bobby Jack had cut his feet in the window glass—and hadn't seemed to notice.

On the far side of the hallway something was on the wall that didn't look right. It was a moment before I understood it. It was interesting how blood splattered on a wall could look so brutal.

Easy. Easy. I peeked around the corner and discovered Chuck on the hallway floor. He was face down in an expanding pool of blood, his legs splayed out, his feet pointing strangely. The back of his bloodied jacket was torn and riddled from the exiting slugs. His beautiful Stetson was crushed and stained beneath his head. He had an arm under him and one reaching forward. And at the end of his stretching arm, his finger pointed at his car keys on a silver ring.

Ching-ching.

Beyond his body there was an open door. A lighted bedroom. I could hear the low hum of an electric fan.

I listened hard for any other sounds. Nothing. I looked behind me and got ready to go around the corner–

"Gotcha!" a male voice said from back there somewhere.

I froze. The voice was not close, but not far away.

I heard whimpering. A girl.

That was a relief. I had begun to worry that she might be dead.

I wiped the sweat out of my eyes, stayed where I was, and listened some more. A slap. The girl cried out. The guy's voice again.

"What makes you so stupid? Try'n hide from me in my own fuckin' house."

I stood there, around the corner, with my pistol at ready and listened to him force the crying girl up the hall from back in the house somewhere. From where I was, my view of the bedroom was narrowly framed by the open door. I could see a box springs and mattress on the floor through that doorway. Not much else.

When I heard Bobby Jack push the girl into the bedroom, I chanced a quick look and saw them. They were both naked. He shoved her onto the mattress and moved out of sight. She curled up and began sobbing.

It was Sherry Beasley: long brunette hair, seventeen years old, five feet tall.

Bobby Jack yelled at her from wherever he was in the room.

"Shut up your fuckin' bawlin' and getcher skinny ass over here. Get over here and do some of this, you lazy slut."

"No more, Bobby Jack." She sputtered through her sobbing.

"Yeah, more. This'll wake you up. Call yourself a good fuck. You don't know jack shit about how to fuck. Get over here."

"I'm gonna be sick."

Sherry saw Bobby Jack coming before I knew he'd moved. She scooted off the bed and out of my sight. Bobby Jack crossed my doorframe view as he went after her. I heard him catch her and saw him drag her by her hair back past the open door.

"You get sick, I'll beat the livin' shit outta you," he told her from the other side of the room.

Sherry was growing hysterical. I could hear her crying and choking. Bobby Jack started snorting. I stepped around the corner and moved as fast as I could. I wanted to take a new position closer to the bedroom. I took care to keep my bare feet out of Chuck's blood as I passed him. I was almost to Bobby Jack's door when Sherry got slapped again. She fell to the carpeted floor in front of the open door.

I put my hand holding the revolver behind my leg and kept moving toward her.

Sherry's eyes widened when she saw me. Her face went from wrinkled and panicked to stunned and disbelieving. Her nose and lips were dusted with a pale-colored powder. She had dark circles under her eyes. Her face was bruised and splotchy, not at all like it was in the pretty pictures that I had of her. She pushed her dirty, matted hair out of her face and opened her mouth to speak.

I brought a finger to my lips, showed her the palm of my hand, and moved out of her sight. I positioned myself beside the bedroom door, hoping that she would do the right thing. I couldn't count on it. I just hoped.

I crouched down on my heels so that if he came to the door I would be below his natural line of sight. That instant might make the difference.

I heard Sherry get to her feet and speak to him using a calmer voice.

"I'll do you good, Bobby Jack. I will."

"Yeah?"

"I got scared for a minute. All those guns."

"What about the guns?"

"Nothing. Nothing about the guns. I just got scared, that's all."

There was a long awful silence before I heard struggling.

Sherry sobbed and groaned and it was quiet again. I wiped the sweat out of my eyes and slowly—carefully, carefully, staying low—I peaked around the edge of the door.

Bobby Jack had his back to me. He stood beside the bed with a hand holding Sherry by her hair. She was on her knees, her face to his crotch. His other hand held a nickel-plated Luger.

That was not good. I stood up and moved into the doorway just as he growled with disgust and pushed her away.

"You don't know what you're doin'." He let go of her hair and jacked one into the chamber.

Sherry screamed and back-pedaled away. He fell to his knees onto the mattress, grabbed her by her ankle, dragged her back, kicking and screaming, and pointed his pistol at her face.

I was going full speed by then, crossing the carpeted bedroom in giant strides.

Before anything else happened, I rabbit punched Bobby Jack with the butt of my snub nose. Solid. Right at the base of his skull.

He grunted, fired a wild shot into the bed, and collapsed on Sherry.

The loud gunshot so near her face ratcheted Sherry into even more of a girl-gone-crazy mode. She screamed louder and began clawing and kicking her way from beneath his limp body.

And then—Bobby Jack groaned, raised himself up, and gave his head a shake.

That really set Sherry off.

She yelped like she'd been jabbed with a cattle prod and pushed away so hard she launched herself off the low bed. She scrambled across the room on her hands and knees like some wild creature.

I gave my boy another hard smack on his brain stem. This time blood sprayed from the gash I opened and he fell face down on the soiled mattress, seriously unconscious.

"And stay there," I told him.

Sherry jumped up and dashed back to the bed.

"Hey, hey," I had time to say before she grabbed his shiny pistol and pulled the trigger. I wrenched the weapon away from her before she could fire at him twice.

She grew hysterical again. "Kill him! Kill him! Kill him!" she shrieked.

"You're beginning to piss me off," I said because that wild shot of hers had hit the electric fan and stopped dead the single decent breeze I'd felt since I'd come into that house. I stuffed the Luger in my belt, wiped the sweat out of my eyes, and looked around the dirty, disheveled room. "Where're your clothes?"

Sherry Beasley, soon to be one of the richest women in Texas, stopped as if she'd had a switch thrown. She just stood there, all ninety pounds of her, naked as a jaybird, her feet planted wide apart in a defiant stance, a thin stream of blood coming from her nose, her dilated eyes bloodshot and wary. She wasn't herself. God only knows what cruel indignities she'd had to suffer the past few days. She shook her head like she was denying a nightmare.

"It's all wrong," she said.

"You're right about that. Where're your things, Sherry?"

I thought I saw something hopeful in amongst the debris and clutter on top of the low dresser and went over to it. I picked up what had to be her pocketbook.

"This is yours, right?"

She snatched the Dior saddlebag from me, opened it, and dumped the contents out on the floor—the expected things, keys, money, lipstick. Taking her posh bag over to a side table, she dragged a pile of grayish powder into it.

"Forget that stuff. Let's get your clothes on so we can get out of here."

Her bruised face was flushed with anger and confusion. "Who the fuck are you to boss me around?"

"I just saved your ass, that's who. Get dressed. Let's move it."

She pointed at a soft leather travel bag on the floor by the dresser, near where the phone jack had been torn from the wall. "Get that," she said.

"Your clothes in there?" I stepped over to grab the bag and saw movement in the dresser mirror.

It was Sherry with a glittery Mexican figurine in her hands, coming at me to use it like a club. I turned, brushed aside her attempt to brain me, and cold-cocked her with a right cross. With a little help from me, she toppled back onto the mattress next to Bobby Jack.

Glancing down at the shattered chalk and glitter—all that was left of Jesus of Nazareth—I wiped the sweat from my eyes and said, "Hallelujah."

4

I'D WRAPPED SHERRY in a bed sheet and picked her up like a baby. She was almost more than I could carry as I staggered past Chuck, around the corner, and down the dark hall toward the glow of the open front door.

I stopped.

That was moonlight coming through the open door. The porch light was out.

"Otis," I said.

"I'm right here." He opened the squeaky screen door.

I began struggling down the hall again, this time toward his suit and fedora silhouette. "How long've you been there?"

"Since you went back there barefoot. Is she okay?"

"You could help me carry her." I stopped again and he came in and relieved me of the unconscious socialite.

Otis was as big as Cecil, a tad older, and maybe a little worse for wear in his own way, but his knees weren't a problem to him. He cradled Sherry in his big arms like she didn't weigh anything.

We started for the front door.

"She was high as a kite. I had to put her to sleep."

"Who used the shotgun?"

"Bobby Jack shot the guys who brought me out here."

"Were they arguing?"

"Who knows? He was so stoned, he'll never remember why he did it."

"How about the pistol shots?"

"Bobby Jack shot his Posturepedic, and Sherry showed an electric fan a thing or two."

"So you didn't kill him."

"Maybe I should have. He's a pig."

"Mmmm," he hummed. "Things here wasn't the way we thought they'd be, huh?"

"This got extra bad. I think we were lied to."

"We'll talk," he said and stepped onto the porch.

I hustled back to the room, where Bobby Jack was still going beddiebye, and gathered up the travel bag Sherry had asked for. I also got the personal items she'd dumped on the floor—and, what the hell, her purse, too.

My next stop was the little dining room to snatch up my purse and boots. I put on the steam, since I didn't want to stay a minute more in that house than was necessary. There wasn't any way to know who might be coming down the road next. I was glad Otis was outside waiting for me.

He and I'd been partners at his private investigation firm over in Fort Worth—the Millett Agency—for a while now. I met Otis when Henry Chin hired him to help us find the men who killed Henry's son and my father. That's a story that's already been told.

Otis was more than twice my age, so I guess anyone could see that I was still learning the trade. He trusted me to hold up my end of the bargain, and I trusted him to tell it to me straight. We were making a go of it.

I grabbed my stuff and went out to join my partner at his old Buick, one of his primer-coated 'invisible' cars. The grass felt good on my bare feet, and I didn't mind the moist night air. The fact was, I was happy to be alive. I never thought it would get away from me in there; however, there's never any way of guaranteeing that. Some of it was experience; some of it was luck, too—if you believed in luck. I could feel the nervousness in my stomach starting to ease back.

Otis saw Bobby Jack's nickel-plated pistol stuck in my belt and said, "Where'd you get that shiny thing?"

"A gift from our host. I've never owned a Luger."

"You sure that ain't a murder weapon you're souveniring?"

"Not tonight, but I'll leave it if you think I should."

He waved his hand. He didn't care what I did with it, so I kept it. I threw my boots and purse and Sherry's purse and travel bag in the front seat and joined him by the open back door. He looked in at Sherry, wrapped in the bed sheet, asleep on the back seat. Her face was still a mess, although sleep had taken some of the anxiety away.

"Let's hope she'll be snug as a bug till we get back. If she wakes up in a fighting mood, she could be a mess of pester."

"Tell me about it," I said.

"Did she recognize you in there?"

"I don't know. She was higher this time."

Otis closed the door without slamming it.

"If she keeps this up, it ain't always gonna end this way," he said as he walked around the car.

"It almost ended wrong tonight," I told him.

On the drive into the city, I dumped the powder out the window. Otis thought it was speed, and I tried just a tiny bit to confirm his suspicion. Months ago, he'd taught me about a number of different drugs. He'd said there was nothing worse than a PI who was ignorant about the illegal stuff.

"You're right. It's amphetamine."

I spit the bitter stuff out the window.

"I hope the little gal in back ain't grown to like it."

"How come it's powdered?" I asked. "Isn't it usually pills?"

"They shoot it, smoke it, and sniff it, too. Why was it

powder, and why did they have so much? Damned if I know."

Farther down the road—since it contained residue—Otis had me get rid of her Christian Dior pocketbook, too. That wasn't as easy as dumping the drug. It was a nice purse. Then came the surprise. I opened the bag that I thought held her clothes and found money.

A lot of money.

I quit counting the banded packets when I could see it was tens of thousands, maybe as much as a hundred thousand dollars.

Keeping my voice down, I told Otis how much I'd counted.

He whistled.

"That's a fortune! A good car costs maybe three grand. Hell, you can buy a nice little house for twenty grand. A mansion for fifty."

"Is it her money? Do you think she brought it with her when she ran away?"

"Maybe this time it ain't no runaway."

"That's what I'm thinking, too. What've we gotten ourselves into here?"

"Well, take a hopped up heiress, a couple a fresh stiffs, stir some speed into the mix along with a hundred G's in cash, and I'd say you're gonna come up with something nasty for sure."

"I'm feeling kind of exposed," I said.

"I guess so. As soon as we show up with her, we've put ourselves at that ranch. Look at us, we'll be saying. We witnessed two of Vahaska's gangsters getting iced."

"This much money's going to be missed."

"You can say that again, Missy."

"We don't have much time to figure this out. When Sleeping Beauty wakes up, she and her pricey lawyers are going to be after some answers."

"Not to mention our pal, Bobby Jack," Otis allowed, under his breath.

"Not to mention him," I allowed under mine.

"Even still, you did right not killing him. Though I'm sure he could of used some killing."

"He's Vahaska's kin. I just figured we didn't need a crime boss looking for us."

"No, no...you're right about that."

He snapped open his Zippo and lit a cigarette. After a long pause, he asked the night, "Who to trust? Who to trust?"

I glanced at Sherry in the back seat as I closed the bag that held more money than I'd ever seen and wondered where life was taking me next.

Man makes plans and God laughs.

"You okay?"

Otis was just checking in. We'd been driving for a while without talking. Neither of us was afraid of silence.

"I'm fine." We were keeping our voices down because Sherry was still napping. "In our line of work these things can happen," I said.

"I know. It's been a spell since you've been so close to nastiness as ugly as that back there, though. I'm serious now, you okay?"

"I don't need to throw up, if that's what you mean."

"That never crossed my mind. I just wondered if you needed to talk about it maybe."

"I'm fine, Otis. Thanks."

I guess he knew, just as I did, that Ching-Ching Chuck and Cecil, the football player, were with me for the rest of my life.

We rode in silence for a while until Otis spoke up. "You know, Missy, I think we oughta take the princess over to Doc McGraw's and leave her there to dry out."

"Good idea," I said.

He often had good ideas. If he hadn't thrown his wife's lover out a second story window and gone on a two-year drunk, Otis might still have been solving crimes as a police detective over in Dallas. It was a job he was good at.

"That'll buy us some time," I added.

"Uh huh. Just a day or two or even three ain't gonna matter. Besides, she needs a chance to get herself back together before she sees her family."

"She'll be a handful," I said.

"Doc'll know how to deal with her."

"I hope so. She tried to plant some religion in my head with a plaster statue."

"Doc handles horses and bulls for a living."

"I know," I said. "But, best of all, nobody'll know where she is."

The moon was so bright I could watch the countryside fly past—vast and solitary Blackland Prairie that reached into the darkness.

"I was thinking, Otis…"

"Yeah?"

"I was thinking about the last time we went after her."

"That was messy, too," he said.

"At least we went in expecting it," I said.

5

IT WAS SIX months ago, during a rain that lasted the better part of February.

The one break we'd gotten on the case was the make and model of a car in which Sherry had been seen. Otis remembered the car from another time she'd run away and thought he knew where we should look.

We ran into a couple of dead ends and then got lucky. If you can call luck finding yourself on the wrong side of Fort Worth on a cold, drizzly night out in front of Delbert's, a lowlife beer joint that catered to guys with nothing to lose.

"Goddamn it," Otis complained. "That car says she's in there."

A tan '48 Chrysler with Mexican plates was parked at the curb near us.

"What's she doing in a dump like this?" I asked.

"Damned if I can understand half the tunes she sings," Otis mouthed under his breath.

We drove around and parked in the alley behind the narrow little stand-alone, two-story brick building. My partner got what he needed from the trunk and chained and padlocked the back door of the dive. I liked the way he moved when he did stuff like that, like he had every right to be there.

I think that was left over from all those years he spent with the Dallas Police.

"Remind me to call the fire department and report this place for locking up their fire escape," he said as he got back in the car.

We drove around front and parked behind the Chrysler. I put on my black stocking cap to cover my blonde hair.

"You understand if she's in this dump and we take her into our custody, we're obligated to get her out of there safe and sound. Now, since we don't know which of the scumbags in there might do her harm..."

"We're going to assume they're all dangerous."

"Right you are, Missy. And remember, when we go in, get out of the doorway and off to where your back's to a wall."

I nodded that I would. I'd heard that speech before.

"We're going in tough, because it's that kind of place. It'll mostly be drunks and bums. We'll know real trouble if we see it. Of course, the barkeep's gonna have a hog leg or something worse."

Bartenders always had hog legs or something worse.

"Cover my back and we'll do fine," he told me. "You always think good on your feet."

He stepped out into the misting rain and started for the front door, looking like a big version of Humphrey Bogart in his trench coat and fedora. I got out and fell right in behind him, looking like a second story man all in black.

There weren't many cars and no foot traffic at all. The blinking red neon above the saloon's front door danced in the puddles on the wet sidewalk, lighting us a fiery path to the entrance, like Satan laughing.

It was dark inside and overheated; it stank of stale beer and vomit. It was one of those long, narrow joints with a linoleum floor and a high tin ceiling. The sounds were some low volume Hank Williams and the hum of refrigeration from behind the bar. There were fewer than a dozen lost souls populating the place—just men drinking.

I went to the short end of the bar, a dark area where I

felt unnoticed in my black boots, jeans, and lamb's wool jacket. I had my hands in my coat pockets, a .38 automatic in each fist.

Otis went to the middle of the bar, grabbed a man by his collar, yanked him off his stool, and dropped him to the floor. The old boy next to that guy started to say something. So Otis dumped him on the floor, too, sparing us his comment.

Everyone looked up. Otis weighs two eighty plus and stands six five plus in his boots. He's not hard to notice.

He waved at the bartender. "Come here."

The bartender, no small fellow himself, made the mistake of moving within Otis' reach. My partner shot out his left, grabbed the big guy by the front of his shirt, dragged him onto the bar, and brought his face up close.

"I understand you're harboring a fugitive minor in here."

"Fuck you," the bartender choked out as he grabbed the edge of the bar in an attempt to break away.

Otis smashed the big man's face into the counter, dragged him over the bar, and deposited his stunned remains on the floor at his feet.

It was getting crowded down there.

Most of the stumblebums were already out the door. There were still a few holdouts here and there, in particular a couple of young guys at a table in the back. They weren't moving, just watching.

The bartender made a sound that Otis construed as argumentative, so he kicked him in the head. The sound of Otis' boot making contact with the bartender's noggin prompted another two or three customers to lurch to their feet and wobble out into the weather.

The population had dwindled. We were now sharing that rank space with just the unconscious bartender and the two observers in back.

The holdouts were in their twenties, just the right age for making mistakes. One fella had a long neck and looked lanky. The other was a compact little guy. My thought was they were hoodlums. It was too dark to know for sure. I figured they were carrying weapons—and had them on their laps aiming at Otis from beneath the table. Why else would they be so calm?

Otis pulled his .45, stepped over the bartender, and walked toward them. I pulled both my pistols and thumbed off the safeties as I slipped out of the shadows and into the big man's wake. At my size, there was no seeing me from the other side of Otis. I was like a submarine running deep and quiet.

Breathe. Focus.

"Drink up, boys. The night's over," Otis told them.

"You a cop?" one of them piped up. "You sure put it on like a cop."

Otis continued walking toward them. "I told you to drink up and get out."

"Why'd you pull your pistol out for?" the same voice asked. "You don't gotta shoot me fulla holes, do you?"

The young thugs laughed.

"Want me to?" Otis's pistol went up to point at them.

I stepped out and into view.

We were close enough by then to see their eyes shift to me. I saw no sign of intelligence in either of their callow faces. I did see surprise. I had appeared from thin air, coming out from behind Otis with two automatics pointed at them. They weren't laughing now. We were almost to their table.

"You're outgunned, boys."

Otis used a reasonable tone of voice, like he was ready to talk things over. However, before we could engage them in a meaningful discourse, he brought up a size twelve and pushed their table into them. He pushed it so hard that it knocked both men backward in their chairs and onto the floor in a flailing tangle of bodies, furniture, beer bottles, and ashtrays.

Before they could do anything, we had kicked aside the furniture and put our boot toes hard in their stomachs and ribs a few times to take the fight out of them.

It ended up with our pistols in their faces.

"Now boys, I want your hands on top of your heads, or there won't be nothing left to do but arrange your funerals," Otis said.

They did as they were told. However, the little guy, the one who'd been doing all the talking, had to say one more thing.

"Listen here..." he got out before Otis whopped him with his big automatic.

That pistol-slap was multipurpose. It left a nasty gash across the talky guy's temple, robbed him of consciousness, and delivered a spray of blood across his lanky friend.

"You wanna add something to that?" Otis asked the one who was busy blinking the little guy's blood out of his eyes.

Silence.

Otis glanced at me. "This one's the brains of the outfit. Get their arsenal."

There were a couple of small caliber automatics on the floor near them that I picked up and shoved in my pocket. I patted down the sleeping guy and found a pair of brass knuckle-dusters and a Baby Browning .25 that I added to my collection.

It was the lanky fellow's turn.

"Put your hands down and sit up," Otis told him.

He did as he was told and my partner slugged him behind the ear with a leather sap the size of a fat cigar. It did the trick. He let out a breathy groan and folded like a rag doll. I found an early issue .32 Colt snub-nose stuck in his boot. It had been blued recently and was kind of cute.

"Nothing but .32s and one of those loud .25s on these guys," I said.

"They was up to something with all that hardware, low voltage or not. Lock the front door and let's go upstairs."

I knew when I walked off that Otis would break a few of their fingers. It was a way of watching our backs.

"Nothing keeps a guy from going after a gun and

coming back to shoot you better'n hands too painful to use," he was fond of saying.

I locked the door and before I returned, I pulled the plug on the jukebox. I'd heard all the country I wanted for one night.

Otis led the way up the narrow stairway, pretty much blocking the dim light coming from the bare bulb hanging from the ceiling in the cramped hall at the top. There were two doors. After listening at both, Otis kicked one off its hinges.

Pistols drawn, we stepped over the flattened door and into the small, overheated room. Sherry sat on the bed, legs crossed like an Indian. She wore a man's hand-knitted cotton pullover and displayed total surprise.

A handsome little guy maybe twenty with shaggy dark hair and a dark complexion sat in a chair near the fogged window smoking a sweet-smelling roll-your-own. He wore nothing but a pair of faded blue jeans with a tiny flower appliqué on the thigh, and he had his bare feet up on the foot of the bed.

Spread around on a small drop-leaf table near him was a switchblade knife, a fistful of marijuana on a torn piece of newspaper, and a few other items. He and Sherry were loaded and, I think, in the middle of a conversation. Our entrance had startled and confused them. Neither knew what to do; they stared at us.

Otis went to the rickety table, picked up the knife, and put it in his pocket.

"What's your name, son?"

"Rico," he said in a boyish voice.

"Rico what?"

"Rico Hernandez."

"You wanna go to jail, Rico Hernandez?"

"No, señor."

"Then get out of here."

"Uno momento," the little guy said.

"Yeah?" Otis cocked his head just enough to indicate his patience was beginning to stretch.

"Are you her friends?" Rico asked.

Otis brought his fist down so hard on the table, it collapsed to the floor in two pieces, scattering debris everywhere. Rico flinched, dropped his lit reefer to the floor, and brought his feet off the bed. He sat up in his chair, but held his ground.

The men stared at each other.

"I ain't telling you again," Otis growled.

"I won't let you hurt her. You'll have to hurt me first," Rico said.

I could tell Otis was starting to like the boy.

He stepped on the smoking reefer near the young guy's bare foot.

"We're her friends. Now, *adios*, Rico."

After the boy gave Sherry a sweet smile and she smiled back, he said, "Adios, señor." He slipped past Otis, moved past me, stepped gingerly over the splintered door, and vanished down the stairs without looking back.

"Come on, Sherry," I said. "We're taking you home now."

"Home again, home again, jiggity pig," she said, stoned out of her noodle.

That's how it went down six months ago.

This time, she was unconscious in the back seat as we drove her to Doc McGraw's. This time things were different.

6

OVER NEAR LAKE Arlington we left the paved county road and followed a dirt road through a forest of blackjack oaks and thick underbrush that surrounded Doc McGraw's place. Coming out of the woods, we entered a large clearing and soon the road crossed a wide, dry creek bed.

Ahead of us were several whitewashed frame houses with shingle roofs that were set out in front of a big barn, some horse corrals, and other animal sheds and enclosures. The spacious area looked magic in the bright, shimmering moonlight.

As we pulled up, several mongrel hounds charged out and chased around the car, baying and barking. The lights came on above the big porch of the main house and Doc appeared, his hair mashed over to the side. He had slipped his feet into untied high-top shoes and was pulling on a light cotton robe over his undershorts as he crossed the porch, squinting out at us.

"How come Doc gave up his regular medical practice?" I asked Otis.

"Big animals was his calling," he said.

That night, he looked more like a farmer than any kind of man of medicine with his leathery sun-browned face, neck, and arms. He and Otis were about the same size—each pushing three hundred pounds. About the same age, too— right at fifty. The big men were imposing figures with their height, broad shoulders, muscular bodies, and no-nonsense faces.

Doc said something in Spanish to stay the dogs as Otis shut off the engine and got out.

"You okay? Who's hurt?"

"We're fine, Doc. It's something else," Otis said.

Doc saw me get out of the car and nodded. I nodded back. I'd lived out there a couple of months with him and his wife Loretta after my dog Jim got shot. That was late '54 into January of '55. My dog and I both needed some healing that winter.

I opened the back door and looked in at Sherry. She was still out. Imagine how exhausted she must've been to sleep with all that amphetamine in her. I got a chill up my back and checked the artery in her neck to make sure she was still alive.

Jesus. She was so close to death out at Bobby Jack's. What if Leon had driven for Chuck and Cecil? Both he and Sherry would be dead. Bobby Jack was a loose cannon that needed to be brought under control.

Both men came over to stare in at Sherry. I could tell by the way they were acting that it was settled. She was staying.

"So, this is the Beasley child," Doc commented.

Most folks in Texas had heard of Sherry Beasley and how she'd influenced old Hiram's will. It had become news again the past month or so as she approached her eighteenth birthday.

"She's a rascal," Otis threw in.

"She's young," Doc countered.

"Don't turn your back on her," I said. "Warn Loretta. She's treacherous when she's high."

"Poor thing," Doc clucked. "Let's get her inside. We'll put her in the spare room. Why don't you carry her in, Otis. It'll be the closest thing to work you've done for a while."

Doc snorted and smacked Otis on the shoulder so hard it

made him take a step forward to keep his balance. My God. That would have brought down a smaller man. Otis gave me a look that I knew meant he didn't want to stay long. He reached in through the door, gathered up the heiress wrapped in her tangled sheet, and brought her out of the car.

The movement woke her up and she became frantic—a wide-eyed, screeching wildcat trying to throw herself out of Otis' arms.

"Don't let him take me!" Her voice sliced across the darkened property.

Doc moved to help Otis. The dogs began yipping and pacing about, and more lights went on inside the house. Little Sherry was about all those giants could handle. They were a while getting her calmed down and into the house.

Loretta, Doc's wife, was up now, looking strange in her bright blue face cream, fluffy slippers, and curlers. She helped get the heiress into the guest room and then stayed with her. The rest of us kind of trailed back through the house. I told Doc that I'd bring his new houseguest some clothes tomorrow, and then Otis corrected that.

"We'll wait till the day after that. I ain't coming back till she's sober enough to jabber."

"We'll see how it goes," Doc made clear.

I said, "Keep her off the phone, Doc. Believe me, you don't want the people she can call to know your name."

"Thanks for the warning," he said.

Otis commented on how late it was and Doc winked at me.

"He's had all he wants of it. It's my problem now."

"You hungry?" Otis asked as soon as we were in the car and on our way.

"I could eat."

"Sylvia's okay with you?"

Sylvia's Steaks was a workingman's meat and potatoes place over near the stockyards. They never closed, the portions were large, and the waiters just brought the food and got out of the way. Their thick mesquite-grilled porterhouse steaks smothered in mushrooms and onions were world class, and that's what we always ordered—with the killer fried potatoes, of course.

I ate with Otis often enough to know that if Sylvia hadn't been so bad-tempered, he would've asked her to marry him.

"I'm going to weigh a ton," I said.

"You're still running now and again, ain't you?"

"That won't cure everything."

I'd noticed my jeans getting tighter, and I remembered my mom saying, "Weight's easy going on." My dad was tall and slim and I'd always thought I took after him, but still.

On the way to Sylvia's, Otis dropped me off at Spurs in Dallas to pick up my car. Virginia had left me her phone number on a note under my wiper blade and a few lines about how I should call her.

Tenacious, my dad would've called her.

I drove on over to Sylvia's, and my partner and I ended up having supper at three in the morning and talking about what we should do about the Sherry situation.

"Here's what I remember," I said. "After Bobby Jack gunned Cecil down, Chuck told him that Vahaska wanted him to lock his guest in the basement and come see him."

"You don't lock up guests, you lock up prisoners," Otis said.

"Exactly. They were calling her a guest while keeping her against her will. That sounds like kidnapping. And a bag full of that kind of money just thrown aside? Come on, Otis."

"So, why did her attorney tell me she'd run away again?"

"What did he say precisely?"

He looked blank for a moment. I could see around his

eyes how tired he was. "I lost my train of thought there."

"You were talking to Hagan Buchanan."

"Right. Day before yesterday he phoned to tell me Sherry'd run off again and he wanted to...how'd he put it? He wanted to enlist my services to find her and bring her home. I asked him if he had any idea where she might be. He said no. It turned out she'd already been gone a day or so. We got that straightened out, and that was that. I started looking and last night you joined in."

"So, as of right now, she's been on the loose three, maybe four days."

"Thereabouts," Otis agreed.

"I wish I'd been there so we could've discussed it right after the call."

"You deserved a few days off. Don't fret about it."

"And the second time he called?"

"He had an idea where she was, he told me."

"I don't remember him ever calling with a lead before," I said.

"Not once. All the sudden this time he knows she's with one of Vahaska's boys."

"Hagan's a country club type. How would he know guys like that?"

"He said someone told him."

"I think Sherry likes bad boys, but it's a big step up to a known criminal. How'd she manage that?"

"Good question, Missy. I'm betting the first call from Hagan was a cover up. For some reason, he didn't want me to know that Sherry'd been kidnapped. I think he wanted to see if we could find her first."

"That's playing fast and loose. Would he do that? What if Sherry ran off with Bobby Jack? That kind of makes sense, and you can bet Hagan wouldn't want to talk about that. Maybe that's what happened."

Otis held his hand up, asking for a moment to think and I gave it to him.

A few bites of steak later, he said, "That business of

telling Bobby Jack to lock Sherry in the basement..."

"Yeah?"

"Well, don't that imply that Vahaska knew she weren't in the basement?"

"A prisoner not being treated like a prisoner."

"If you'd kidnapped her, wouldn't you just keep her locked up till you got your money? Then you give her back, or kill her, or whatever you're gonna do?"

"Having sex and doing drugs with Bobby Jack puts an odd twist to it."

"It's like she's in on it one minute and the next she ain't. Makes her slippery as a fresh caught trout, don't it? Well, we got her off the hook because that's our job. Maybe before we throw her back she'll tell us a thing or two."

"What do you think's going to happen next out at Bobby Jack's?" I asked.

"Old man Vahaska ain't gonna be happy to find out Sherry and the money's gone and he's got two men dead. I can tell you that."

"Bobby Jack's going to lie through his teeth."

"I can tell you what he ain't gonna say. 'Oh, sorry, Uncle Vahaska. I sucked some dope up my nose, lost my head, and killed two of your guys.' He may be dumb, but he ain't stupid. He ain't gonna say that."

"He's going to have to blame somebody," I said. "Those guys sure are dead."

"You'd know. You was there."

"How can he explain any of it? Especially the money being gone."

"He lost the money and their little millionaire. It serves him right." Otis yawned big. "You know, I can't take anymore."

"Before we go," I said.

"Yeah?"

"If we're careful...or lucky...Bobby Jack and Vahaska may never know we were there."

"We were careful. So now it's about dadgum luck."

"Sherry was there, and she knows who killed Chuck and Cecil."

"And Bobby Jack knows she knows, Missy. That's why we're keeping her stashed away till this thing gets worked out."

"Our Miss Beasley may have something to say about being stashed away," I said. "If we don't watch our step, her lawyers will have us for kidnapping."

Otis sighed and indicated Sylvia's glowing front windows. "Hell, these nights ain't very long. We'll get on this like a duck on a June bug later this afternoon. Agreed?"

"Agreed."

We got up and started for the door.

"You staying in town?"

"No, I'm going out to the homestead."

"You just spent a week out there."

"I miss my dog. What can I say?"

The homestead was a section of Texas tallgrass prairie out northwest of Sweetwater that belonged to Henry Chin. I claimed a large, one-room adobe in back of his house that I called my *hacienda*. It was quite a distance to and from the office in Fort Worth. Even so, getting away to Henry's was a piece of sanity for me, and well worth the drive. I got out there as often as I could, since that little adobe was like my real home.

I'd moved out to Henry's and into the *hacienda* when I was seventeen and had lost my father. I liked the seclusion and the calm of country living. And I loved it for my big German shepherd who had the freedom to chase rabbits, prairie dogs, and other varmints on the open acreage.

The sun had been up about an hour by the time I left the highway and aimed my new Olds 88 down the dirt road that led to home. It was going to be another scorcher. I looked out across the tall grass waving at the cloudless sky. It was good there was a little breeze.

Jim heard me leave the highway and came down to wait under the three twisted old jacaranda trees near the gate. He stood up and gave himself a shake when I drew near. I stopped the car and he got in—all hundred and twenty pounds of him. After a lot of wagging and wiggles and licks, he settled down and rode like a good boy with his head stuck out the window for the final quarter of a mile.

I loved that dog more than I could say.

Henry's homestead had a deep well that provided enough water for a sizable pond that Jim liked to wade in, a grove of large pecan trees, and a scattering of even larger cottonwoods that shaded his tile-roofed, thick-walled adobe buildings that included a main house, a woodworking shop, a big, barn-like garage, and my *hacienda* that was set back past the vegetable garden. The only new structure was the awkward-looking TV antenna that stuck up from the garage like Martian hardware and the wires that drooped across to Henry's house.

I saw Henry in his overalls and straw hat leave the house. He was a small, wiry man, strong and in good shape from having been a carpenter all his life. His sturdy stride got him to the garage by the time I drove up.

He slid the big door open so I could pull in. I'd had my car's original shiny paint job covered over with a dull, dark gray primer coat finish so it wouldn't reflect light at night. Even without a nice paint finish, Henry and I both thought it was better to park in the garage out of the Texas elements.

"Want breakfast?" Henry asked when Jim and I got out.

"No, thanks. Otis and I caught a bite at Sylvia's."

"Porterhouse."

I felt fat when I nodded yes.

"See full moon last night?"

"Yeah. It was bright enough for Otis to follow me with his lights turned off."

"That Harvest Moon."

Henry knew the names of all the full moons—a lot of the stars, too. He closed the garage door.

"Find rich girl?"

"Yeah, we did."

"She have birthday soon."

"That's true," I said. I guess everybody in Texas knew that.

We walked over and stopped between the main house and the hacienda. I explained in broad strokes what happened at Bobby Jack's, and about taking Sherry to Doc McGraw's to dry out and rest up. He listened without comment. He would have things to say later after thinking it all over. It was his way.

"It almost six thirty. You sleep now?"

"Yeah. I'll head back early afternoon. Will you be around?"

"Go see Madame Li today. Maybe see you at office later."

Madame Li owned the Mandarin Palace Restaurant in a blue-collar section of Fort Worth. The Millett Agency was upstairs in the same building. She was Otis' landlady and Henry's friend.

"I have some shopping to do for Sherry. So I may be a while getting there."

"Maybe see, maybe not see."

"Fair enough." I headed off for bed.

"Sleep tight, don't let bedbugs bite," he called out.

He learned a lot of his English from radio shows.

"Thanks," I said over my shoulder. He had more to say. I paused. "Something else?"

"Madame Li introduce friend."

"About work?" I asked, but I knew better.

"Social issue."

"Oh. Another lady friend."

"Maybe Henry like." He laughed and slapped his knee.

"Good luck, Casanova."

"Casanova," I heard him repeat as I went inside my little house.

I left the door open so Jim could come and go.

On the backside of my place, the roof extended to cover a large patio. I had a Mexican rope hammock out there that I sometimes slept in after pulling a night shift. The patio roof plus all the shade from our trees helped keep the temperature down through the hot months. Any little breeze helped during the humidity we'd been suffering through.

As I drew my bath, I thought about Madame Li's efforts to get Henry married. He was a widower in his fifties with a successful custom furniture and cabinet business, and Madame Li felt he needed a wife—a suitable Chinese wife. She had over the past two years—no, make that almost three years—introduced him to many ladies.

"When romantic meetings begin," Henry told me, "I know it take special woman replace Lilly."

He'd lost his Lilly to cancer over six years ago.

Madame Li prepared a delicious dinner for the potential mates as part of each introduction. So Henry always met the women at the Mandarin Palace.

"Home cooking." His name for Chinese food. "And good practice talk. My Chinese not much better my English anymore."

I fell asleep in the big tub.

When I woke up, I dragged my wrinkled body out and set the alarm. I slipped on underpants and a big t-shirt, aimed the electric fan through the open door onto the patio, and got the wool sock that held the .38 automatic that I slept with. The tiles were cool on my bare feet as I went out and curled into the hammock.

Sleep was elusive. I found myself mesmerized by the sparkling moments of morning sun flitting through our rustling cottonwoods, and I went over the Sherry Beasley case and the danger she'd gotten herself into. I thought of the honky-tonk waitress that left me her phone number.

Virginia was her name.

The cottonwoods rustled with every little breeze and clicked like nests of castanets. I listened to that clatter a while and to the hum of bees mixing with the scent of honey-suckle.

What was I thinking?

Oh, yes—Virginia.

She'd been helpful by seating me with Leon. Maybe she'd be helpful again.

7

THE NEXT DAY, late in the afternoon, I walked into the office and found Hagan Buchanan sitting on our new leather sofa. He was impeccably tailored, as usual.

He showed me his pearlies and stood up. "Miss Van Dijk."

"Mr. Buchanan. Please sit down."

Hagan was the senior partner at Buchanan, Farnley, Meadows and Meadows. He'd been Hiram Beasley's personal attorney, was the executor of his will, and the person we spoke to when Sherry was on the loose.

He remained on his feet. "Been shopping?"

I was lugging several bags full of clothing. I gave him a shy laugh.

"A girl has to do what a girl has to do."

"We're chawing about finding Miss Beasley," Otis said from behind his big desk. "You wanna join us?"

That was Otis' way of telling me to go in the other room and listen in.

"I will if you want me to, Otis. Although, I have some work to catch up on in the darkroom."

"That's right. Well, you go ahead with that then."

"Nice seeing you, Mr. Buchanan."

"A pleasure seeing you," he replied in that practiced tone of voice he so often used.

I paused near the door. "And Mrs. Buchanan's well?"

"Why, quite well." His brows hiked up with faux surprise at my good breeding. "How kind of you to inquire."

I had met her once when I was at his office with Otis—she was maybe too young for him, maybe too much makeup—polite and sincere enough, as I recalled. Strong-minded, Otis had commented.

"Please tell her that I asked about her."

"Bless your heart," he said. "I will. I will."

Once in Otis' apartment with the door closed behind me, I tossed aside the shopping bags and went back to where I could stand with my good ear near the crack of the ill-fitting door.

Otis was talking about our efforts to locate Sherry Beasley. It was dangerous business to lie to a client as powerful as Hagan Buchanan; on the other hand, things about this case smelled to high heaven. We wanted some answers before we rolled over like lazy hounds.

Last winter, after we took Sherry home from that open gutter, Delbert's, Otis had had me start some research. He wanted us to learn everything we could about the Hiram Beasley family and Sherry's background in particular. He said discretion was easy to understand, while secrets made things complicated. His gut feeling was that Hagan's reasons for the way he behaved concerning Sherry Beasley were more than likely okay.

"Be that as it may," he'd said, "just because a big law firm hires us to do something don't always mean what they're asking us to do is the right thing. Or even a legal thing to do, for that matter. Ever hear that song that goes, 'tain't necessarily so'?"

"The things you read in the Bible," I said.

"That's the one. It don't matter who says it or where it comes from, it's safer if we find out for ourselves."

The thing was, Otis was curious why a young woman as wealthy as Sherry would find it so appealing to run away and get in trouble with people so far below her station. I was curious why a seventeen-year-old with her money, education, and connections wasn't free to come and go when she pleased without having to resort to running away.

"Isn't that the issue?" I'd asked Otis. "At seventeen, some girls might need a chaperone. That's a given, but plenty of seventeen-years-olds are married with children, too. My question is why does Sherry have to *escape* in order to go somewhere?"

My research turned up some interesting information without answering our questions. First of all, there was a lot of money to be considered.

Hiram Beasley owed his enormous fortune to being in the right place at the right time. He lived in Beaumont, Texas, at the turn of the century. And anyone who knows Texas history knows what happened there in January 1901.

Spindletop.

I'd read to Otis from a biography I'd checked out of the library, "Hiram was in his early fifties and an investor in both land and oil when the Spindletop Oilfield was brought in."

Otis said, "That discovery was so big, so important, it changed world history, not just Texas history. And it made Hiram Beasley and a corral full of other Beaumont citizens richer'n skunks."

Otis was right about that. Hiram Beasley suddenly had enough money to change wives and lives when he felt like it. By the time he died in 1942, he had run through four wives and produced five children.

"Sherry was the last of the bunch," Otis had said. "And she was his favorite, too. Everybody knew that."

I kept reading to him.

"Hiram Beasley's fourth and last wife, Lynette, was a voluptuous, twenty-two-year-old, gold-digging party girl the oil millionaire met when he was in his nineties. She gave him a child so promptly it put wags to counting their fingers. The blessed bundle she delivered to the proud old man was a daughter. He was thrilled to finally have a female heir after siring nothing save boys for years. Lynette named her baby Sherry Louise."

"How old was she when the old man died?" Otis asked.

"She was four."

"He died in the spring of '42, didn't he?"

"That's right. And Lynette, Sherry's mother, died two weeks later."

"The papers had a field day with that one," Otis clucked.

Otis was right. Her death created a lot of interest. And the newspapers showed neither respect nor restraint. It was known around town that when Lynette learned she had come into millions of dollars, she took out a credit line at a Dallas Savings & Loan and launched a spending spree that had the better retail stores salivating.

I read some more from that same biography.

"Lynette Beasley's shopping extravaganza included the purchase of a beautifully conditioned 1939 Aston Martin four-litre. The same day she took ownership of the spirited British sports car, she broadsided a gasoline tanker truck at the estimated speed of 107 miles per hour. The resulting conflagration cremated the driver of the tanker truck, Lynette Beasley, and her two passengers—a Mexican pool boy from a *déclassé* local hotel and a champagne-colored toy poodle inappropriately named Lucky."

"Now, mind you, Missy. There was a war going on, and Sherry's mama got front-page coverage. Nothing sells better'n gossip about rich folks."

Not even war.

After Hagan left, Otis got himself a fresh cup of coffee. "That was something."

It was quiet in the office except for the antique electric fan on a tall stand that hummed and rattled from the corner over past the desk.

"He seemed edgy to me," I said.

"Nervous as a shady lady in church," Otis said and sloshed coffee on his new mahogany desk. He turned that small mess into a big one with a soiled dishtowel, threw the damp cloth aside, and sat down without another thought about it.

When I became his partner, I insisted on and got a lady to come in every two weeks to clean the office and Otis' apartment. While a weekly cleaning would've been more realistic, twice a month was a victory of sorts. I'd been careful to never complain.

Otis said, "This deal has him wiggling. I heard it in everything he said and everything he didn't say."

"Sherry's a big responsibility and she's been gone for a while," I reminded Otis.

"It's more'n that. There's something going on he ain't ready to tell us. You hear that business about the private hospital?"

"No. What was that?"

Otis began digging around in the pile of papers on his desk.

"I think that's where she might've been when she walked away. He didn't say that, but that's what I got."

"Why was she in a hospital?"

"You got me, but he's fit to be tied about something."

"The money, maybe?"

"You could be right, Missy. He didn't say a word about money, but he did say he'd make some calls to help us locate Bobby Jack."

"He can do that? He can just call around about a known criminal's nephew?"

Otis shrugged.

"Why not? He's on a first name basis with plenty of defense attorneys. All them shysters at City Hall know each other."

"It seems cozy to me, but I guess you're right."

"Here it is." He brought up a scrap of paper. "Lemme see here. Cambridge Court. That's the name of the...he called it a sanitarium, not a hospital."

"Have any idea where that is?"

"Not a clue, Missy. But it's gonna smell like rich folks, I'll bet."

We found Cambridge Court Sanitarium in a neglected Dallas neighborhood that didn't smell a bit like rich folks. Let's not bother with the prevailing odors. A sign near the front door of the rundown three-story brick Gothic structure stated that the institution had been at that location since 1927. Given its age, it was reasonable to believe that the building had not always been squeezed between a hockshop and a low rent apartment building with wash hanging out of the windows.

"I've seen snappier addresses," Otis said.

I turned down a side street and drove around so we could get behind the place. Just as we pulled up to park, a long black hearse drifted away from the back door and disappeared up the street. With our windows up and the air on, the departure of the hearse played out in a dreamy silence.

"I just felt a possum trot over my grave," my partner said.

There was something about the anonymity of it, the fact that things could happen *privately* in a place like that; a place that seemed so sinister with all its windows behind wrought iron bars.

"I bet that's a lovely place inside there," Otis said.

"How'd she escape?" I wondered, remembering she'd had her purse at Bobby Jack's.

BABY SHARK'S BEAUMONT BLUES

"I don't see it as likely myself...unless she had help."

"Well, yeah, with help maybe," I said.

"You know, Missy..."

"Yeah?"

"I was just thinking. Maybe the reason our Sherry was stark nekked when we carried her out of Bobby Jack's was because she didn't have no clothes on to begin with."

It took me a minute. "You're saying she left this place here wearing a hospital gown."

"Sure, and it didn't take Bobby Jack long to get her out of that."

"What's missing..." I began.

"...is how he got holt of her to begin with," he finished.

"That's it," I said.

He stared out the window for a moment before coming back to me. "You know, she told me one time how hard it was for her growing up. Sure, sure. A poor little rich girl. Money, as you might know, don't always make things right. Seems like she didn't know for a long time how different she was being treated."

"How do you mean?"

"Oh, she knew she had more'n most folks. She'd always had private teachers. Hell, private everything and trips around the world. All that stuff, but what she came to see was she was being treated like...mmmm, what did she say?"

"Like a rich girl," I offered.

"No. Like a potted geranium is what she said. No one in the family paid attention to her. She never had friends. She couldn't even have a car or learn to drive. She had a driver if she needed to go some place. She couldn't go to town to see a movie. She had her own theater, why'd she need to go to town? Or shopping? She just had to order it and it got delivered."

"Poor thing."

"Well, you can say that. At the same time, as independent as you are, you know how fast that would get old. She got tired of that crap, and her and Nadine began going round and round. So, Sherry quit discussing it. She just walked away."

"That's when they called you?"

"Not yet. First time she ran away, they called the Rangers."

"You're kidding me. The Rangers?"

"Uh huh. They brought her back in a matter of hours, and it made the evening news."

"I'll bet it did," I said.

"Hagan was asked to hire a private investigator after that."

"Discretion," I said.

"Or secrecy...depends how you look at it. Anyway, I rounded her up twice alone and twice now with your help. Sherry told me once she was ready for home by the time I showed up. She said she could almost time it."

"I wonder why she can't get along with her Aunt."

"You'd get ornery as a fried toad, too, if you was locked up all the time."

"I suppose. But why is Nadine so protective of her?"

"She told Sherry there'd been threats. That was cow hockey, of course. I would have known about threats. Hagan would have called me first off if there'd been anything like that."

"Except this time."

"Yep, except this time. Let's go," he said. "We been here long enough."

I pulled away and drove up the street the way I'd seen the hearse go.

"There's something not right," I said. "That place doesn't make sense for people as wealthy as the Beasleys."

"Unless they wanted a Beasley to go unnoticed," he said. "Might could be like a country club inside."

"A creepy country club, maybe."

"We'll get to the bottom of it. What time're you meeting that red-headed waitress?"

He'd heard me give her a call from the office.

"Eight thirty. You want me to introduce you?"

"That depends. What color are her eyes?"

"When did you start noticing that part of a woman's anatomy?" I asked.

Otis chuckled and dragged out a Lucky.

8

VIRGINIA, THE WAITRESS with hazel eyes, had asked me to meet her outside a picture show in Dallas.

"You're not working at Spurs tonight?" I'd asked her on the phone.

"I called in sick," she'd told me. "I got bigger fish to fry than slinging hash. That's what I wanna talk to you about."

I pulled up to the curb and saw her standing back under the marquee. She wore baggy shorts and a baggy tee shirt. Her thick red hair sprouted out at all angles from beneath a disreputable floppy felt hat. If she was trying to downplay her considerable looks, she was succeeding.

She snatched up a denim overnight bag at her feet, worked her way around some rambunctious teenage boys, and came striding across the wide sidewalk. I was as tall as she was; still, I wondered if my legs looked as long as hers. She tossed her bag into the back and snuggled into the seat next to me. Her scent was *Evening in Paris*. Everyone seemed to be wearing it. She looked over and frowned.

"It's like December in here."

"You'll get used to it. See a movie?"

"I walked out. People don't sing and dance through life. Let's take a drive, okay?"

I pulled away.

"Leon got home okay last night?"

"I guess so. Angel takes care of that."

"Angel?"

"Yeah, Angel. How do you know those guys?"

"Which guys?"

Virginia shot a warning look across my bow. "Which guys? The guys who hired you instead of Leon to do their dirty work. Who the hell did you think I meant?"

"Hold on now," I said. "What dirty work? They needed a driver. As it turned out, there was no job. So, they just dropped me off, and that was that."

She sniffed to let me know she didn't believe me. "How'd you get such a new car?"

"My grandmother died and left it to me," I made up on the spot.

She hiked an eyebrow, changed her mind about the first thing she felt like saying, and said instead, "Sorry to hear about your grandma."

"I appreciate your thoughtfulness."

Virginia pointed. "Go that way." I made the turn she suggested as she clicked on the radio and found a popular music station. "You mind?"

I assumed that was rhetorical. I said, "How do *you* know those guys?"

"Cockroaches like that are always around. You can't exterminate them fast enough."

"It's good I didn't get mixed up with them," I told her.

"What're you talking about? You did business with them. I saw that guy Chuck slip you some money."

That reminded me—I'd thrown those jeans in the laundry with a fiver in the pocket.

"That ended up not meaning anything," I said. "You can do me a favor and forget that."

"Why should I do you a favor? And besides, if they dropped you off and there was no job, why do you care whether I remember it or not? Turn left."

Virginia was older than I first thought—twenty-four,

twenty-five. I kept my face blank and made the turn she asked for.

"The reason you care, of course, is because they didn't drop you off, and you did do some dirty work with them," she said.

"You ever shut up with all your theories and finger pointing?"

"Not often," she said, not in the least annoyed. "You think I'm stupid, don't you?"

"No. I don't think that."

"Sure you do. You thought you could pay me off to get you next to Leon last night and then pretend being next to him wasn't all that important to you."

She'd summarized that pretty accurately, so I said, "That's not true."

"Sure it is. And you've agreed to meet me because you need something else."

"You asked for this meeting."

"Uh huh, and here you are trying to bullshit me into saying I didn't see you with Vahaska's boys. You not only think I'm stupid, you don't care what happens to me, either. Those boys play rough. I stuck my neck out for you."

"Well, exactly. That's why it's better if you buy what I'm telling you and not worry about the rest."

"Uh huh. Well, I heard Leon talking about what happened out at Bobby Jack's last night."

That stopped my heart for an instant. She had gone of her own volition where I'd hoped to lead her.

"You know Bobby Jack?"

"I know who he is," she said, choosing her words.

"And Leon talked about him?"

"Leon likes to talk. He talks about a lot a things."

"Yeah? Like what?"

"Oh. You wanna know, do you? What a surprise. See over there? Pull over."

I stopped at the curb, left the car idling, and waited to

hear where her latest sarcasm would take us. Doris Day sang *"Que Sera, Sera."*

Well, yes, Doris…you might say that.

"I'll tell you what, Christian…"

"Kristin."

She paused. "Leon said it was Christian."

"He did, huh?"

"Look, I'll make you a deal. I didn't see you with Vahaska's hoods, and I'll tell you what Leon said. How's that?"

"For what?" I asked.

"You shoot my pictures."

"We're back to those pictures."

"You want a favor and information, don't you?"

Why hadn't I noted before the intelligence that was so evident in her eyes and face? My mind had been on other things last night.

"You know Vahaska?"

"Nope. Never even seen him. He stays down in Beaumont, mostly, I think. I just know a few of the numskulls that work for him up here. The ones that hang out at Spurs."

"Like Leon?"

"Forget Leon. He's not one of them jerks. He just does an odd job for them now and again. Leon's a baby. You know that. He talked his head off to you, didn't he?"

Virginia struck me as telling fewer lies than I did. Not that she was more honest; she just seemed too straightforward in her approach to bother with lying. Me, I was always covering my tracks. "All right," I said. "Let's hear this picture deal."

She didn't hesitate. "A PI I know has a client whose husband's cheatin' on her."

"Yeah?"

"The husband's got a good business, and the wife wants the big bucks when she dumps him."

She was describing a variation on the Millet Agency's core business. Feuding husbands and wives kept our doors open. Ahhh, finally—Miss Day was finished. I turned the radio off.

"And your PI wants pictures of what?" As if I didn't know.

"Naughty stuff."

"Uh huh. And you're doing what? Finding a photographer for him?"

"Something like that. It's a business proposition. I'm like an enterpernaur."

"An entrepreneur," I said, pronouncing it correctly.

"You think that's funny?"

"Calm down. Who's the woman the husband gets caught with?"

"Me."

Of course.

"You know him? This businessman?"

"Not yet," she said.

"You're going to pick him up."

Virginia pointed. "And we're going there."

I looked across the street at a seedy hotel. Blinking blue neon signs at top and bottom.

"That's where you get the pictures," she said.

"Naughty pictures," I confirmed.

"And I'll bet you know naughty pictures when you see them, don'cha?" she shot back.

"You're always spoiling for a fight, aren't you?"

"I know when I'm being taken seriously."

"You're an interesting character, Virginia. When's all this supposed to happen?"

"Tonight."

That took me off guard. I shook my head in disbelief.

"What's the matter with you?" she asked.

"Me? What's the matter with you?"

"What about me?"

"Look at you," I said.

"Look at what?" she asked.

She had no idea what I was talking about.

"You're saying you're going to pick up some big time

businessman tonight. How's that supposed to happen? Pretty as you are, you look like a refugee."

I watched her freckles darken as she glared at me from below the wide brim of her old, gray floppy hat.

"Kiss my ass, Christian. You worry about holding up your end of the deal. I'm just guessing anyway that you know one end of a camera from the other."

She had a point. She'd never seen a picture that I'd taken.

There was a long silence—long enough for the single-minded businesswoman to cool her irritation.

"So, we have a deal?"

"Not so fast. Let's be clear about your end of this bargain."

"Absolutely," she said. "I'm gonna tell you all the stuff you can't hardly wait to hear about Vahaska's scummy thugs and what happened at Bobby Jack's."

Her nonchalance about what occurred at that ranch made me wonder if we were talking about the same thing.

"Leon told you what happened out there?"

She read doubt in my face. "Leon's my boyfriend."

"I thought he was Angel's boyfriend."

"She thinks so, too. Just goes to show you, huh? Now, let's talk about your end of the bargain."

A little later, I dropped Virginia off at a lounge, where she was to seduce her businessman. Down the street, I phoned Otis from a booth outside a filling station.

"I got snookered," I told him.

"How's that?"

"I'm trading some sleazy photography work for information about Bobby Jack."

"You're taking pictures of her with a mark?"

Otis was quick like that.

"That's it."

"At some hotel?"

"A real flea bag, yeah."

"Where is it?"

I told him and he sighed. "That was a nice hotel before the war. Back then the neighborhood was nicer, too. Anyway, when you're all done with your chores there, come on by. We have some things to discuss."

"Will do," I said.

There was a pause.

"You trust her?"

"Sure, I suppose so. I'll tell you this, I've stopped under-rating her."

"Why's that?"

"Well, she changed clothes in the back seat of my car and ended up looking pretty darn good in a little black nothing of a dress and some sling backs that cost more than everything else she wore combined."

"Women and their shoes."

"She knows her stuff. She mussed up her hair until it looked sexy. I could never do that. She knows about lipstick and eyes; her jewelry was subtle. When she was ready to go, she was bare shoulders, full bosom, lipstick, and hair, and she knew how to work that combination, too…along with a spaghetti strap that just wouldn't stay up."

"I'm sold," my partner said.

"I'm going to be cautious around her in the future. She's not just pretty. She's bright, clever, and from what I can tell, without any scruples."

"Sounds like Dixie, my ex-wife."

Nelson Algren said, "…never lie down with a woman who's got more troubles than you."

"You don't often speak of Dixie," I said.

"That don't mean I don't reflect on her. And you think your waitress has some inside stuff on our boy Bobby Jack?"

"Uh huh. I won't know how good it is, though, until after I've let her see how few scruples I have." That was a slip. "Sorry. I didn't mean anything by that."

"Don't worry about it, I opened the door. And don't be too rough on yourself doing what you have to do sometimes. Just remember, we're trying to protect a girl's life."

"I'll keep that in mind."

"You gonna be all right there?"

"Come on, Otis. It's a photo shoot. What can go wrong?"

9

AS I CROSSED the dingy hotel lobby with my camera bag slung over my shoulder, I heard a preacher's voice haranguing from one of those stations in Del Rio. The night manager, a grubby old codger in overalls sitting near his radio in a rundown comfortable chair, looked up and let fly a brown stream into a Folgers can. He wiped his mouth with the back of his hand and watched me from below bushy white eyebrows.

I didn't look at him again until I'd entered the elevator and was closing the door. I pushed the roll handle down, and the old machine lurched upward. During the hotel's better days, there would have been a handsome young operator in a uniform to do that.

A bell clanked when the car stopped at the top floor. I leveled it, got out, and started down the gloomy hall, checking room numbers. The only sound was the groan of the elevator behind me as the motor wound up and the car began its trip back to the lobby.

I used the key that Virginia had given me to open the door.

The room was larger than I'd expected. It held a bed, a chair, a bedside table, a lamp, a tall chest of drawers, and a flimsy door that wasn't a closet—it led to the adjoining room. It was locked.

Blue reflections from the blinking neon on the roof sporadically permeated the space.

I closed the hall door, put my bag on the bed, got out a camera, and moved over to an open window. Staying back in the shadows, I checked my pocket watch. It was half past two.

Out the window, I could see across an open space into a lighted room in another wing of the same hotel—thirty-five feet or so away. I saw there a middle-aged man, balding, glasses, and a woman with her back to me.

The woman was the aggressor, but the man was willing as she removed his shirt. I couldn't make out their conversation, but I could tell that the woman in the sexy black nothing of a dress was doing the talking. I put my camera to my eye, brought the back of her head into tight focus, confirmed that it was Virginia, and snapped off a few shots. I adjusted focus until it was the man's excited face that was sharp.

I had gotten to the window right on schedule.

The soft click of the camera and the slide and snap of the film advance mechanism played against the silence of the room as I took a series of pictures. After Virginia had her mark undressed, she began shedding her clothes. She kept herself off at an angle to allow me the shots she wanted. With her back to me, and the businessman's attention focused on her, she provided me full-face shots of him without identifying herself. Their pale skin glowed soft blue from the neon light that intermittently invaded the rooms.

Virginia displayed her long legs and removed her nylons with what appeared to be a decent amount of passion. At least her slow moves were without excess. I reflected on my own affairs, which didn't take long, since they were so few and far between. And anyway, this wasn't an affair. What this was I'd seen plenty of in Otis' darkroom.

However, watching Virginia at work, I could almost believe that I saw foreplay, but of course what was really on display was a lie unfolding. Virginia took her time to give me opportunity, and she was good at what she was doing. She was a calculating performer with a little frog tattoo on her ass cheek.

I retired my camera to my side, having recorded enough to hang her mark. I neither needed nor wanted to see any more of their performance. I was turning away when the door to Virginia's room crashed open and Leon stormed in, dressed in his cowboy clothes.

Leon? This was something Virginia had neglected to mention.

Virginia backed up as Leon went to the bed. Before the naked businessman could get to his feet, Leon punched him in the face. I got a picture of that, and I got a couple of shots of the man standing in the doorway, a neatly dressed little fella with a black patch over one eye.

An eye patch…What next?

Leon moved from the bed to Virginia, but she wasn't as easy to smack around as the mark. They yelled at each other as she blocked a couple of his attempts to slap her. She was able to push him away, but he caught his balance and grabbed her.

I'd seen enough. She needed help.

I stuck my camera in my bag, left it on the bed, and opened the door to the hall. I would have been on my way, but a man stood there. A swarthy guy with blond hair—not tall, not heavy—blocked my way.

He stepped toward me, and I moved back into the room. My heart rate threatened to get involved, but I wasn't excited yet.

"You're coming with me," he said.

"You've got the wrong room, *Guero.*"

"Don't call me that."

Guero was a nickname for fair-haired Mexicans. I guess some didn't like it.

He came farther into the room and showed me a Walther P38. The sight of it was supposed to scare me. It didn't.

He stepped to the side to give me room to exit.

"*Vamos.*"

He motioned with his pistol.

I stepped toward the door. After getting the man moving, I turned, pushed his pistol aside, jabbed a hand into his throat, and shoved as hard as I could. That took him backward a few steps and into the chest of drawers.

He fired off a wild round—a loud round in that closed space.

We lost our balance as the piece of furniture slid away and along the wall. It crashed into the corner of the room. We fell to the floor, him on his back, and me to my knees. I grabbed his gun hand hard and bent some fingers back.

He yowled and dropped his weapon.

I got to my feet, charged for the hall, and ran into a large man there.

He straight-armed me with a fist to my chest. I flew back and landed hard, sitting down next to the bed. I saw *Guero's* P38 near me and grabbed for it. He grabbed for it, too, but I got it and brought it up shooting.

How could I have missed a corn-fed bruiser that big? He was framed in the damn doorway. But at least my effort drove him back into the hall.

Guero grabbed at my hand, but I got off two more wild shots before he pulled the pistol from me. I threw a fist hard into his eye and knocked the gun away before he got a proper hold on it. He cursed at me and dived for the weapon.

I scrambled to my feet and kicked *Guero* as hard as I could in his ribs. The sound he made said I'd hurt him. Now, for sure, I couldn't let him catch me.

My choices were the hall door, the window, or the flimsy door that led to the adjoining room.

I charged full out, rammed my shoulder into the thin wood, and tumbled with the demolished door into the next room. I got to my feet faster than I would've thought possible and dashed for the door to the hall.

I knew I couldn't go back toward the elevator and stairs, so I ran for the open window at the end of the hall that let out to the fire escape. I had a head start on them. I wanted the pistol in my ankle holster, but how the hell was I supposed to get to that?

I dived head first through the open window, scraped my shins on the sill, and got a jolt of stomach-sickening vertigo when I suddenly stared down seven stories through the steel slats of a rusty, old fire escape.

As I scrambled around on my hands and knees, I heard one of the men arrive at the window right behind me.

"Shit!" I let out when I realized I'd crawled away from the stairs that would have taken me down and away from the men.

I'd left myself a ladder that led to the roof.

I snapped to my feet, saw the Mexican crawling through the window behind me, and stomped on his hand. His was the kind of scream that wakes the dead. I hoped that I'd bought enough time to get to the roof. I wanted the high ground.

I grabbed the ladder and scrambled up a rung or two before the old piece of steel pulled away from the wall. The bolts that held it were letting go.

"Jesus!" I yelled, and dropped back to the fire escape landing.

Guero got to his feet, and behind him the big man came through the window. I began climbing like a monkey—hand over hand, up the wobbly ladder. I prayed that it would stay attached to the building for the short distance I had to climb to reach the roof.

"*Su madre!*" the Mexican shouted as he grabbed my foot.

I kicked hard. Got loose. Started climbing again.

Guero shouted something else in Spanish as the ladder reacted to the big man starting up behind me. A bolt near my face popped out of the wall and scared me half to death. The ladder twisted slightly, and I felt every movement of the big man as he climbed after me.

The steel railing at the top of the ladder had snapped loose and slid left and right in rhythm with the heavy guy's changing handholds. My heart thundered as I grabbed for the roof edge.

I missed.

I grabbed for it again, but the shifting ladder pulled me away from it.

"Shit!"

I was going to fall before I could get over the low wall and onto the roof. Another bolt popped out, and one side of the metal bands that fit over the low wall scraped up and over with a loud screech.

The ladder was giving way. It twisted horribly.

Guero shouted again.

I let go of the rung I held just as the top of the ladder bent up with a screech of tortured metal.

I grabbed the edge of the roof as the whole thing snapped over the edge.

The ladder flashed past me and was gone.

I gasped with fear.

From below—the sound of metal colliding with metal—a scream of pain.

My handhold on the roof edge slipped. My stomach rolled over, and I fell.

With my heart in my throat, I dropped the short distance to the fire escape landing. I took an awkward tumble and got to my feet expecting to be in the middle of a fight.

But I discovered something quite different.

The collapsing ladder had caught the Mexican. He was folded backwards over the steel railing, his spine broken. He was pinned like a rat in a trap. His face was a grotesque death mask. One of his arms stuck straight out like he was hailing a taxi to Hell.

The big man was in trouble, too. The ladder that he had

ridden down—the ladder that had crushed his partner—
extended out and down at a slight angle with him near the
end of it. He dangled seventy feet above the dark alley.

We locked eyes, and I spoke to him in a quiet voice.

"See what happens when you chase young girls."

His attention went back to his challenge. He took his time
letting go with one hand, but he did it. He jerked forward
and grabbed the next rung to move his enormous weight
toward me.

He glanced at me again as he gave a little swing, let go
again, and grabbed the next rung. He'd made progress, but
he was sweating heavily. A hand slipped off, and he swung
there by one arm, grabbing air with his free hand.

Our eyes met one last time before his other hand slipped
and he fell—he fell fast. I watched him all the way to the
alley. He never uttered a sound.

*"Look at my little brachiator," my dad used to say when I played
on the monkey bars.*

I was a moment pulling myself together. My memory
was getting a bit crowded with dead guys.

I sighed and turned to the blond Mexican's misshapen
corpse. "Not your lucky day, huh, *Guero*?"

I took his Walther P38 from his shoulder holster and
checked his jacket pocket where I found an extra magazine.
I reloaded, put one in the chamber, and eased the hammer
down. I tossed the half-empty magazine after the big guy and
stuck the pistol in the back pocket of my Levi's. Tight fit.

My heart had almost settled down by the time I climbed in
through the window and started down the dimly lit hall.

Where was Virginia, I wondered?

I saw a man down the hall in a pool of light. He leaned
against the wall across from the elevator. A small man—shiny
loafers, creased slacks, a fresh shirt. A tenant, maybe?

When he turned his head, I saw the black patch that
covered his left eye.

10

GUERO'S P38 WAS in my right back pocket, and I didn't want the guy down by the elevator to see me get it. Also, I wanted to look behind me to make sure there weren't more of those vermin in the hall. I did two things at once.

I pushed my left shoulder forward to turn my body so I could look back over my right shoulder. At the same time, I pulled the automatic from my back pocket. When I brought my gaze forward again, I held the pistol behind my leg, and I knew that I was not surrounded.

I cocked the hammer and thumbed off the safety.

After I'd taken a few more steps, the guy pushed away from the wall and turned toward me. I stopped. A featherweight. Everything about him said quick.

No mistakes.

"Where do you think you're going?"

He had a reedy voice, a nasal twang.

"I beg your pardon."

We were less than twenty feet apart. I saw when he realized I had a hand behind my leg. He hissed as he grabbed his pistol from his belt. When our weapons came up, we were in a Mexican standoff, our arms extended.

Our hands were steady.

He owned the firepower with a Colt .45, but it didn't

matter, as close as we were. If a trigger was pulled, we were both wearing toe tags. He knew it, too.

Beyond the bad end of his cannon, I stared at a dark, squinty eye, a pointy little nose, and a horizontal line for a mouth. He was no youngster—forties someplace. A jagged, dark brown scar seemed to pour from his ear to disappear behind his eye patch.

The prominent sound in the hallway was the whirring coming from the elevator shaft. The car was in motion.

"What're you doing carrying a gun?" His voice was calm.

"I keep it to shoot cockroaches," I replied in a voice equally as calm.

"Maybe you oughta be changing diapers instead of packing heat."

"You need your diaper changed, do you?"

"I don't like sass, Blondie."

"I don't like you, One Eye."

His face twitched like a raw nerve. I could see the sheen of a light sweat on his forehead. I was sweating, too. It was a hot night.

"You got a mouth, ain'tcha?" He pointed his chin up the hall behind me. "The guys that went out there with you... where'd they go?"

"To a warm place. You wanna go there, too?"

He ground his molars for a moment.

"You're that girly they call Christian, ain'tcha? The one that drinks with Leon."

"Who's Leon?"

His mouth twisted down. "Good thing Bobby Jack wants you alive."

"Oh, yeah? Maybe you kiss Bobby Jack's ass, One Eye. But me? I don't care what he wants."

He cocked his head like a dog that's heard a whistle.

"You're a cool customer, Blondie." He almost whispered it.

I gave him a sweet smile. "You wanna start this stunt over and play nice?"

I put it to him with a little appeal in my voice, and I'll be damned if it didn't work some magic. I saw his demeanor change—just a hair. He either relaxed a little, or he wanted me to believe he had.

"Good idea. Why don't we crank her down a notch?"

"Maybe two notches," I said

"No sense in us havin' no accident," he said, baring his teeth in what was probably a smile.

We could have nattered all night, but the elevator caught our attention. The old bell clanked, and the car groaned to a stop at our floor.

One Eye was a southpaw, and he had his left arm extended. That meant he had to look over his left shoulder to see the elevator, and he just had his right eye to do that with. His lips curled with nervous distaste. The door opened, and he knew he had to look.

"Be careful now, Blondie."

He shifted his whole body as he shot a glance into the elevator car. His attention came back to me with his body turned so it wasn't such a task to see two directions.

A heavy-set guy in a wheelchair rolled out and into the hallway, a smoking butt dangling from his lips—one of those long ones, a Pall Mall maybe—no sissy filter. The door closed behind him, and he sat for a long moment sizing up the situation, his hands resting on his wheels.

He wore khaki pants and a sweat-stained, olive green tank top that was in need of mending. He had USMC DEVIL DOGS tattooed on his shoulder in several colors. He had the dark look of a guy down on his luck, a tough customer that had been doing some drinking.

And another thing—I'd seen him somewhere before.

He was staring at me when he said in a deep, raspy voice, "You need some help? She looks kind of mean."

One Eye wasn't in the mood for it.

"Shove off, Wheels, before you get hurt."

His jaw tightened as he turned his head to give the vet a quick, nasty take from his good eye before getting it back on me.

"I guess you're right," the vet mumbled, but I saw in that hard, unshaven face that he wasn't going anyplace.

Some veterans I'd known in wheelchairs had terrific upper body strength, and this guy appeared to be one of those, with his meaty shoulders and bulging arms.

I got ready.

He tossed aside his cigarette, spun his chair, and backed toward me in a quick, positive move that brought him up beside One Eye's gun hand. He sent a big fist up, grabbed the featherweight's left arm, and pulled down hard.

I moved to the side fast, expecting what happened. One Eye fired off a deafening blast that gouged a hole in the floor a dozen feet past where I'd been standing.

That should've rousted a tenant or two.

The arm pull was powerful enough to bring One Eye's body down and forward, and the vet chopped him in the side of the head with a right cross that Marciano could've been proud of. The little guy let out a gruff bark and went to the floor like a sack of oats, never having seen the punch coming. He wasn't quite out, however, and exhaled a groan.

The vet spun his chair around, leaned down, and gave him another shot. That one to the back of his head, which did the trick. One Eye's face hit the floor with a splat, and he was through making any noises. So much for his pointy little nose.

I thumbed the safety on, eased the hammer down, and stuffed the Walther in my hip pocket before stepping over and toeing the .45 out of One Eye's limp hand.

I picked up the big automatic by the trigger guard and offered it to the vet.

"To the victor go the spoils."

"That's swell," he said, and made it disappear.

"You mind keeping an eye on him?"

"I mind if you're going for a beer."

I smiled. "I'll just be a minute. Why don't you pat him down while I'm gone. He might have a few other collectibles."

He smiled back, showing me a bright silver incisor among the gray enamel.

I ducked into the untidy room where my camera bag was still on the bed. I looked across the way where Virginia had been and saw that the lights were still on. The room was empty, and the door was open. I grabbed my bag.

Back in the hall, I heard someone singing, "I'm so lonesome I could cry," and noticed a few curious tenants out of their rooms. The vet and One Eye were how I'd left them, except One Eye's pockets were pulled inside out and the vet now had an unlit cigarette dangling from his lips.

When I walked over to him, he snagged the butt from his mouth before he took the hand I offered. His hand was rough and calloused, his grip strong.

"You shoot pool at Wally's, don'cha."

I gave the guy another smile. My face was going to ache from so much conviviality. "I thought I'd seen you someplace."

He released my hand. "You owe me a game."

"I'll owe you three if you forget you saw me."

"Who was that middle-aged man?" He let go a guttural sound that was his laugh.

I walked past him and looked back before entering the stairwell. "Some shit's gone down here, Marine. I'd make myself scarce if I were you."

"And miss all the fun?" He snapped a kitchen match off his shiny front tooth.

I descended seven floors. I listened, but I detected no sounds in the old building. It was three in the morning, but on the other hand, why hadn't someone called the police? Were gunshots an everyday occurrence in that hotel?

The stairwell let out around the corner from the lobby. I found my way to the alley and walked out to the street. There were sirens in the distance.

Leon's Studebaker was parked at the curb in front of the hotel. The top was down, and the passenger door stood open. I didn't rush it. When I was sure the coast was clear, I went over and looked inside the car.

There was Leon sprawled across the front seat—asleep, unconscious, or dead, and Virginia's perfume was in the breeze.

11

I ROLLED DOWN my windows to hear better and glided around the block and down a couple of side streets. I caught the scent of her perfume before I saw her. She was up ahead, carrying her shoes, walking fast, and trying to keep to the shadows.

"Virginia," I called out as I pulled up to the curb.

She skipped over like a jackrabbit when she saw who it was, tossed her shoes and denim bag in the backseat and got in. My God, the odor of her perfume was overpowering. That was when I realized her bag was soaked with *Evening in Paris.*

We drove off.

"Spill your perfume?"

"I slugged Leon with my bag…broke my bottle on his head."

"That's a classy blackjack."

"Tell me about it."

She leaned her head toward the open window like my dog Jim. In the distance the sirens arrived at the hotel.

"Was Leon supposed to show up at the hotel?"

"That nincompoop? Of course not."

"How'd he know where you were?"

"He did it with me last time. But everything he shot was

out of focus. I think he tried to use the camera with one hand. He's worthless."

"Who was the guy with the eye patch?"

"Joey Loco. He's one of Vahaska's idiots."

"What did he want?"

"Leon said he wants to know what happened at Spurs last night."

"What happened at Spurs?"

"You and Leon," Virginia said.

"What about Leon and me?"

"Quit acting dumb, Christian. They're looking for you."

Otis got his wish. I drove Virginia over to the office, marched her up to his desk, and introduced her. She captured his attention since she was still stuffed to overflowing into her little black dress.

"Pleased to meet you," she said and fooled with her delinquent spaghetti strap.

Otis just stared at us, a pinched expression on his face.

"Vahaska is for sure looking for me," I told him.

"He's looking for me, too," Virginia chimed in as she glanced with curiosity around the office.

"Okay, I wanna hear this from the beginning, but first, who's got on all the toilet water?"

Virginia and I jumped to it. We emptied her denim bag of everything except the broken glass and put the smelly thing out in the hall. We were all glad the fan was running.

"That's gonna take a dry-cleaning," Virginia admitted.

"You may have to bury it in cow manure," Otis said.

Virginia looked uneasy.

"He's just teasing," I told her. "Have a seat."

"Coffee?" Otis asked our guest as she made herself comfortable on our new leather sofa.

"Is it strong? It'll keep me awake if it's strong."

"I wouldn't say strong," Otis ventured.

"You'll be happier skipping the coffee," I advised her. "Let's talk about the information you owe me."

Otis refilled his cup and watched Virginia cross her legs as I took a seat in one of our straight back chairs meant for serious clients.

"You got pictures, didn't you?"

I nodded yes. "I even got pictures of Leon and...who was the other guy?"

"The mark?"

"Well, yeah, I got pictures of the mark. But I meant the one-eyed guy."

"Joey Loco," she said.

Otis spoke up with interest. "He's back in town?"

"Well, I guess so," Virginia sniffed. "He was there. And he's meaner'n a skillet full of rattlesnakes, too, I'll tell you."

"Couldn't have said it better myself," Otis said.

She widened her eyes at me. "I owe you what Leon talked about. But I'm looking at Otis there with his pistol and all, and I'm wondering why you folks wanna know."

"We can't tell you," I said.

"No?" She looked at my partner.

"Sorry," he said.

"You're not cops, are you?"

I smiled at her.

"I mean you don't act like cops. You do in a way, but not exactly."

"We're private detectives," Otis told her. "Licensed by the sovereign State of Texas. You wanna see some paperwork?"

She shook her head. "So, you're working on a case or something. Like Dragnet."

Neither Otis nor I spoke.

"You keep that to yourselves, I'm guessing."

We remained silent.

"You know, Christian. Vahaska's guys do bad things."

Otis glanced at me when she called me Christian, but she didn't notice.

"Those guys are real thugs."

"I'll be careful. Thanks for your concern."

"Okay. You kept your word and shot my pictures, and you came looking for me when you could of just cut and run. So, I owe you twice."

"Thanks," I said for a second time, since we were being so simpatico.

She sighed. Otis and I waited.

"Okay. Leon got a call last night. Maybe four in the morning, from a piece of shit named Floyd Gutt. Leon's head was killing him, and he didn't wanna talk on the phone, much less pull himself outta bed. He said that, but Floyd told him to get up and get dressed. I heard Angel ask Leon where he was going, and he told her out to Bobby Jack's because something bad happened out there."

"Did he say what?" Otis wanted to know.

"He did when he got back."

"When was that?" I kicked in.

"Floyd dropped him off early afternoon. Look… am I telling this or are you two gonna third degree me to death?"

Otis smiled.

"Sorry. We're just trying to understand," I explained.

"Okay then," she said.

"One thing first, though," I said. "You, Angel, and Leon live together?"

"It's Angel's place, then Leon moved in. I was last. I sleep on the sofa. You don't get rich slinging hash."

"I know that," I said. "Go ahead."

"Well, the phone's in the living room. That's how come I heard so much."

Otis took notes like he always did.

Virginia went on.

"Floyd Gutt is low on the totem pole. Not as low as Leon, but damned near. So, he likes to lord it over Leon every chance he gets. He was in the Army and thinks he's tough, but he's just an asshole. Anyhow, Leon said that a couple of Vahaska's boys got killed out at Bobby Jack's ranch..."

It went on like that while Otis and I kept our traps shut. Leon had come home with all the details about what happened out at the ranch. He'd said Vahaska had a bunch of his boys out there—local boys and boys who'd come up from Beaumont.

"You remember any names?" I asked.

"Mmmm, well, he mentioned Joey Loco and a big guy. And some tommy taco named Jose or Juan or something. There was another jerk or two. I don't know how many more. Floyd and Leon had to do the heavy lifting, getting the bodies out back, and digging holes for them in the garden. But it was while they were cleaning up in the house he heard Vahaska yelling at Bobby Jack."

"About what?" Otis asked.

"He was pissed off," Virginia said. "He told Bobby Jack that his problem was he was weak seed." She grinned. "He said Bobby Jack's father had been too old, and his mother was a worthless whore, and that was why he was nothing but weak seed. Vahaska's Bobby Jack's uncle. Did you know that?"

"Yeah," I said.

"How'd the men get killed?" Otis asked.

"They got gunned down. Leon said it was nastier'n the south end of a skunk around that house. The dead bodies were starting to stink...and they let their bowels go when they die. Did you know that? I didn't know that. Makes sense, though."

"Who did the shooting?" I asked.

"Bobby Jack blamed some girl," she said and laughed. "I thought that girl might've been you."

Neither Otis nor I reacted.

"I mean, I know you went out there."

"No, you don't," I said.

"If you say so," she sniffed. "And another thing, Bobby

Jack was under the weather. Leon said he was damp with sweat and shaking and kept getting sick at his stomach."

"Had he been taking drugs?" Otis asked. "That'll make you sick."

"I don't know about that," she said.

"How come Bobby Jack didn't get killed with the others?" I asked.

"I don't know," Virginia shrugged. "Leon didn't mention that. But that is strange, isn't it?"

"Seems strange to me," I said. "He said a girl killed the men."

"It wasn't just the killing. There was money taken, too. Bobby Jack blamed her for everything. There was a lot of noise about her. Cherry, Leon said her name was."

And we know Leon always gets his names straight.

"Anybody say how much money got took?" Otis asked.

"Got me," she said. "But it must've been a shit load the way he said they carried on."

"Mmmm," Otis hummed.

"When Vahaska accused Bobby Jack of letting a teenage slut beat him up and steal from him, Leon said he got as jumpy as a barefoot kid on a sidewalk in July. He claimed she had help."

"Did Bobby Jack say who that might've been?" Otis asked.

"Nope. Leon said Vahaska was royally pissed off. He told Bobby Jack if he didn't find the girl quick and get back his money, he should pick out a spot in the garden."

"That's clear," I said. "What else?"

Virginia thought for a moment.

"Leon talked about how heavy one of the dead guys was. How they had to roll him into a blanket and drag him off the porch and around the house. He said the flies was awful...swarms of them. That was the worst, he said."

Being dragged in a blanket was easier on ol' Cecil's knees, I thought—even though I knew it didn't make any sense to think that.

After Virginia fell asleep on the sofa in the office, I joined Otis in our darkroom. I watched as he developed my night's work.

"What's that?" he asked, as an unusual image emerged on the blank paper he was swishing around in the chemical bath.

"A frog," I said as the highly contrasted image sharpened.

"Damned if it ain't," he said and leaned forward, his attention drawn to the tight shot of the small tattoo on Virginia's firm backside.

"It's a fake. I watched her lick the thing and paste it on when she changed clothes in the car."

"She's clever," Otis allowed. "That businessman can't bullshit his wife about these pictures because he has to be with some strumpet. Nice girls don't have tattoos, just like they don't pierce their ears."

"Tell me about Joey Loco," I said when he pulled a picture of him out of the soup.

Otis tightened up. This guy was something or somebody to him.

"Joey Kilgore. I met the rat when I was a patrolman, a lotta years ago. I arrested him...well, my partner and me arrested him and a couple of other slimy thugs. They was causing trouble in a part of town where they never should've been. They wouldn't go peaceful, so we had to rough them up. They all had a lot to say, but Joey made the most threats. He was a friend of Vahaska's even in those days and thought that carried some weight."

"Why the nickname Loco?"

"Well, the way the story goes, one night Joey slammed

around some gal. Him and some other Einsteins was in a house trailer over east of town, drinking and making like fools. So, Joey wallops the girlfriend and gets attacked by her dog."

"Big dog?"

"Nah, just your average mutt. But he bit Joey in the face. He opened up the side of his head and dragged his eyeball out."

"Damn. That had to hurt."

"You could say that. And, with the bloody thing hanging out of the socket by its connections, Joey grabs the mongrel and bites its ear off. I don't mean no little piece. With the animal fighting and squealing like a pig being slaughtered, he gnawed the thing clean off its head and made the woman eat it. All the while bleeding all over the place and screaming like a maniac with his eyeball dangling about on his cheek like a Christmas ornament."

"Jesus," I said.

"Uh huh. And over the next few months, that woman, her dog, and both of her brothers disappeared. That sneaky sonofabitch Joey Loco was brought in along with his friend Vahaska, but nobody could make it stick because the bodies was never found."

There was more. I could always tell with Otis. I waited.

"Butch Stovall, my partner, went missing, too."

That hurt me to hear, so I knew how it made Otis feel.

"You were patrolmen?"

"Yeah. Had a patrol car. Had a section of the city we worked."

"Your partner ever show up?"

"Nah, we never found him, Missy. Like all them others, he just disappeared. The old man where he bought his cigarettes was the last to see him. Stopped there on his way home one night. Swell guy. Tough guy...though he was small, you know. They used to call us Mutt and Jeff."

"And you think Joey Loco got him."

"Ain't no doubt about it. We knew it was him and Vahaska.

But we never could get nothing on the sneaky bastards. I knew it weren't my fault, but I couldn't help feeling I'd let my partner down somehow. He went too soon to the other side, and I was a long time getting over it."

"Those guys ever make a play for you?"

"There was a couple of times I thought I'd been staked out, but nothing ever went down. I guess Joey and Vahaska got tired of being took downtown every time they farted in public, so they up and moved to Beaumont. It was like a disease had left town. Anyway, it was a dog dragged his eye out. That's the stunt that got Joey the moniker."

"I'm sorry you lost your partner," I said.

That was weak. But I had to say something.

"Thank you, Missy. And I'm sorry to hear Joey Loco's back in town. I thought I was finished with him when he moved away. Haven't seen him for years."

"I don't think he's moved back. He just came up with Vahaska for this Bobby Jack business, don't you imagine?"

"I hope you're right. What you gotta know about him is he'd just as soon rip your liver out as piss on the drapes. He's never taken a fall I know of, but he's been up for a half dozen gun charges...shootings he's always managed to get out of. My advice is to avoid him if you get a choice. But if your back's against the wall, kill the tricky bastard right away. You might not get a second chance."

That was when I told Otis about the big guy and Guero and my meeting with Joey Loco.

Otis heard me through, shook his head, and said, "Vahaska's boys are dropping like flies around you. What's going on?"

I shrugged. How could I answer that?

"Two a night. You keep that up, there won't be nobody left by the end of the week and our problem's solved."

"Bobby Jack got two, and the other two were accidents," I said. "My hands are clean."

"Try explaining that to the police," he said.

I wanted no part of that.

"Well, lemme tell you how it is," Otis piped up. "Our waitress in there and Joey Loco and a pool-shooting vet in a wheelchair…and we don't know who the hell else…can put you at that hotel."

"So what," I said. "That gang's put me together with Leon at Spurs, too. But they don't know who I am. And they don't know for sure I was out at Bobby Jack's."

"But they suspect you was out there…whoever you are… or they wouldn't be interested at all. Would they?"

"I agree," I said.

"But after the long haul, it ain't you they want anyway, is it, Missy?"

That was rhetorical. It was Sherry Beasley and the money they wanted.

"Bringing in a runaway girl has turned into something else," I said.

"A bag full of hot potatoes," Otis suggested.

I shrugged. He was right, of course.

"When your waitress wakes up, you wanna find out what she told that Leon fella. You know for sure she told him you was gonna be with her at the hotel. Otherwise, how'd them snakes know which door to knock on?"

"Virginia talks to Leon as much as Leon talks to her," I said, feeling foolish for not realizing that earlier.

"Sauce for the goose," Otis said. "In the meantime, let's put these pictures away."

"In with the Barefoot Contessa," I said, referring to the autographed pinup of Ava Gardner that Otis kept inside a beautiful old Murray Allenby, Boston series, triple hard-plate safe he used as a bedside table.

As he gathered up the prints and negatives, I went ahead of him and opened the heavy door. The combination was Ava's birthday.

"You ever had this much money in your safe before?" I asked him, looking in at the neat stacks of banded hundreds that we'd brought back from Bobby Jack's.

"Never," he said. "And won't it be interesting to find out who it belongs to."

"I'm going shopping if nobody claims it," I said and Otis gave me a hard stare. "I was kidding, for chrissake."

"It ain't that," he said. "I don't give a rat's ass what happens to that money. It's that tow-headed mop of yours. It's how all them witnesses are gonna remember you...the blonde."

Two years ago when we got new furniture for the office, Otis moved the old sofa into his apartment. That night, Virginia slept on the office sofa—where I usually spent the night when I stayed over. Otis said he would sleep on the old sofa, and I could have his bed. But I wouldn't allow that; I slept on the old sofa.

Something woke me later that morning. Otis was snoring. That wasn't it. Someone was moving around in the other room. I glanced at my pocket watch. It was a little after eleven. What was that? Six—six and a half hour's sleep? I thought it was Virginia, but just to make sure I picked up my .38 and sat up.

At that moment the door opened, and a scent of *Evening in Paris* wafted in from the office. Following that was Virginia, looking like an aspiring starlet in colorful Capri pants, a low-cut peasant blouse, and flat shoes. Her thick red hair looked like a tossed salad. Sunglasses with pink frames would have completed the picture. She glanced around the room, found me sitting on the sofa, and took a stance with her hands on her hips.

"You smell like a cat house," I told her.

"Well, you can just live with it. Besides, we're not stopping any place between here and my house, are we?"

We had agreed the night before that I would drive her over to where she lived with Leon and Angel so she could get her things. Further, I'd agreed to let her stay with me until this Vahaska business blew over.

I had been in a weakened state.

Virginia and her two roommates hung their hats kind of close together in a tiny one bedroom, wood frame house in an older section of Dallas. Theirs was one of five rustic rental units in a cozy bungalow court arrangement gathered around a dry Mexican tile fountain and an abundance of blood-red bougainvillea. All charm and neglect.

However, seeing Bobby Jack and Leon walking out of the courtyard canceled any real notion of charm.

"Scoot down," I told Virginia.

She saw them, too, before sliding to the floor.

"Get your hair down," I said.

She scrunched down more until her pile of red hair was below the window level.

"Who's that with Leon?" she whispered.

"I don't know," I lied. "You didn't recognize him?"

"Who knows? One of Vahaska's nimrods," she said.

The men paid no attention as I drove by. Down the street, I pulled over to the curb and watched in my rearview as they got into Bobby Jack's big pickup truck and drove away. I was glad to see that Bobby Jack had a bandage showing on the back of his head.

"Okay," I said.

She sat up and looked out the back window. "That green Pontiac's Floyd Gutt's car."

She meant the shiny two-door parked near where Bobby Jack's truck had been.

"So, he's at your place. Is Angel there?"

"Probably," she said, under her breath.

"Is there a back way in?"

"Off the alley. You think something bad's happened, don't you?"

"Can't hurt to be cautious," I said.

I sure could call them sometimes.

96   —

12

VIRGINIA OPENED THE back door, and we heard gruff, foul-mouthed insults coming from the other room.

"That's Floyd," she whispered.

I wiped the sweat off my face and glanced across the kitchen toward the doorway that opened into a short hall.I knew that the old, discolored linoleum floor squeaked.

"Walk fast into the other room. Call out to Angel as you go," I whispered.

"You sure?" she asked.

"Go ahead."

"Okay," she said.

I held the torn screen door open, and she charged into and across the kitchen with real purpose.

"Angel," she called out like a proper actress. "Angel. You home?"

I let the screen door slam behind us.

Virginia moved down the short hall and into the living room with me right behind her. I had a snub-nose in my ankle holster in case I needed it.

We discovered Angel splayed back on the sofa. Her flower print, rayon housecoat was torn away, exposing her naked upper body. Her face was blotched and bruised. One of her eyes and her cheekbone were swollen, and blood ran from her nose.

Floyd Gutt was hunched over her, holding her by her long, dark hair. He had a fist doubled up and ready to fly.

Just to the right of the doorway, on a skinny little three-legged table, I saw the telephone Virginia had mentioned earlier. It gave me an idea.

"What're you looking at?" Floyd snarled at Virginia.

"I'm looking at you, you ugly moron. What d'you think you're doing?"

I liked her brass.

Floyd was twenty-five or so. Average guy, a hundred fifty, maybe. Curly hair the color of coal, low forehead. He had an unpleasant smile that seemed drawn on his pasty face. He dropped Angel to the sofa and aimed his awful smile at us.

"I'll show you ugly," he growled.

He took the step or two that would have brought him to Virginia if she had still been there. But I pushed her to the side at the last moment, grabbed the telephone hand receiver, and swung the heavy piece at Floyd's temple.

The cord wasn't long enough for that action, however, and shortened my swing when it tightened up. Instead of hitting him in the side of the head, the receiver swiped across his face and broke his prominent nose. Blood spurted down the front of his white polo shirt.

He grunted with surprise and stopped. His vacant, deep-set eyes were like dark marbles behind blinking lids. His hand went to his face. I dropped the phone and kicked him hard with the heel of my boot just below his knee. Grunting again, he hopped back and collapsed, crushing a cheap blond wood table as he went to the floor.

"Oh, my God," I heard Virginia say.

"Get Angel," I told her. "Take her in the other room and close the door."

"Come on, honey," Virginia cooed. She got the battered and confused girl by the hand and led her away from where Floyd snuffled blood as he struggled to his feet.

It was a small room, and the girls were in my way, or

I would've kicked him again while I had the advantage. I didn't know if he carried a gun. I knew I should have had mine in my hand, but I could get it if I needed to. Gunfire with neighbors so close would bring the police for sure.

I watched his hands. He would make the gun decision. I heard the bedroom door slam.

Floyd breathed through his mouth; his face was covered with sweat and smeared with blood. He emitted a throaty sound as he dragged the back of his hand across this mouth.

"Get out of here, Numbnuts. Go home."

His waist was short and thick, his hips broad for a man. The way he wore his pants up high gave him a bottom-heavy, goofy look. But there was nothing comical about the way he pulled a switchblade from his pocket, snapped it open, and moved toward me.

My guess was he thought that I was an unarmed girl who had gotten in a couple of lucky hits. But I carried knives, one in each boot. The move it took to put a scalpel-sharp blade in my hand was quick and sure.

I could tell from his moves that Floyd had been in the service and from how he held his knife what his training had been. Mine hadn't been so different. I thought I knew what he would do. All that was missing was how well he could do it. I couldn't count on his injured knee helping me. Adrenaline had a way of erasing shocks like that.

He was accustomed to pushing women around. So I held my knife like a brave amateur and took a stance that I knew he had been trained to defeat. His angry face gave nothing away, but the way he advanced told me he had gone for my fake.

At the last moment I blocked his thrust with a hand to his forearm. I pushed his arm up, stepped inside, and jabbed him twice to the hilt under his short ribs. Very fast.

I dodged a predictable, but whisper-close counter move, and struck again.

This time I sliced him, high across his chest and shoulder. He stepped back and took a couple of steps for balance. He bled badly.

"Give it up, Floyd. Get out while you still can."

He took a gasping breath and came at me, flinging blood like a dog from a bath. He aimed at my throat.

I shifted my weight and took the point of his blade in my shoulder. I cut him in return, a diagonal swipe across the inside of his outstretched knife arm—then leaned in and used my legs to shove him hard, back away from me. He flailed out as he caught his balance, but he was out of range.

I had cut his arm clear to the bone. And so clean it was nothing but a thin line for a heartbeat or two before beading up and gaping open. When his dark blood came rushing out, he dropped that arm to his side.

I'd severed muscle, ligament, and artery. He stepped back, wobbly on his feet. I pressed forward. His reaction was to shift into the defensive stance I expected—the one that left his groin exposed.

I snapped a kick hard into his manhood.

He exhaled a grunt and jerked forward. I stepped in and stabbed him in the chest. I moved back as he went limp. He sank to the floor and came to rest on his ample haunches. He paused there with his mouth wide open, pink bubbles forming around his lips.

The gates of hell are open day and night.

His eyes went wide, and he gagged and shuddered before his head fell back, carrying his body with it. There he was in an expanding pool of blood, a useless switchblade near his fist, and a more than useless smile on his face—all ready for his trip to Hades.

I stood for a moment, soaked with sweat, my heart tripping against my ribs. I had no illusions. I could've been the one on the floor if Floyd had been better, faster, smarter—hell, luckier—if his knife had gone into my heart, instead of mine into his.

It was just business, as my knife instructor Sarge used to say, but he never mentioned the raw terror that is part of being attacked with a knife. I caught my breath and willed my heart to slow down.

The truth? I was tired of tough guys pushing people around.

Floyd was right-handed. So I fished in his right pants pocket for his car keys and dropped them in my handbag. Next, I took off my blood-spattered blouse and used it to clean my knife, wipe my prints off the telephone receiver, and to open the bedroom door.

The girls were sitting on the edge of the bed holding each other. Angel was sobbing. She was beat up, of course, and more frightened than Virginia. However, neither of them appeared to take much comfort in seeing me in the doorway in my jeans and bra with blood all over me.

I said to Virginia, "I'm going to need your help with this cut. And I'll have to borrow a blouse."

To her roommate, I said, "Start packing, Angel. It's moving day, and we don't have a lot of time."

It was right that Angel should inherit Floyd's Pontiac, but she was hesitant.

"It's like stealing, isn't it?"

"Take it, for God's sake," Virginia reasoned with her. "Who's gonna report it missing, Floyd?"

So we packed up the new car with her belongings, and forty minutes later she was behind the wheel, ready to head back to Newton County. She was still teary-eyed and looked like an accident victim.

"I'm just barely a Texan," she said. "My hometown's so close to the border, if you miss our stop sign you're in Louisiana."

We smiled. It was something her grandpa used to say. Angel appeared to be happy to be leaving the Dallas big city life behind. Just out of her teens, she was pretty, busty, and long-legged like all the waitresses seemed to be at Spurs. But more than that, she was a sweet-natured young woman who didn't deserve being beaten.

"Bobby Jack thought I knew the name of the girl Leon had drinks with at Spurs," Angel said.

"But you didn't, did you," I said.

"I was so busy I never saw her. I told him Leon called her Christian. But Bobby Jack kept slapping me and saying that wasn't good enough. When it got through to him that I didn't know who the girl was, he quit hitting me. That was when he told Floyd that I was expendable and to finish the job."

"He said that? Expendable?"

"His exact words."

Killing Floyd was the right thing to have done.

Angel went on, "They're looking for you, too, Virginia."

Virginia shrugged like she didn't care and threw a glance at me.

"So, that was Bobby Jack," she said, referring to the guy we'd seen leaving with Leon. "He didn't look like so much."

"He didn't, did he," I agreed.

Angel said, "Bobby Jack told Floyd if he found the slut that slipped Leon the Mickey, he'd find that other slut Cherry who killed those two men."

Virginia shot me a look I could have done without.

"We're wasting time. Start the car," I said.

When Angel had the Pontiac purring, she grinned slyly and confessed that she'd never owned a new car.

"I don't know how to thank you," she said.

"By forgetting any of this ever happened," I said.

She pulled a face and said, "I'm worried what Leon's gonna do when he comes home and finds me gone and Floyd deceased in the parlor."

Always the realist, Virginia said, "Better him than you in the parlor."

"Leon knows where you're from?" I asked Angel.

Virginia snorted. "Leon doesn't know where he's from."

Angel offered an embarrassed nod of agreement.

"Whose name is on the lease here?" I asked.

"Heck if I know," Angel said, and then understood what was behind my question. "I inherited the house last year off a barmaid. She was on her way to Hollywood to be in pictures. Maybe her name's on the lease."

Luck favored the prepared...so to speak.

"You take care of yourself," I said.

Angel put on some big sunglasses that hid her half-closed, black eye.

"Don't slow down till you're home," Virginia advised her.

We both stepped away from the car, and Floyd Gutt's last victim drove away. Well, next to last victim. I'd forgotten for a moment that he'd stabbed me.

Virginia had thrown me some real looks while Angel sang like a bird. But she didn't let out a peep herself until we were in my car and had put some distance between Floyd's fly-covered remains and us.

She said, "Scary as all that was, I'm glad that evil turd's dead. He was gonna kill Angel and me, too, maybe."

"Forget all that," I said.

"I'll try, but come on, Christian. I've never seen a PI work before. First you carve up Floyd like a pork roast, then you Band-Aid a knife cut cool as a cucumber."

The knife cut that she thought I was so casual about was a puncture wound, hurt like hell, and still bled.

"A lot of funny stuff's happened since you showed up," she said.

"Coincidence. Don't start blaming Vahaska's business on me."

"Maybe. Maybe. Nice for me and Angel, though. You

pulled our fat out of the fire, and you didn't even break a sweat."

"Next you'll have me leaping tall buildings."

"You're a mixed blessing," she said. "You saved us from that jerk Floyd, sure, but now I have no home and no job, either. Unless I want those pickle brains that work for Vahaska to find me. I'd better be careful showing up at Spurs again."

"Count your blessings, dear," I said.

"Oh, yeah? And how are you in any better shape?" she reasoned. "It's you they're talking about. Because you *did* slip Leon something, and you *did* drive off with those guys who, by the by, got themselves dead that same night."

"Slow down," I told her.

"Uh huh. Well, I know for a fact you can make people dead."

That was closer than I cared for.

"You ever see me kill anyone?"

"The last time I saw Floyd he looked like rare roast beef. How do we suppose that happened, Cupcake?"

"Did you see me do that?"

"See you? Oh, you're gonna start that stuff."

"Did you see me do anything to those guys out at the ranch?"

"No and no."

"No and no, see? So stop telling me what you know. You don't know squat."

"There's nobody in this car but the two of us, and you want me to pretend I don't know you sliced out Floyd's gizzard. Is that what's happening here?"

"That's not a bad idea," I pointed out.

"And I'd started to like you," she said and exhaled, loudly. "Tell me the God's truth for one half second, if you can manage it. Any fool would know your life's in danger because of something that happened out at Bobby Jack's."

"That's what you say," I pointed out.

"Well, okay, that's your affair, but Angel got the crap

kicked out of her because they're looking for you. And my life's up for grabs, too. Same reason. You. Don't you think you owe me more than five bucks and a kiss-my-ass?"

"Okay. Okay," I said. "Take a step back. Let me think for a moment. There are more lives at risk than just yours and mine."

Virginia didn't have much in the way of possessions. Roving gypsies claimed more belongings. She had clothes, some jewelry, some bathroom items, and a small, iron kettle candle she enigmatically called her dowry. All of which she kept in an open-topped cardboard box and two bulging pillowcases.

"This is some kitchen," she said as we entered the back door at my place. "Look at that stove. Old but nice."

She crossed the room with her pillowcases clutched in her arms, her head pivoting like she was at a tennis match, and continued her appraisal as she entered the living room.

"What d'you got here? Two? No, three bedrooms, I'll bet."

"You should take up real estate," I called after her.

I deposited her cardboard box on the kitchen table and turned on an electric fan that was nearby.

"Look at the size of this living room," she said as I entered behind her. "And my gosh, it's like a bookstore in here. You read all these?"

"Every one of them," I told her and turned on another electric fan, the one on the table in the corner.

"You live here alone?" she asked, gawking in all directions.

"Don't get any ideas," I advised her.

It *was* a large apartment. For fifteen years, it had been the home of the couple that owned the building, Maude and Wally Kowalski. They'd lived above their business—Wally's—a popular pool hall, lunch counter, and newsstand.

A couple of years ago, they decided to move into a Victorian farmhouse set on a six acre avocado orchard down near Waxahachie. Wally told me they were going to retire in four or five years. Maude stayed home more, and he didn't mind the drive. When I learned about their plans, I spoke to Maude. She spoke to Wally, and I moved in over a year ago.

"We knew your dad. We're glad to have someone we can trust taking care of things," Maude had said.

"You're here shooting pool all the time, anyway," Wally had tossed in. "Might as well live upstairs."

There were two entrances to the spacious apartment, one through the pool hall and the other off the alley. The enclosed stairway that went up the outside wall at the end of the building started inside a two-car garage and led to the apartment's kitchen door.

It had been a safe arrangement for Maude and was perfect for me, too. Having that back entrance helped keep my comings and goings private.

I showed Virginia the bedroom that she would be using *temporarily* before going to my own room and getting out of my blood-splattered clothes.

"Make yourself comfortable," I told her. "But stay off the phone. It's better if you and Angel just disappear."

"I might've been born at night," she said. "But I wasn't born last night."

After my shower, I cleaned my cut with alcohol, painted it with iodine, dabbed it with alum, and taped on a new bandage. I put my stained things in cold water to soak and put on fresh clothes. When I was ready to leave, I found my houseguest standing at the hi-fi, thumbing through my jazz albums.

"If I call, I'll ring twice, hang up, and call back. Otherwise, don't answer the phone. Got that?"

She turned away from the records. "You're the boss. All I wanna do is peel off these Capris, take a bath, and wash this perfume away. See you later."

What had it come to, I wondered while descending the back steps to the car, when someone being agreeable gave me a reason to worry?

13

I STOPPED AT Ivy's Beauty Shop on the way back to the office. Ivy was pricey, but good with my hair, and candid about what was right for me. It was that honesty that caused some of her customers to move along. But I appreciated it, since I'd learned from magazines most of what I knew about cosmetics and fashion, which meant I didn't know crap. Ivy was like a big sister who didn't want to be embarrassed by me.

"That's just silly," she'd say, or simply shake her head about my *beauty* ideas.

Ivy had the prim appearance of a Sunday school teacher but could embarrass a sailor with her bawdy laugh. She was a little thing with a skinny figure, but nobody messed with her. She was delighted to color my hair, as long as she picked the color.

"A pixie cut like yours won't take any time at all," she said.

My hair was longer than a pixie. I had what she'd told me once was a tousled, natural look. Ivy always left me enough hair to cover the cauliflower ear I'd gotten from a beating. The guys who murdered my dad had given me that—along with a couple of other memories.

"How'd you hurt yourself?" she asked when she saw my bandaged shoulder.

"Oh, you know, life on a ranch," I said. "Nothing serious."

It took less than an hour and a half for Ivy to turn me into a new woman. Chestnut, she called the color. It felt strange to not be the pale blonde I'd been all my life, but I liked the way my hair shone when it caught the light. The eyebrows were going to take some getting used to, but I told Ivy that I liked it even before I was certain, because I knew that was what she wanted to hear.

"It's a good thing you always have a suntan," she said. "With your pale skin you'd look a little too contrasty. You'll need some new things," she told me in the mirror.

"Damn. I hadn't thought about clothes."

"Of course not," Ivy said. "Well, you'll look sensational in browns and reds and best of all navy blues. Want me to write that down?"

She had more to say about how breathtaking I'd be, but I was on my way out the door. Finally, she said what I wanted to hear.

"You look so different," she called after me. "No one's gonna recognize you."

Back at the office Otis did a double take.

"That was quick. You still have them glasses with the black frames and the clear lenses?"

I told him I did.

"Wear them things sometimes, too. I'm telling you, nobody'll know who you are."

"I think secretly you've always wanted me to look like a librarian."

Otis grinned, stood up, and grabbed his jacket.

"Let's go."

I started for the door, but he stopped me.

"Missy."

"Yeah," I said, turning to face him.

"Your hairdo looks swell."

I felt my face heat up. "You sweep a girl right off her feet," I told him.

He came around his desk with his jacket wadded under his arm.

"Why don't you drive," he said. "Unless that shoulder hurts too much."

I shook my head. I wasn't going to whine. It was clear to me that until the heat spell broke or my partner bought a car with air conditioning, I was the Millett Agency's chauffeur.

On the way to Doc McGraw's, I told Otis what else I'd learned about Leon's experiences at Bobby Jack's.

"We knew they was looking for you," he said.

"But they still don't know who I am."

"Goddamn it! We save Sherry's life and get ourselves involved in something that's none of our doing, none of our business."

"There's more," I said.

"Saved something for last, did you?" He punched in the lighter. "What now?"

"It just happened. I don't know how I could've told you any sooner."

He dragged a butt out of a crumpled pack and straightened it out. "Come on. Let's hear it," he said, firing up his smoke.

I laid out what had gone down with Floyd Gutt. I told him everything. He frowned a time or two but didn't interrupt. He let me finish.

"So, the other gal skipped town and the one I met is hunkered down at your place."

"Yeah," I said.

"Vahaska's got his boys out looking for you, and now this thing. How long ago was this knife business?"

"Mmmm. I stopped to have my hair done. Let's say three…no, maybe four hours ago."

"You got your hair colored *after*?"

"There wasn't time before."

Otis groaned.

"You got the bleeding stopped?"

"Pretty much. I taped it up at my place."

"You see the Doc about that," he said in that paternal tone he took on sometimes.

"I plan to."

"You know the address where you left that guy?" I nodded that I did. "And you're sure you cleaned up after yourself?" I nodded again.

Otis was up to something.

"Pull over at the next gas pump, I'm reporting this to the police. I'm saying the dead guy over there is Vahaska's man. Maybe the Dallas PD will catch them trying to clean up after their selves. You got some nickels?"

Chauffeur and financier.

When he came back to the car, he told me he'd also called a couple of reporters. He'd told them about Floyd and also to look into the accident at the hotel in Fort Worth.

"I want Vahaska busy covering his tracks instead of lollygagging around looking for you. And if he's as pissed off at Bobby Jack as that young hoodlum Leon says, maybe all the noise'll make him put a slug in his nephew just to close the books."

"Ohhh, I wouldn't count on that," I said. "The way that guy Chuck was tiptoeing around Bobby Jack makes me think he's the favorite nephew."

"Well, even if the police and the press just slow them up, that's good for us."

"I'm sure you're right, but they aren't going away," I said. "Not with Sherry and all that money on their minds."

"Plus five dead now and two knocked silly. Jesus—five dead. You're like the grim reaper in disguise."

"Thank you. That's nice to hear."

"You know what I mean." He waved a big, dismissive hand like he was swatting at flies. "Let's get on over to Doc's and talk to our debutante. Maybe she can tell us the name of the game we're playing."

We had given Sherry back to Hagan last winter wrapped in a blanket and smelling of marijuana. But this time we were determined to help her preserve a degree of dignity. There was a possibility that she wouldn't appreciate the time we'd allowed her at Doc's and the shopping I'd done for her. I'd never seen her off drugs, so I couldn't swear what she was really like.

"Rich girls have a reputation for snotty behavior," I'd mentioned to Otis.

"We ain't been hired to judge her character," he'd said.

Sherry's home was with Nadine Beasley, the one of Hiram's ex-wives still living. Nadine was in her late sixties, still attractive, vain, and self-centered. She'd thought of herself as an actress when she was younger, and Hiram had done his best to promote her career.

"She didn't have a lick of talent," Otis informed me when we'd first discussed her months ago. "After enough folks laughed at her, she retired to one of Hiram's ranches and became known for drunken barbeques and swimming nekked in that big pool they got out there. Hiram was forced to get a divorce. But he was still bighearted with her, providing what I heard Hagan call a 'significant yearly income' for the rest of her life."

"He rewarded her bad behavior," I said.

"And ain't women funny. After old Beasley died, Nadine just up and stopped her rowdy ways. It was like she'd done them things to spite him. He couldn't have been nicer to her."

"Maybe he was too nice," I said.

He shrugged. "That's what I'm saying. Women're funny

that way, ain't they? Like that lizard that changes colors."

"The chameleon."

"Yeah, like that. Don't matter what age they are, neither. Women are like that lizard." He glanced over at me and added, "No offense intended, Missy."

"None taken," I said, because I knew he was right.

As we drove up to the main house, Otis said, "There's just something plain ol' good for the spirit about coming out here to Doc McGraw's."

There was something. Something kind of apple pie about the dogs running out barking. It was like— "Arriving at Grandma's," I said.

I remembered hanging out the car window—barking dogs. The rutted red clay road that led up to my grandma's farm near Shawnee, Oklahoma—and the sun-bleached wood corrals down past the next farm where the laughing boys chewed tobacco and broke horses and ignored me.

"That's it," Otis agreed. "It's like being out in the farm country...like where I grew up."

As I opened the car trunk, Otis waved at Doc's wife, who had come around the house and was walking over to greet us.

Loretta was an imposing woman, large and tall. And the breeze catching her colorful, full-cut housedress made her a formidable object as she came sailing toward us, a spinnaker in farmer's boots.

She had a wide smile and large eyes the color of pecan shells. Her best feature, though, was her thick auburn hair that cascaded over her broad shoulders in waves and curls. Today, the breeze had her holding her hair out of her face.

I handed Otis the bags of clothing I'd purchased for Sherry, and acknowledged Loretta as she walked up, nodding happily. She was mute but could hear as well as anyone. Otis asked where the phony doctor was hiding, and we all had a laugh at Doc's expense.

She tipped her head toward the barn and signed: "With the horses."

When we asked about Sherry, Loretta let us know that she'd moved from the guest room. She was in one of the three little clapboard bungalows that were set back away from the main house. They were nestled under some big oaks in a park-like setting of blooming hydrangea and pyracanthus.

These cabins were hospital rooms. Doc didn't often have stay-over human patients, but when he did, this is where he put them up. Loretta walked with us out toward the little houses. She noticed my hair, of course, and signed to me that she liked it. But I could tell she wasn't quite sure yet.

We hadn't gone far before we saw Sherry under the rustling trees, sitting in mottled sunlight at a picnic table. She wore pale green pajamas, a light cotton robe, and slippers. I'm not sure what I'd expected, but the times I'd seen Sherry before were never in a peaceful, bucolic setting.

She looked up, put down her book, and smiled as we approached. There was stress apparent around her eyes, and the bruising from Bobby Jack's manhandling was still visible on her face and neck. But overall she looked relaxed.

Or, rather, she looked as if she wanted to be relaxed. Her long, dark hair was clean and shiny. That helped with the illusion. But I knew she wasn't the carefree teenager she might have wanted to appear to be. She kept her eyes on Otis as we approached.

"Mister Millett," she said. "How nice to see you."

Otis smiled big.

"I do declare, as my mama used to say. You look rested."

"I'm feeling fine," she replied with the poise of an older girl. "I'm told I have you to thank again."

"Well, me and Kristin. You remember Kristin, I'll bet."

She gazed at me with a pleasant expression and shook her head. "Well, maybe I kind of do. I'm sorry."

I saw in her eyes that she knew who I was. "Don't

worry about it," I told her. She was reading Peyton Place, so I commented on that. "Enjoying the book?"

"I understand why some places have banned it," she said.

"Same reason it's popular," I said and we exchanged a smile.

Otis gave me a look that I understood.

I turned to Loretta and said, "I've got a little place on my shoulder. You think Doc has time to see me?"

She nodded yes.

"Catch up with you later," I told Otis and Sherry.

I walked off toward the main house with Loretta beside me, quizzing me about my shoulder with concerned facial expressions. Behind us I heard Otis telling Sherry he had some new clothes for her.

Loretta helped me off with my blouse and had me sit on the edge of a large stainless steel table in the middle of their air-conditioned operating room so she could clean the wound.

"What did this?" Doc asked when he came in and looked over Loretta's shoulder.

"Knife," I said.

Loretta finished cleaning the area, and he began his examination.

"Brachial plexus. A puncture," he mumbled. "Any shortness of breath?"

"I haven't noticed any," I said, shivering a bit. It was cold in the room and, except for my bra, I was bare from the waist up.

"Loretta's going to administer some antibiotic."

Doc meant she was going to give me a shot. Near him was a table on wheels that held surgical instruments in trays. Loretta placed a small bottle and a syringe on the roll-about before getting a light blanket to put around me.

"Your shoulder's sore?"

"Yep."

"This happened when?"

"Oh…a few hours ago."

"Broke your neck getting here. You're not allergic to anything, are you?"

"Handsome doctors."

I winced as Loretta administered the penicillin. I'd learned to dislike shots during my recovery period after that affair in '52.

"Let me see you use your hand, wise guy," Doc said, looking me in the eye.

Doc had dark, intelligent eyes—the single handsome feature in his fearsome face. It was all the pretty he needed, he was so all man.

"How do you mean?"

"Wiggle your fingers."

I did that.

"Give me some wrist movement."

I did that, too, and he poked around some more.

"There's an artery in there," he said.

"That's not my fault," I said.

"Is that right? Well, you're lucky the blade didn't go any deeper."

"I was moving away, and he'd lost his strength by then," I explained.

I thought of the mountain lion that had clawed Loretta's throat open and wondered if she'd been moving away. The reason she survived was because it happened in front of Doc in that very room.

Using his fingers, he probed around the wound, which hurt like hell. Next he used the turkey baster-looking thing to wash the area some more, which also hurt like hell. I wanted to complain, but I didn't. Hell, I wanted to cry like a baby, but I wasn't going to do that, either.

When he picked up a curved needle that was already threaded, I said to Loretta, "Here comes the fun part."

"Under your collarbone there, it could have punctured your lung," he said.

It could have been serious, but it wasn't—that's what he meant. Loretta winked and made a face to make sure I understood. He squeezed an ointment from a tube and smeared it around the wound, which, again, hurt like hell.

"This is a local so the stitching won't sting so much."

First, do no harm.

I was dreaming, of course. Every stitch he took stung more than the last, and he took six all together. I'm lucky I didn't snap a molar the way I clinched up. Jesus, give me a knife fight any day over a doctor.

"You'll have a scar," he said.

"I'll wear it like a medal," I said, "for surviving medical attention."

"Loretta will give you something for the pain now, and I'll scratch you out a prescription. But you be careful if you're gonna drive. You hear me?"

"Gotcha," I said and swallowed the pills that Loretta offered me with a glass of water. The pills couldn't work too soon for me.

"I'm writing you some paper for antibiotic, too. Take it when you're supposed to. And take every last one of them."

"Yes, sir," I said.

Loretta had bandage and tape ready, and when she finished, my shoulder felt mummified.

"When does this pain medication kick in?" I said, and Doc nodded at Loretta, who gave me two more pills.

"Come back and have Loretta change that dressing later this week. But if you commence bleeding, get back pronto. Don't wait all day like you usually do. Understood?"

"Understood," I said.

He stepped back and gave me an even stare.

"What were you…nineteen when you brought Otis in here with a bullet wound in his belly?"

I nodded.

"And you've been working with him all this time? Going on two years?"

"Uh huh."

"And you haven't had enough yet? Look at you. A knife wound, for goodness sake. Thugs use knives…and what's this bruise on your other shoulder?"

Doc McGraw was a grown man and a doctor; I figured he deserved the truth.

"I broke down a door to get away from a man with a gun."

Loretta's mouth fell open, and Doc narrowed his eyes.

"And the bruise on your sternum?"

I looked down. I hadn't noticed that.

"That must've been from that guy that knocked me to the floor," I told him. Doc heaved an exasperated sigh. "But later he took a fall himself," I added.

Doc had something to say but shook his head instead. I glanced at Loretta and motioned for my blouse. "Help me on with that before he finds something else."

"A pretty, young girl like you," he got out. "You oughta be thinking about meeting some nice fella with a future and settling down, not rubbing up against the criminals and good-for-nothings Otis hangs out with."

"He has some nice friends," I said.

Doc saw Loretta grin and his jaw tightened.

"Okay. That's it. You and Otis have in mind taking Miss Beasley off our hands?"

"She's been a bother?" I asked.

Loretta shook her head and continued buttoning my blouse for me.

Doc said, "No. No bother, but she's not ready to go. Not in my estimation. Poor thing screams in her sleep. She got tranquilized at one place, and then God knows how long she was knocked around and fed amphetamine at another. She was more damaged than you realized when you brought her here. She's not well yet."

"But we need to take her home one of these days," I pointed out.

"When she's ready," her doctor said. "When she's ready."

14

I FOUND OTIS sitting alone beneath the rustling trees. The shadows were getting long.

"Sherry's trying on clothes," he said. "How's the shoulder?"

"Stiff," I told him.

"I don't take to this knife business."

"I know."

"You should've just plugged him. As good a shot as you are, you would've hit him right between the eyes, and it woulda been over with before it started."

"Neighbors don't hear knives, Otis."

He dropped his cigarette and put a foot on it. "It was damn sure self-defense."

I reminded him that he'd taught me quiet in, quiet out. But he still didn't want me taking so many chances. He said it might be wise if we stayed closer together until we'd worked through this case.

I agreed to that because I could see that he was troubled. I sat down across from him at the redwood table. We didn't speak for a while, but I knew he wasn't finished.

I glanced up at the moving tree branches and said, "We may've seen the last of this heat wave."

Otis glanced up and, almost under his breath, he told me that he hadn't been sure at first.

"About what?" I asked him.

"About you working at the agency. I mean, I asked you because I thought you had it in you, but…"

"But what? It's been almost two years, for crying out loud."

"I know it has. Don't get'n a stew. Maybe I didn't expect you to stay. That's all. It's not everybody's cup of tea."

"No, I can imagine not. I'm probably the only female PI in Texas."

"The whole southwest, more'n likely," he said.

I didn't see how that mattered if I was doing a good job. He assured me that it wasn't any of that.

"What is it then?"

"It's you catching all the heat."

"So what? Nobody planned any of that."

"I don't like you getting sliced up with a pig sticker."

"I wouldn't like you getting hurt, either. But look, pal, I just had to listen to a lecture from Doc about how I should be husband hunting. So, no more of this. Okay?"

Otis looked surprised. "He thinks you oughta get married?"

"You think it's odd, me getting married?"

"Are you nuts? A man would be lucky to land you. It's Doc preaching at you. That's what's strange. You see, I ran with that lady-killer in his wilder days." He grinned, shook his head, and added, "He was a hard dog to keep on the porch."

"Enough," I said, knowing he was about to offer details. "We're going to stick closer and cover each other, and that's the end of it. Okay?"

His smile turned into a laugh. I waited. He took a deep breath.

"Oh, Missy, if you knew how funny that is."

I waited again while he shook his head and grinned.

The breeze brought the earthy fragrance of the surrounding fields. I looked over at a grass pasture where a couple of mares were standing shoulder to shoulder at the fence. They had all the space in the world, and for some reason those horses wanted to be close together. Like Otis and me, maybe—joined at the hip for our own reasons.

"Anyway," my partner said, "let me bring you up to speed. Sherry told me she called Hagan several months back and asked him how much she was gonna inherit on her eighteenth birthday. She said he got all twisted up and wouldn't discuss that over the phone."

I had to smile. She had some nerve, that one.

"She's a pisser, ain't she?" Otis said. "So she asked him to meet with her. When he asked what for, she told him that she was considering changing lawyers when she hit eighteen."

"She's clever."

"He was over to the house and ready to palaver faster'n a dog eats breakfast. She said it was the straightest talk he'd ever had with her."

"When did this happen?"

"Back after we got her out of that upstairs room with that kid…"

"Rico," I said.

"Yeah, that's the one."

I began to put some things together. "So after that talk, her attorney and Nadine had her committed to the hospital."

"Not right away, but they got around to it. And they could do it because she ain't quite eighteen yet. She still has to do what they tell her."

"So maybe that sanitarium was punishment."

"That's what Sherry says, and I ain't thinking she's lying." He looked past me. "She'll tell us herself."

I looked around to see Sherry walking toward us.

"She'll talk in front of me all of a sudden?"

"I reminded her we was partners."

My fashion sense wasn't too bad. Sherry looked cute in a full skirt and slim-fitting blouse and a pair of the colorful flat shoes that were so popular. But I could tell when she accepted Otis' compliments that she would have rather done her own shopping.

She saw that I'd caught that, and smiled at me.

"You've never seen me dressed, have you?"

"No, I guess I haven't."

"For shooting blind, you did fine. Though you spent more than I would have on the underwear, I love it."

Sherry's reaction to my shopping was more gracious than I'd expected, which said as much about me as her.

"Thanks," I said, and we were past it.

Otis didn't waste time. He asked her how she ended up in the Cambridge Court Sanitarium.

"I kind of asked for it in a way," she sighed.

"How's that?"

"Well, my friend Rico was by one night a couple of weeks ago. He wasn't supposed to be there, of course, but he's so good with the dogs he comes and goes all the time without any fuss. No one ever knows he's been there."

"Nadine found out?"

"Yeah, but it's the way it happened. We were playing around the pool, and I fell in while I was laughing. I swallowed some water and choked. That started the dogs up."

"And woke your aunt," Otis said.

"The old cow turned on every light on the property and yelled at us from her bedroom balcony...acting all shocked. She carried on like she'd never gone skinny dipping with her friends."

"What did she do?" Otis asked.

"You mean after the usual hysterics about my safety?"

Sherry stared off past us for a while before she spoke again.

"She claimed I'd nearly drowned because I was on drugs. We'd been lighting up, you know. Big deal. Anyway, she had Hagan stick me in that sanitarium—she said so they could keep me safe from myself and treat my marijuana addiction."

"Before the sanitarium," he said. "Nadine kept you pretty much holed up at home anyway, right? And Hagan went along with it."

"That's right."

"Why?"

"You know my daddy's last will and testament becomes effective on my birthday, Mister Millett."

"Everybody in Texas knows that," he said.

Sherry shrugged.

"Everybody thinks they know. The magazines like to say I'm going to be the richest woman in Texas. But that's not true. Everyone in the family is supposed to inherit the same amount. No, my birthday has another significance."

"And what's that?" Otis said.

"My daddy knew I was just a baby, and my mama was a wild thing. So, he wrote it up to make sure I'd make it past childhood."

Otis and I exchanged a glance, adjusting to what we were being told.

"Lord have mercy," Otis intoned, since her life sounded like a Greek tragedy.

"My daddy knew his wives and children," she said. "And Hagan made sure they all understood it was hands off me if they expected to inherit anything."

"There's a passel of you Beasleys, ain't there?"

"It's at twenty-two right now. Aunt Nadine, nine half-brothers, seven grandchildren, four great-grandchildren, and me."

"And I bet there's plenty of inheritance to go around."

"Oh, my, yes. But you know how some folks always want it all."

"Ain't that the way it is."

"Anyway, the idea was everybody got a little something when Daddy passed away. But nobody was to get their full amount until I turned eighteen."

"What's that been? Fourteen years and some?" Otis

figured. "I guess that might seem a lot if you was the one waiting for your nag to cross the line."

"It wasn't just the wait, Mr. Millett. There was another detail in the will. Just a little clause that added some spice."

"And what was that?" he wanted to know.

"I have it memorized. It reads that if I die, become mentally or physically incapacitated, or disappear before reaching the age of eighteen, all Daddy's money goes to Joshua Scurver."

Otis wrestled a moment with that. "The radio evangelist."

"That's right."

"Brother Joshua can't still be alive." There was real doubt in his voice.

Sherry shrugged. "As far as I know, he is."

"Never heard of him," I said.

"Years ago he had a late night ministry out of Del Rio," Otis told me. "Put your hand on the radio, he'd say. You'll feel my prayer coming through."

"You know your Bible thumpers," Sherry said.

"Everybody knew Brother Joshua. My God, that was a long time ago. If he is alive, what age do you suppose he'd be now?"

"I couldn't say, but that old radio preacher gets all my daddy's money, and none of my kin know that but me. What they do know is they don't get an Indian head penny unless I'm there, in person, to answer questions and sign a paper on the day the will is read.

"On your birthday."

"That's right. And there is no grace period."

Otis shook his head. "Your daddy not only loved you, little girl, he had a sense of humor, too." Sherry gave Otis a brave smile. "And your birthday's pretty quick now, ain't it?"

She nodded yes.

"So, it's been in everybody's best interest to keep you healthy," I suggested.

She looked me in the eye. "They've protected me all my life to safeguard their inheritance. Pure and simple."

"You're still alive, so I guess your father's plan worked," I said.

"It has, but with no love lost. They despised my mother and figured me to be a hindrance to the family since I was born. They've never let me forget who she was or who I am for one solid minute of my life."

"Not one of them ever tried to be your friend?" Otis asked.

She shook her head. "Ever since I was little...really too young to understand...they've gone out of their way to insult me and my mother."

"That ain't a pretty picture," Otis said.

She gave Otis a wry smile. "In a few days, after that will is read, trust me, there won't be a single soul in my family who'll give a damn what happens to me."

"Me and my partner give a damn."

"And I know that, Mister Millett, and I'm thankful you do."

"Okay, so a few days ago they stuck you in the hospital to keep you safe from yourself...so they said. But that didn't turn out so good. Let's talk about this hospital you was in and the drugs you was on and how you ended up out at Bobby Jack's. I ain't clear on all that."

"Do you mind if I smoke? I've been dying for a cigarette."

"Well, that sure ain't gonna hurtcha." Otis reached for his Luckies and shook one out for her.

Sherry fired up and exhaled a stream of white smoke. "I wasn't there under my own name, you know. I was checked in as Sheryl Miller."

"Doc McGraw said you was on tranquilizers. Were they drugging you?"

That question caused Sherry to clam up, and Otis couldn't get another word out of her.

I thought I saw something in her eyes, something I recognized from my mirror. I stood up. "Let's take a walk. Break in those new shoes."

She got up to follow me, and my partner stayed where he was.

I waited until we were out of Otis' earshot before I spoke.

"I don't know what happened at the hospital, but I saw what you had to go through at Bobby Jack's. And I know how hard it is to talk about these things."

"Do you?" She wasn't so sure.

It was hard to talk about those things. I wasn't so sure I could, but I had to if we were going to get what we needed from her. "I was your age when I was beaten and raped by three men," I started, and felt my heart rate pick up.

"I know what you've gone through," I told her. "They took away my free will, my freedom. They tried to steal my self-esteem." I had to pause and take a deep breath. She waited. "A rapist wants you to hate yourself, Sherry. But you can't let them make you do that. It's not about sex, you know…it's about who has the power."

Sherry's eyes clouded with tears. "You do know," she said.

"Look at my face." I put my finger here and there, pointing out the almost invisible scars. "See the pale lines? Surgery." I showed her my cauliflower ear, and she looked pained and averted her eyes.

"Oh, my."

"They left me for dead, but I fooled them. It took a couple of years, but I made them pay for what they did."

"You got them back?" she asked in a voice that approved of payback.

"Oh, yes." I recalled the revenge I'd exacted. "Look, Otis

just wants to know what's happening, Sherry. The more we know, the better we can protect you. We took you away from some dangerous men who weren't happy about losing you."

I told her who Vahaska was and how Bobby Jack had killed Chuck and Cecil that last night she was at his ranch. Her memory of being at Bobby Jack's was spotty. Some of it was clear as could be, but much of it was fuzzy.

She loosened up some as she talked, but it wasn't easy for her, and I understood why. She cried as she told me about her stay at the Cambridge Court Sanitarium, how she was treated while she was there. It was dreadful. She'd been sedated and abused. She told me the names of the orderlies who had mistreated her, and I put that information to memory.

She also shared with me how she was taken from her room at the hospital and how she ended up at Bobby Jack's.

It sounded like spy novel stuff.

When she finished talking and had recaptured her composure, we went back to where Otis waited at the table outside her bungalow.

"We had a good talk. She doesn't need to repeat what she told me, but there is one thing I wanted her to tell you herself."

"What's that, Sherry?"

"I got a chance to use the phone while I was at Bobby Jack's."

"You did? Who'd you call?"

"My attorney, Hagan Buchanan."

Otis shot me a look.

"Is that a fact? You tell him you was kidnapped?"

"Yes, I did, and I told him who had me. That was all I had time to do before Bobby Jack caught me and tore the wire out of the wall."

Otis glanced at me again, and I warned him with a look to finish it up.

"Do you know who Vahaska is?"

"Kristin said he's a gangster."

"Uh huh, from down Beaumont way. He's Bobby Jack's uncle, see. The reason you have to stay hunkered down is because you was out at their ranch house when Bobby Jack killed a couple of men."

"I didn't see him do that."

I said, "Unfortunately, Sherry, that doesn't matter. You were still there."

Otis said, "The problem is if dumb was dirt, Bobby Jack would cover about a half acre. He's in trouble with his uncle because he lost you. So we want you where he can't find you."

"He's looking?"

"I'm afraid he is," I told her.

She mulled that over and then said, "Thank you for helping me. I know I can trust you."

"You're right about that. But we ain't so sure who we can trust. That's why where you're at has to be our secret until we get things sorted out. So, no phone calls. That includes Hagan."

"Hagan," she repeated, her voice even.

"Him included. Understand?"

She thought a moment. "He didn't tell you I'd been kidnapped, did he?"

It wasn't a question.

"Not in so many words," Otis hedged.

"I see. Thank you again, Mister Millett...and Kristin. I don't know what would've happened to me without the two of you."

I knew.

"It's strange," she went on. "After that last talk with Hagan, I'd promised myself to not run away again. And then I got stuck in that awful place and kidnapped. Funny, huh?"

Robert Fate

"It's a laugh a minute," Otis commented under his breath as we walked off. "Five dead so far, we don't know up from down, and it still ain't over with."

Otis waited until we were in the car, but we hadn't outrun Doc's dogs before he asked what Sherry had said about her stay at Cambridge Court Sanitarium.

"They mistreated her," I told him.

"How do you mean that?"

"She said they did things to her. They touched her in ways they weren't supposed to."

"Inappropriate ways," he said.

"They'd say it was an accident and then do it again. When she complained, they laughed at her."

"Who did that?"

"The orderlies, but the nurses didn't do anything about it. She said the orderlies walked in on her when she was in the shower. When she refused to shower, they forced her to and stayed with her. If she gave them any trouble, they'd give her a shot."

"They knocked her out?"

"That's what she said. Early on she wasn't sure what happened while she was sedated, but she was certain that the head orderly, a guy named Nelson, did things to her."

"More touching stuff?" Otis asked.

"More serious than that was the implication. She said that she could tell by the way he treated her and the way the other orderlies smirked and whispered."

Otis' eyes narrowed and his jaw clinched.

"Who runs that dump? How can they get away with crap like that?"

"She said the Director was a cold fish and always polite to her. But still, she suspected him of knowing how his orderlies were acting."

"I agree with her," Otis growled. "That place sounds

130   —

rotten from the top down. Okay, she was in there under an assumed name, so maybe they didn't know who they was messing with. But that kind of stuff's wrong, no matter who it is. What about the nurses? The women there should've put a stop to it."

"They were afraid of the orderlies, too. It was the nurses that gave her pills to make her sleep."

"The nurses gave her pills and the orderlies shot her up?"

"An older nurse showed her how to cheek her pills. It was when she began pretending to be sedated that she discovered what the orderlies were doing to her." I could see Otis' anger building. "She said it was awful, but that's how she learned their names."

"You know them names?"

"I do. And the head orderly, the man named Nelson, was the worst of the bunch."

"Nelson, huh? I want all them names. I want every one of them names."

We rode in silence for a while before Otis asked what I'd learned about the kidnapping.

"It was an inside job. She told me Bobby Jack came into her room late one night. Nelson called him BJ."

"What happened then?"

"Bobby Jack told Nelson that he didn't have to worry about Sherry's personal items. He said she was okay the way she was. She wasn't going to be gone very long."

"What did he mean by that?"

"Got me. I'm telling you what she told me."

"So she was in her hospital gown when they took her out of there." Otis gave me a nod to validate his earlier point about her not having any clothes at Bobby Jack's.

"She said Nelson carried her in his arms down the back way to a waiting car."

"Just like that? He took her out of the hospital?"

"She said before they left her room, she grabbed her purse and wouldn't let go of it, so they let her keep it."

"Uh huh. And no one stopped them from leaving the hospital?"

"I asked the same thing. She said there was no one around. She didn't see anybody."

"She must've been scared to death."

"She was and she wasn't," she told me. "On the one hand she was glad to be getting out of there. But on the other hand she had no idea who BJ was and where he planned to take her."

"Bobby Jack was alone?"

"Yeah. She said he put her in the front seat with him. Before they drove off, Nelson told him she was sedated and not to worry about her being any trouble. He said she didn't know what was going on."

"But that weren't the case."

"No. She hadn't taken the pills they'd given her earlier. So she was alert, and Bobby Jack didn't know it. She said she watched for a chance to jump out of the car and run. But a chance never came, and they ended up out at the ranch house."

"And then?"

"Bobby Jack carried her inside. She said he was rude to her and pushed her around from the beginning. But he didn't hit his stride until he went after the money and came back with the speed."

"He went out and got the money?"

"And the drugs. She said she tried to fight him, but he kept her high. It was just speed and sex, she said. Food and sleep weren't part of the program. When she tried to resist or get away, he'd knock her around and then do what he wanted to her. I saw some of that myself."

"I don't have to hear no more," my partner said.

He seethed. He fired up a cigarette and didn't say another word for miles. He had a streak of Southern Baptist country morality in him concerning women. It wasn't so much in his manners—they were rudimentary. But it came out in a pugnacious way when it concerned the mistreatment of the fairer sex.

In school, he would've been the brother the boys dreaded if they'd been impolite to his sister.

The sun was slipping past the horizon by the time we got back to Fort Worth. I glanced over at Otis. He was more relaxed and gave me a wink.

"Feel like Jalisco's for supper? I'm buying."

15

I'D INTRODUCED OTIS to Jalisco's. My dad and I used to eat there. It was a dilapidated little fan-ventilated joint with curling strips of carcass-covered flypaper hanging about and bare bulbs. It always had south-of-the-border radio music wafting out from the tiny kitchen along with the mixed aromas of Mexican cooking.

There were chairs for a dozen customers. We stood outside until it was our turn. The place was always open, always busy, and no matter what time you dropped in, the owner was there in a long white apron with a bottle of beer in her hand. I don't think she ever slept.

She came over to our table. "I pray for your father," she said.

"I do, too," I lied.

It was a ritual.

"He was a good man," she added.

He was a good tipper when he won. I think that's what she meant.

"Coffee and a chorizo and egg burrito," she recited because that's what I always ordered unless it was Sunday morning. On Sundays I had a bowl of *cocido de res*.

"*Por favor*," I said.

"And you, *Señor*?"

"Coffee and four...no, make it five of them beef tacos you do so good. I can already taste 'em."

"We have *cabrito*, if you prefer."

Otis hiked his eyebrows at me. "That's goat, ain't it?"

"Young goat," I said.

"No, plain ol' cow will do it," he told her.

She was just scaring him and showed him her gold fillings to make sure he knew it. She walked away, waving her longneck bottle in time with the music. Her son who stood at the stove turned an ear toward her as she repeated our order. He then glanced at our table and smiled.

"There ain't no shame in being a gringo," Otis said.

"They're just teasing," I said.

Soon we were served hot black coffee in chipped clay mugs, and after that our food arrived on paper plates. I liked everything about Jalisco's.

Otis spread salsa and tiny green rings of jalapeños over his tacos and dug in.

"It's like being there," he told me with his mouth full.

It was after eleven by the time I pulled into the alley and drove up to the back entrance to my apartment. It was still breezy.

The building was dark. Wally closed the pool hall at ten, and Virginia must have already gone to bed. I was glad about that. She could be a handful, and crawling under the covers without having to deal with her would be a blessing. My shoulder was stiff and aching. Pain pills and a solid night's sleep was all I wanted.

But, even as bushed as I was, I followed my routine. There was a checklist that I set up when I first moved to my downtown apartment. Better safe than sorry. Each time I locked my sliding garage door, I left the thick chain and heavy lock in a particular way so I would know if they'd changed position while I was gone. That night I noticed they'd been moved.

My heart rate picked up as I stepped away from the door. Without making a show of it, I checked the alley in both directions, walked back to my car, got in, and drove away. The obvious came to mind. Virginia had moved the lock and chain when she came down the back way, thinking she could leave for a while without anyone being the wiser.

Well…maybe.

I knew there were other explanations, too. The one that concerned me was that someone had picked the lock, entered, and re-locked the door to sucker me into a trap. It seemed a little too sophisticated for Vahaska's men; but they were the ones looking for me, and I wasn't in the mood to play it loose.

I drove out of the alley and circled the block, noting the parked cars that I knew were regulars. I discovered one vehicle that I couldn't account for: a red and white '55 Chevy Bel Air hardtop. I jotted down the license number and drove back down the alley to my garage.

Before getting out and opening the garage door, I shifted the .32 snub nose I carried at my ankle to the waist of my jeans where it would be hidden by my shirt. I turned on the garage light after opening the door and had a look around before driving in and locking the door behind me. I retrieved my .38 from the trunk where I'd put it while I was with Doc and Loretta.

At the top of the stairs, I switched the garage light off, cocked and locked my .38, and stood for a moment, allowing my eyes to adjust to the dark.

It didn't matter about the noise I made if they were waiting for me. They would have heard me arrive, leave, come back. They would be listening as I entered the kitchen and locked the door behind me. Whoever they were.

I hated the idea that someone should be in my home. I'd left my big dog Jim in the country because I thought it was better for him. Maybe I'd rethink that decision.

I smelled someone—not strong. Man scent. Behind that there was still the aroma of Virginia's perfume.

I felt a slight throb at my temples as I crossed the kitchen and moved up the short hall that led to the living room. I moved without making a sound, but if they were there and listening, they knew where I was. Also, it wasn't dark like it was out at Henry's. There were enough windows and sufficient city light from outside that it was never completely dark in the apartment.

That's how I knew there was no one in the section of the living room that I could see from where I was in the hall.

To see the rest of the living room, I would have to look around the edge of the doorway.

I eased up to where I needed to be and stood still, listening to the silence, and feeling the ache in my shoulder.

I caught the man scent again.

Someone—or maybe more than one person—was in the living room.

If I had had sharper hearing, I could've listened for breathing, the rustle of clothing, or some other telltale sound. I couldn't trust my ears, but my eyesight was perfect. And I had a keen sense of smell.

I thumbed the safety off my .38.

Easy. Easy. I bent my knees, sank to my haunches, and leaned my head over until one eye cleared the doorframe and I could see the rest of the living room.

My heart slapped against my ribs when I saw the man sitting in the comfortable chair beside the table where I kept my record player. I didn't see anybody else, but there was enough light to tell that he looked at me.

"Hey, Shorty. By yourself?"

A chill went up my back. He had spoken in a hushed voice, almost a whisper. Did that mean that he knew Virginia was asleep and didn't want to wake her? Or was Virginia dead, and I was left with the sick dog that had done it?

I stood up, keeping my back to the wall and used a tone of voice that matched his. "What do you want?"

"I wanna talk. You alone?"

"How about you, mister? You alone?"

A pause.

"Yeah, I'm by myself, and I just wanna talk to you." He paused again, maybe waiting to see if I had anything more to say. "I'm a police officer. I just have a few questions."

That sent my mind spinning. I had been witness to and had engaged in so many illegal acts over the past day or so, speaking to the police right then teetered between stupid and dangerous.

I knew that killing Floyd Gutt was self-defense, but walking away from it the way I did made it simple homicide by the police who found him. In my heart, I knew I was on the side of right, but the police might not see things the same way I did.

"Since when do police break and enter?"

"I can explain that. Why don't I turn on the lamp here and show you my badge? Then you can come in and we can talk for a minute. Okay?"

"Not even close to okay. What have you done to Virginia?"

"Your roommate?"

"Yeah. My houseguest."

"I haven't done anything to her."

"I want to know she's safe."

"She's asleep in the front bedroom. Or she was until we started talking. I don't know now."

If what he said was true, she could still be asleep. We were continuing to speak quietly.

"You've just made yourself at home here? Gone everywhere, seen everything?"

"I'm turning on the light..." He switched on the table lamp.

I slipped an eye past the edge of the door and saw that he was a dark-haired guy, dark slacks, and light green short sleeve shirt. He held his wallet badge out where I could see it, but his other hand was hidden beside his leg.

"You're not so short after all," he said.

"And you're not so clever. What've you got in your other hand?"

"My service revolver. I'm investigating a homicide, and I don't know that I can trust you yet. You wanna come on in here? Let's meet each other proper."

"You've started off on the wrong foot with me. Maybe I should call the real police and have them explain to you the penalty for breaking and entering."

"You can do that if you want, but it would mean more people in your business and probably going downtown. Why would you want either of those things, especially at this hour? I'm trying to be friendly here."

Friendly is how the con starts, Harlan the grifter told me once. But this was a standoff, and it was clear I was going to have to do something.

"Okay. Let's say you are a police officer and that you are investigating a homicide and you did just break in here to be sociable. What's this got to do with me?"

"This is not working for me," he said. "I need you to come in here."

"Maybe it would work for me if you didn't have a loaded gun in your hand."

"All right. Here's the trade off. You come in where I can see you, and I put the revolver away."

"You put the gun away, and I'll see about coming in there."

"You want it all your way."

"I'm not the second story man," I reminded him.

I heard him sigh. "Let's do it in steps..." he started, but I interrupted him.

"Let's do it my way, or we don't do it at all." I had to believe that headquarters would disapprove of him breaking and entering. "Put it away, or I call the police."

He paused, and then finally agreed. "All right, Shorty. Peek around and watch."

I put an eye around the edge of the doorframe and

watched him lift his shirt and slip his pistol into his hip holster. He held up both his hands.

"May I invite you in?" He gave me a big smile.

I kept my eyes on him as I came around the corner with my pistol in my hand. It threatened him enough at my side without pointing it. He kept an eye on the hall entry. He wasn't certain I was alone.

"Stand up. I don't want you in that chair anymore."

"You have a permit for that?" he asked as he stood up.

"I do, as a matter of fact. Go over there and sit." I indicated a chair at the dining table. He hadn't looked quite so tall, sitting in the comfortable chair—or as broad shouldered.

He went over and sat down.

"Pulling a gun on an officer of the law is a bad idea."

"If he's a burglar, he takes his chances."

Watching him, I reached down and pulled the cushion from the chair where he'd been sitting. The move hurt my shoulder, but I found that there were no guns hidden there.

"Satisfied?"

"Don't get righteous. I still don't know who you are."

He chuckled. "I like your style. But you have to put that piece away now."

I walked over to the table, still holding my .38 at my side. "Put your I.D. on the table and push it over here."

"That thing's cocked, for God's sake. Is the safety on?"

"It is now." I thumbed the safety so he could watch me do it and lowered the hammer.

"Jesus," he said and pushed his I.D. across the tabletop.

He was Dallas police, all right. His name was Carlos Leandro Pierson. 175lbs., 5'11" – DOB 10-30-29. I pushed his I.D. back, sat down across from him, and put my pistol on the table within easy reach. I looked into his eyes—the color of polished walnut. Maybe his best feature.

"Okay, Officer Pierson. I'm all ears. Why did you break in here?"

"That's Detective Pierson."

"Oh, a detective."

"I didn't mean it like that. There's another Pierson."

"Uh huh."

"And you said you have a permit for that?"

I pulled a thin wallet from my hip pocket, opened it, and pushed it over to him. I showed him my private investigator's license and, next to it, the permit for my weapons. Only Otis and Henry had seen those things. I'd never had to show them before.

He looked up. "Is this a joke?"

"Where's the joke?"

"You...a PI, I mean. You're a..."

"I'm a what?"

"They're letting girls be PI's now?"

"You live a narrow life, do you, Detective Pierson? Don't keep up with what's happening in the world?"

I liked his smile. Or maybe what I liked was his appreciation for my sarcasm. At any rate, he bared his even white teeth in a pleasant manner. "Do you mind if I call you Kristin?"

"I don't care what you call me if it'll move this along. I'd like to get to bed."

"Lee is what I go by."

Of course he wouldn't use Carlos...not in Dallas...not on the police force.

"I thought it was Detective Pierson."

"You're not going to forget that, huh?"

"Lee it is."

"Okay. So, you're a private dick..."

He blushed and I smiled.

He shut his eyes and shook his head. "Your boyfriend. Where is he tonight?"

"What boyfriend would that be? The one you thought I was with when I came in?"

He thought about that for a moment and decided to change directions. "Your houseguest...when did she move in?"

"If this is about her, why are you hassling me?"

"I didn't know who you were going to be. And, besides, why wake her up when we're getting along so well?"

"You're starting to piss me off."

"Wait a minute. I thought I was okay with this, but I'm not yet. Who are you an investigator with? An insurance company, maybe? An oil company? I mean, who do you work for?"

"I'm a partner at the Millett Agency in Fort Worth."

"Otis Millett?"

"He's my partner, yeah. You know him?"

"I knew him when he was on the force. I was a rookie then."

"Not Detective Pierson yet, huh?"

"You're a hard case. You know that?"

"How does Virginia figure into your homicide?"

"I thought I'd ask the questions."

"Just moving it along. It's been a tough day."

Detective Lee Pierson paused a moment and gave me a chance to study his face while he studied mine. I liked what I saw, but I knew I shouldn't be thinking things like that.

"Okay, I'll tell you what. Since you're Otis' partner, I'm going to trust you on this…"

"You're going to trust me?" I smiled. "Are we forgetting who slipped two locks to get in here and creep around?"

"I thought you wanted to move this along." A moment of silence between us and then he said, "What happened to your shoulder?"

My heart turned over. The edge of the bandage showed.

"I sprained it playing tennis," I lied.

"When did you do that?"

"A couple of days ago. Look, can we…?"

"I know. I know. Okay, we'll do this tomorrow if…"

"If?" I asked.

"If you tell me your roommate…sorry. If you tell me your houseguest is going to be here tomorrow. I need to talk to

her, and I don't want to chase her across the state to do it.
Okay? You'll see she sticks around?"

"What if I tell you I'll do my best? She's an adult, you
know."

The detective threw his hands in the air and stood up.

"I can't take any more of this. Show me out of here before
I sign my house over to you."

Downstairs, standing at the open garage door, he said,
"What if I come by around one or so tomorrow and we walk
over to The Skillet for lunch? We can get our business done
there."

"One o'clock it is."

"How do I come to your door? Through the pool hall?"

"You didn't have any trouble earlier tonight." He tilted
his head and gave me a look, appealing for a truce. I gave
in. "Let's meet downstairs."

"Wally's at one," he said.

He stood for a moment like he didn't want to leave.

"Something else?" I asked him.

"A small thing."

"Yes?"

"Your tennis equipment. Where do you keep that?"

I felt it in the pit of my stomach. He was a detective, all
right, and he had been through my things.

"At the club. And you owe me an apology for searching
my apartment. You had no right to do that."

He exhaled a resigned breath. "How long have you been
with Otis?"

"Goodnight, Detective Pierson."

I put my hand on his chest to give him a gentle push out
of the doorway. Okay—I wanted to touch him, too.

When he put his hand over mine and held me with his
steady gaze, I knew he felt the same confusion that I was
feeling. And, worse than that, I could tell that he knew,
too.

And another thing. He wasn't wearing a wedding ring. I eased my hand away from him.

"Goodnight, Shorty," he said and stepped back.

When he smiled, I saw a dimple I hadn't noticed before.

I slid the door shut, locked it, and stood for a moment while my heart settled down. I listened for his footsteps. But he was standing on the other side of the door just as I was. I wasn't going to let this get crazy. I got myself up the stairs and inside as quickly as I could.

I called my partner from the phone in the kitchen. I knew he would still be awake. Otis and the vampires. I gave him the license number of the Bel Air to run down and asked him if he remembered a rookie officer named Lee Pierson.

"Pierson. There was a couple of them. One was older. You mean the younger one?"

"I guess I do."

"Yeah, I remember him. Smart, as I recall. Good-looking little guy."

"He's not little. He's five eleven."

"It's all relative now, ain't it? What about him?"

"He visited me tonight. Your phone call paid off. The Dallas police are all over the Floyd Gutt matter."

"And he shows up at your door?"

"He was here waiting for me when I walked in."

"Bring me up to speed."

I gave him a play-by-play of my midnight visit from Detective Lee Pierson. I left out the part about liking his eyelashes.

"It's that top-heavy waitress. She got out of there while you was gone and brought Pierson back with her. The real questions are where else did she go, and who else besides your detective knows she's staying at your place?"

"I'll take that up with her in the morning."

"And, Missy."

"Yeah?"

"Did he say he was looking into the Floyd Gutt killing?"

"No, but he said homicide, not homicides, and he's interested in Virginia."

"So, you're guessing. Be careful. Don't assume a damn thing."

"You're right."

"How's your shoulder?"

"I'll live," I told him and we hung up.

Who did I have to blame? I knew Virginia was trouble, but what the hell were my choices? Better to have her inside the tent pissing out, than outside pissing in, as Churchill sort of said under vaguely similar circumstances.

While I brushed my teeth, I thought about the next challenge—the meeting between Virginia and the detective.

I couldn't see a way to avoid it—even if he was observant and she was reckless. That's just the way it was.

I took the medicine Doc prescribed, plus two pain pills, and wondered if that would be enough. I put a glass of water and all the pills beside the bed in case.

Of course—Virginia had the self-assurance of an armed robber. Maybe I didn't need to worry so much. And look how she slept. Like she had a clear conscience—perhaps she did have. After all, she hadn't done anything wrong—well, nothing terribly wrong.

I set the alarm and turned out the lamp.

I expected to fall right off, but I didn't. What did that say about my conscience?

I thought about Detective Lee Pierson for a while—his broad shoulders—his dimple—until my eyes got heavy.

In my half-sleep, I walked with Satchel Paige. He showed me a serious face. *"Don't look back,"* he warned me. *"Something might be gaining on you."*

16

THE NEXT MORNING, I found Virginia sitting at the kitchen table having toast and coffee. We both wore shorts and t-shirts. Another scorcher was on the way. She had the fans running.

"You were sleeping like the dead," she said.

She should talk. I poured myself some coffee.

"I like your hair. That's a good color for you."

"Thanks."

"Is that what kept you away so long? It got boring around here."

I looked her in the eye. "Save your tall tale. I know you left here and went somewhere."

"Oh, you know that, do you?"

That gave me my first taste of attitude for the day. I joined her at the table. "I thought we had an agreement."

"What agreement would that be?"

"The one that said you could stay here if you kept it to yourself where you were. That agreement."

"I didn't say shit to a single soul about where I'm staying."

"Besides the police, you mean."

That led her to a moment of silent reflection and a softer tone of voice. "What're you talking about?"

"The police were here last night, looking for you. That's what I'm talking about." Now I knew what it took to shut Virginia up. "Where did you go?" I asked her.

She gave me a long stare before mumbling, "Spurs, to get the money that was owed me."

I would have staked out that place, too.

"You came straight back?"

She sniffed to let me know I was prying. "I got some stuff I needed at a drugstore."

"How'd you get around?"

"Taxi. He waited for me everywhere."

"Everywhere?"

"The two places I went in. I already told you. Two places."

"Spurs and a drugstore?"

"Yeah, that's right, and I had a burger and a shake downstairs before I came back up. It was okay if I had some supper, wasn't it? Hell, I hadn't eaten all day."

"You asked Wally to open the door, or you couldn't have gotten back in. What did you tell him?"

"The old guy?"

"Yeah. The owner. My landlord. What did you tell him?"

"I told him I was your cousin. He was okay with that."

"But you didn't notice the detective who picked you up at the honky tonk and followed you back here, huh?"

"No, but I'm sure you're gonna tell me all about it."

She scraped her chair back and went over to the percolator.

"I'll take some more, too," I told her.

She brought the coffee over to the table. "There's not much left. I didn't know when you'd get up, so I didn't make a full pot."

She poured us each a half-cup, put the empty pot aside, sat down again, and sighed. "Last week Leon tried to get me to drive to the coast with him. I should've said yes, and I wouldn't be here right now."

"From what I've seen, you two couldn't make it to the city limits without going for each other's throats."

"He's a big disappointment to me in many ways, but he's hell on wheels in bed."

"Look. We're going to have to talk to the police today," I said.

"Why's that?"

"Because if we don't cooperate, it'll get nasty. It's better when it's agreeable."

"I don't get what's happening. What do the police want with me?"

"There was a man killed in the house where you were staying," I reminded her. "I'm not certain, but I think that's what this is about."

"I didn't do that."

"And no one will ever say you did. But we need to be very careful what we say to the police."

"What do you think they know?"

"That's the right kind of question. If this is about Floyd Gutt, then what they know is a guy who worked for Vahaska was killed in a knife fight. They also know that the two women who shared the house where he died both moved out yesterday. They know you're one of the women and you work at Spurs."

"How'd they find all that out?"

"Your neighbors know more about you than you think."

"What am I supposed to say?"

"Stick as close to the truth as you can. You and your roommate came home. You found Floyd dead in the parlor. You were scared. You grabbed your things and got out."

"What about Angel?"

"Just like you, she packed up and left. You don't know where she went. You called me and asked to stay over here for a while."

She nodded. "I didn't see it happen, and I know nothing about it."

"Perfect. Now, they may or may not know about Leon. But they will, sooner or later."

"Leon doesn't know what happened there."

"Okay. So he can't harm you if he talks too much."

"If his name comes up, what do I say about that idiot?"

"The truth. He works for Vahaska's guys sometimes..."

She interrupted me. "I say that?"

"Sure. Because they'll already know it. Just tell the truth about Leon. He wasn't there. You don't know where he is."

She smiled. "He could be dead, the way I smacked him with my perfume bottle."

"Don't open that can of worms."

"I know better'n that. So, when're we seeing the cops?"

"In a couple of hours. A detective is taking us to lunch."

I would've paid good money for a picture of Virginia's face when she heard that.

"We're breaking bread with an officer of the law?"

"That's what I'm telling you. It's going to be friendly, as long as we keep it that way. The police probably think they're dealing with a mob killing. They're pulling in loose ends right now. Eliminating things. Looking for leads. And remember, I'm just guessing this is about Floyd Gutt. So, don't volunteer anything. Just answer questions."

Virginia stared at me for a long moment.

"You know, Christian...I miss the good old days before I ever met you."

That should've been my line. How like Virginia to get in there first with it.

I'd made more coffee and was reading the morning paper when Otis phoned around noon. He confirmed my suspicion that the '55 Chevy belonged to Carlos Leandro Pierson.

"Tell Lee I said hello." He added a few other things for me to pass along and ended our conversation with, "You've always been good at saying nothing."

"Being discreet, you mean."

"That's right. Keeping your pretty trap shut. Be extra good at it with Pierson. He's building a case."

Before he got away, I asked about a plausible tennis club where I might claim to be a member and explained my need.

He knew of one in Fort Worth and told me about it. A bookkeeper there, a divorcée, owed him a favor. "I'll get her to arrange a membership for you. Let's say you've been a member for about a year."

Lies on top of lies...

"They serve a decent lunch there. Chicken salad and ice tea on the patio while you watch gals in short skirts play tennis."

"You better go with me, check out their eyes," I said.

He was laughing when he hung up, and I went back to my newspaper.

The morning news featured the Floyd Gutt murder in Dallas and referenced the two deaths at a Fort Worth hotel. Gutt and the men at the hotel were identified as known criminals and associates. The hotel deaths appeared to be accidental due to a faulty fire escape ladder, though homicide had not been ruled out, since residents at the hotel reported hearing gunfire during the night.

No witnesses had yet been found to any of the deaths. A police investigation was ongoing.

After finishing the paper, I went downstairs to speak to Wally while Virginia dressed and before Lee Pierson showed up. I had on business clothes, boots, slacks, and a full blouse that hid my bandaged shoulder.

My landlord was behind his counter. I headed over, threading my way between the tables. I saw some fellas I recognized. "Don't you guys have jobs?"

"How come you ain't somewhere washing baby clothes?" one of them shot back.

Everyone was trying to get me married.

"Afternoon, Kristin," my landlord greeted me as I walked up.

"How's it going, Wally?"

"Something different about you. I can't pinpoint it...but something."

I didn't help him.

Wally could've been anyone's uncle. He had that average older guy look. Otis and I were at the fights one night, and he said he saw Wally; it took me forever to pick him out of the crowd.

"I met your cousin last night," he told me. "I fixed her a burger. If she's staying with you long, we should get her a key."

"She won't be here that long. And, Wally, just to keep things honest between us, she's no relation."

"I knew that. Why does she call you Christian?"

"Long story," I said.

He shrugged. "I don't care if you have guests. That's up to you."

"Thanks. How's Maude?"

"Well, she's starting to collect cats, you know. I guess older women just do that. We got four so far."

"No mice, though."

"I never thought about it like that," he said, and moved away to take care of a customer.

I heard the place go quiet and knew before I looked that Virginia had come down. I glanced around and confirmed that every lustful eye in the place followed her progress as she sashayed over to join me.

Nobody told her to go hang wash.

She already had her sunglasses on, and her red hair was stacked up with a yellow scarf holding it together. She must have had an inexhaustible supply of colorful Capri pants, each tighter than the other, each making her shapely legs look longer.

The bright yellow low-cut, off the shoulder blouse she

wore attested to good engineering in the undergarment industry. Otherwise, who knew what might happen with a bosom like hers?

"She sort of looks like a bass lure, don'cha think?" the voice behind me observed.

"Why Detective Pierson, is that any way to talk?"

We both laughed.

"I think we better get her out of here before someone has an accident and gets a cue in the eye," he said.

We started for the front door and let Virginia catch us.

For Virginia, crossing the street had its similarities to crossing Wally's; guys couldn't keep their eyes off her, and potential traffic accidents became an issue.

In a way it was good, because if it was the Floyd Gutt murder Lee wanted to discuss, Virginia appeared way too girly to have been involved in a mess like that. I had to think that she knew what she was doing when she struggled into that outfit.

The Skillet was crowded, but we got a banquette and ordered from their breakfast/lunch menu. When Virginia asked for a banana milkshake, Lee changed from coffee to a milkshake also—pineapple.

"Haven't had one of those for a while."

He apparently felt the need to explain himself. There were things I could've said, but I'd vowed silence and caution during this meeting.

"So. Did you see the morning papers?" he asked us. I nodded. Virginia ignored the question and studied her polished nails. "There was some excitement at your former address," he said to her. "Did you happen to notice that on the front page?"

"I'm so busy working on my memoirs," she said, sweetly. "I hardly have time to keep up with day-to-day events."

Detective Pierson looked at me. "It's gonna be one of those days." To Virginia, he said, "Let me bring you up to date. I need some questions answered." Out came the little spiral notebook and pencil. "Okay, I wanna get your name straight. You're Trudy Blanchard?"

"I don't use that name."

"You go by Virginia."

"That's right."

"Why's that?"

"It's where I'm from. It's a nickname that stuck."

He wrote in his little book. "You ever been arrested, Trudy?"

"Call me that again and I'm gone before our food arrives."

"No problem," he said. "Ever been arrested?"

"Do I look like a convict?"

He didn't respond. He just waited until she replied, "No."

He quoted an address and asked her to confirm it as hers. She pointed out that she didn't live there anymore. He asked her why. And she asked him if he planned to question her about stuff he already knew. He asked her why she'd gotten so hot under the collar.

It went back and forth that way for a while. When I realized I was holding my breath, I tried to relax.

"So that was your address until yesterday?"

She nodded yes with a lot of attitude.

"What do you know about the murder that occurred there?"

She didn't miss a beat.

"Not a damn thing. My roommate and I came home, found that mess in the living room, and got the hell out. That's it in a nutshell. Are we finished?"

"Your roommate's name is Angelica Shaw?"

"Angel, yeah."

"And about what time was that?"

"Christ, I don't know…after noon…before one."

"Talk me through it. You came in, saw the body, then what?"

"We got our butts in high gear, packed our stuff, and moved out."

"Did you think about calling the police?"

"Oh, sure. And wait around to see who got there first, the murderer or you snails?"

"Where did Miss Shaw go?"

Virginia told Detective Pierson she didn't know where Angel had gone, but that Las Vegas had been tossed around. He said he understood why they moved out, but why had they both quit their jobs at Spurs?

She told him that they recognized the dead guy as a regular at the honky tonk. To find him dead in their house made it a possibility that someone in his gang might think of them as witnesses. "He's a gangster, for God's sake," she said. "You put it together."

"Have any ideas about why that should've happened in your house?"

"Not a clue."

"You don't own a car. How'd you get over here?"

"I picked her up," I said.

His eyes came to me.

"Did you see the murder victim?"

I made a face appropriate to the experience. "I'm afraid so."

"And you didn't report it, either?"

"How do you know I didn't?"

I knew that an anonymous tip had opened his case. So I understood it when he paused to see if I would add anything.

"You knew the murdered man?"

"I saw him for the first time in that room."

"How about you?" he said to Virginia.

"We didn't go to Bible school together. Is that what you wanna hear?"

"But you know his name."

"Like you don't."

He waited while she stared at him and tapped her fork against her water glass.

"Floyd Gutt," she said. "He was an asshole. I'm not sorry he's dead."

That was more than the detective had expected, but he didn't react. He just wrote in his little book while the waitress put our food on the table.

I widened my eyes at Virginia to let her know she'd talked too much. She sniffed to let me know to mind my business.

"Milkshakes were a good idea," Lee said, pleasantly.

I smiled and Virginia ignored him. After a few bites of lunch, he started up again. "Do you know where your other roommate is?"

Virginia gave him a blank stare that didn't work.

"That would be Leon Hodges," he told her.

She used her innocent voice. "That's Leon's last name?"

"Did he have something to do with Floyd Gutt's murder?"

"How would I know?"

"But you don't see it as, uh…out of the realm of possibility?"

"I already said I don't know."

"Where is Leon? Do you know that?"

"He's Angel's boyfriend, not mine."

"That may be so, but that doesn't answer my question."

"You know what you should be doing instead of slugging down milkshakes with us?"

Lee and I stared at her. I held my breath again.

"There's something you wanna say?" he asked her.

"You should be talking to Bobby Jack," Virginia said, and wiped a forkful of French toast through syrup before putting it in her mouth.

My heart rolled over.

"That would be Bobby Jack Vahaska?" Lee asked, giving her a hard stare.

"That's right," she said, chewing away.

"Go on."

"When Angel and I got home, we saw him coming down our front walk."

"Bobby Jack Vahaska was leaving your house as you arrived?"

"You should get your hearing checked. I just said that."

"And you didn't think this was important enough to tell the police?"

"Who're you?"

"I mean yesterday. Why didn't you tell the police yesterday, a little closer to the occurrence?"

"And end up like that turkey brain Floyd Gutt? I don't think so."

"Don't go anywhere," he said to us. He slid out of the booth and walked toward the back.

I pushed my lunch away. Any appetite I had was gone. "You just made yourself a witness in a murder investigation," I told her.

"I don't care," she said.

"Now they're going to want Angel, too. Do you think she'll hold up when the questions start?"

"Leave me alone."

She put on her sunglasses. I glanced toward the back. Lee was talking on the phone.

"This is going to get real stupid real fast, Virginia. All you had to do was answer questions."

"I didn't do anything. I shouldn't have to put up with this shit."

She slid out of the booth and started for the door. I glanced back at the detective. He was talking and not looking our direction, but I knew it was just a matter of time.

I watched out the front windows as Virginia snarled traffic. She was heading back to Wally's.

Goddamn it!

I had to choose sides or at least appear to.

I stood up and started for the back of the room.

Lee noticed me coming but kept talking. When he looked past me and realized that Virginia was no longer in the booth, his eyes shot around the restaurant.

He ended his phone call by dropping the receiver, and reached me in two strides.

"Where'd she go?"

"I think back to Wally's. She's scared."

"Come on."

He threw some money on the table as we hurried past our half-eaten meals.

I'm a runner. I had no trouble keeping up with him as we crossed the street, rushed down to the pool hall, and dashed inside.

I saw Virginia first. She was going out the back door. By the time Lee looked that direction, I don't think he caught more than the door closing. But that was enough.

He broke for the rear of the big room with me right behind him. The normal hubbub of the place stopped, cues froze, and everyone's attention focused on us as we dodged around the tables, hell bent for leather.

Lee tore open the back door, and we darted outside. Up at the end of the alley Leon's old Studebaker convertible spewed smoke as it turned into the street and sped away.

That moron, Leon. That idiot, Leon. The lady doth protest too much.

Detective Pierson shrugged philosophically. "I think we've put on enough of a show down here. Do you mind if I come up to your place to use the phone?"

"Not at all," I said, and got out my key as we re-entered Wally's.

17

STANDING AT THE phone in the kitchen, Lee clarified for the dispatcher that an APB was already out on the light green '48 Studebaker cabriolet. He reported seeing it and gave a location and possible direction of travel. He also made clear that Trudy "Virginia" Blanchard and Leon Hodges should be detained for questioning regarding a homicide.

"No, they're not suspects," he told the dispatcher. "They're potential witnesses. Bobby Jack Vahaska is a suspect. He's to be approached with caution, considered armed and dangerous."

When he hung up, he turned to me and said, "I'm sorry our lunch got interrupted. How about if I make it up to you with dinner?"

I liked how his interest in me made me feel, but I wasn't so naïve as to think he wasn't still working his case. "Lunch. Dinner. Are you trying to fatten me up?"

To move him toward the front door, I strolled off down the hall and into the living room.

He followed me, saying, "You shouldn't have to worry about weight since you play tennis. Where is it you play?"

"You're the detective. You tell me."

"Well, at least give me a hint."

"You're a big baby that needs help, huh?" I stopped in the middle of the living room and faced him. "Okay. My club's in Dallas," I lied.

"Not so many details, please. You'll make it too easy."

"I'll tell you what. If you ever figure it out, I'll take you to lunch on the patio there. You can sip a pineapple shake and watch girls in short skirts play tennis. That's an offer that should inspire some police work."

"You're a hard case."

"You've used that line, Detective Pierson."

"It bears repeating."

"I'd love to talk more, but like you, I'm working a case."

"You are, huh?"

"Yes, and I have things to do."

"You're throwing me out."

"You need to follow up your lead, don't you?"

"I'm gonna enjoy dragging that Beaumont poobah's nephew in for a little talk."

"Well…" I guided him toward the door.

"Oh, one other thing," he said.

"A piece of advice," I said. "Your habit of remembering something as you're leaving has lost its charm."

He smiled, and I had to wonder if his mouth might not be his best feature instead of his eyes.

"I have two things."

"And what would they be?"

"Why does Virginia call you Christian?"

"When did you hear that?"

"Last night when she told Wally she was your cousin."

"You were that close and she didn't notice you?"

"They call me The Shadow. So, why Christian?"

I shook my head. "I don't know. I've never understood it myself."

"Really?"

"Really."

He shrugged.

"It's usually a man's name."

It took a moment, but I got it. "That's why you asked about a boyfriend last night?"

He gave me some credit by twisting his mouth down and cocking his head. "You have a good memory."

"And strong intuition, as well. And number two?"

"You wouldn't happen to know another friend of hers or maybe Angelica's...a blonde?"

My heart rolled over. "A blonde?"

"Yeah. A neighbor said a girl was with them when they moved out."

"A young girl?"

"A woman, I suppose I mean."

"Another waitress, maybe?"

"Nope. I tried that. No platinum blondes."

"Neighbors can make mistakes," I said. He frowned as if he were considering my remark. "Sorry," I added. "I don't know Virginia all that well."

"And you let her move in with you?"

"She was desperate and scared."

"Mmmm. You two are so different. It's hard seeing you as friends."

I shrugged.

"So? Did you call in the murder?"

"No." I smiled. "But it could be I know who did."

He nodded in a way that said the subject would come up again and managed to look pretty darn cute at the same time. I opened the front door.

"Well, save your money," he said.

"Why should I do that?"

"Surely they serve lobster and champagne for lunch at tennis clubs. You did say you were buying."

I rolled my eyes and said, "Good luck with Vahaska's nephew, Detective Pierson."

He paused because I wasn't holding the door open wide enough for him to leave.

"Yes?" he asked.

"I'm going to tell you something, but you can't come back

at me about it, because I'm working on a case that I won't compromise."

"That means you'll deny telling me."

"I will deny telling you." He inhaled a big breath and nodded for me to go ahead. I said, "I heard that there are bodies buried in the garden out at Bobby Jack's ranch."

He wrinkled his brow. "Recent bodies?"

"That's what I heard."

"Solid source?"

"Solid."

"You're into something heavier than helping housewives get divorced."

"That's what you think I do?"

He smiled. "Don't get sensitive. I know how PI's pay the rent."

"My case isn't about infidelity. But that's as much as you get to know about it."

We were standing so close I noticed his scent—a masculine aftershave and clean sweat from our run.

"So if I should go looking in the garden?"

"Who knows what you might find."

He gazed at me for a long moment. "Every time I see you I wanna kiss you more than the last time."

"Oh?" I said calmly, as my heart turned over–yet again.

"But I'm a romantic, so I'm waiting for the perfect moment."

"Good idea."

"Kissing you or waiting?"

"Both."

"Mmmm," he said, and I opened the door so he could leave. But he didn't move, and that played havoc with my blood pressure. Finally, he said, "Thanks for the tip, Kristin," and started down the stairs.

I closed the door and stood for a moment. I wanted to take a stab at thinking things through. Try to get a handle on where I was.

Over the past couple of days I'd witnessed the murder of two gangsters, stolen a hundred thousand dollars without meaning to, and been involved in an altercation with three other gangsters—two of whom ended up dead, and the third stood in a hotel hallway holding a gun on me while he studied my face like he was practicing for a lineup.

The trading of blackmail photography for information was such an insignificant event it wasn't worth mentioning. And the Floyd Gutt matter was self-defense. So why was I on the run? Because it was better to be invisible when you knew too much, that's why.

I had recently advised two witnesses to lie to the police while assisting another to get out of town to avoid arrest. So what if it was self-preservation? Wasn't it still breaking the law?

And, let's not forget, I was complicit in sequestering a minor from her legal guardian and family. It seemed like a PI's work was never done—if flirting with a policeman and dodging gangsters could be considered work.

There were a dozen ways my life could turn unholy awful, and what was I doing? —thinking about Detective Lee Pierson's dimple.

I almost came out of my skin when the phone rang.

It was Otis.

"Come get me. And wear something you don't mind getting messed up."

Otis stood in front of the Mandarin Palace having a smoke.

"My next car will have air conditioning," he said when he got in.

"I saw in the paper we're expecting rain," I said. "So don't look for the humidity to go away."

He had on more clothes than he needed—as usual. He wore one of his old suits with a vest and a fedora. I'd grabbed a two-year-old lightweight jacket that was Salvation Army bound—pale blue linen with a tear in the lining. I wore it over my usual black Levi's and man-tailored blouse.

Otis and I were never what you'd call a fashion show, but that day we could've been featured on the cover of Hobo News.

"Virginia's on the run," I told him. "She and that Leon have an APB out on them."

He frowned and cocked his head. "Why's she running from the police?"

"She told Lee Pierson that she saw Bobby Jack coming from her house just before she said she found Floyd Gutt's body."

"I thought you said she was smart."

I sighed. "Maybe I meant she knows her way around an argument. She sure talked me into a corner."

"This Floyd Gutt fracas ain't looking so good now, is it? You should've plugged him, explained it to the police, filled out the paperwork, and been done with it."

"You've forgotten all the reasons why I couldn't do that," I reminded him, and then I told him that I'd sent Lee Pierson out to Bobby Jack's to dig for bodies in the garden. "I figure if he's busy enough with better leads…"

"He'll let the waitress slip away, and you'll dodge a bullet. You watch out, Missy. He ain't your waitress. He is smart."

It was late in the day by the time we arrived at the Cambridge Court Sanitarium, gotten past the reception desk, and up a rickety stairway to the second floor. This was some country club, all right. It was old wood floors, high tin ceilings, faded wallpaper, and that hospital aroma no one likes.

Otis had told me on the way over that our goal was to determine if the sanitarium was involved in the kidnapping. I knew him well enough to know he was after revenge, as well. "You got all the names?" he'd asked me. He wasn't going to forget how Sherry was drugged and abused.

We were shown into the Director's office.

The Director, a small man in his fifties in a white doctor's coat, asked us to take seats in the ladder-back chairs that faced him across a large desk. Edwin G. Sealy, MD, was carved into one of those triangular strips of wood facing us.

Otis thanked the Director for seeing us so late in the day and presented a card as proof that we were in the business of legal research. He introduced himself as Arthur Wilcox and me as Gloria. He said that we were representing the Miller family in a matter that required that we speak privately to Miss Sheryl Miller.

"I was told by the family that she's a guest here," Otis confided in the Director.

"It is the policy of Cambridge Court Sanitarium to extend every courtesy to our patients and the families of our patients…"

"I'm glad to hear that," Otis cut in, taking the wind out of the dapper little man who was just getting puffed up.

"However," the Director exhaled, "that courtesy is limited by our primary concerns: the health, comfort, and privacy of our patients."

"Of course. We'll keep our interview short."

"Mmmm," Doctor Sealy crooned. "I'm afraid there won't be an interview granted today, Mister…" He leaned forward and read from the card that Otis had given him, "Mister Wilcox."

"You can call me Arthur," Otis assured him.

"Yes, well…"

"And why's that? Why no interview?"

"Why? Mmmm…she's not well enough at this time."

"I'm not sure I understand," Otis replied. "I was told by her family that she was here for a little rest. No one said she was sick. You wanna explain that?"

The doctor offered a condescending smile. "You will not be allowed to interview Miss Miller today."

"Okay, no interview," Otis said in a voice that tightened up. "But I will need to see her in order to fill out my report."

The Director rose from his chair. It might have been an

impressive gesture, had his desk not been quite so large and he quite so small.

"I'm rather busy, sir. I wish you and your associate a pleasant evening."

We stood up, too, and Otis leaned forward, placing his hands flat on the desk. "I don't dismiss quite so easy, you little twerp. I go nowhere till I see Sheryl Miller."

The Director bristled, but tried to feign casual, as he flicked a toggle switch on the polished oak intercom box on his desk, and spoke toward it. "Margaret, have Nelson come in, please."

"That's a good idea," Otis said, and crossed his arms. Nelson was a name he knew.

The Director pretended disinterest and turned his gaze toward the windows during the wait for Nelson. I looked out the windows, too. The sun had set while we were there, and lights had come on in the neighborhood and on the street below.

The door from the anteroom opened, and a white-coated orderly entered. He was a tough-looking guy, average height, stocky, with a head of thick, wavy brown hair. He glanced over at the Director and took a position near the door.

There was procedure being followed. It felt military.

A moment later, Nelson arrived. His lab coat had his name above the pocket. He was not as big as Otis, but physically imposing and younger than I'd expected. Maybe thirty.

"This is gonna be fun," Otis voiced *sotto voce*, as my dad would've said.

Two more orderlies arrived, a dark-skinned guy with a crew cut, and a wiry guy with a long face and red hair. Both were tall and broad.

"Hilarious," I told Otis and felt my heart rate quicken.

It was already four to two, and there was a pause that meant we were waiting for more orderlies to arrive.

Sure enough, a moment later, a rather slight, older man with a sunken chest entered. He was red-faced and peculiar looking with thick glasses that made his eyes appear distorted and weird; he had a rowdy thatch of gray hair and carried a hefty hypodermic needle like it was a Bowie knife.

The five men, who looked ready for battle, took positions between the door and Otis and me. I assumed that was the entire army, since the Director piped up again.

"I implore you one last time to leave, Mr. Wilcox. Leave of your own free will, and I wish you good riddance."

"I ain't leaving without Sheryl Miller, you slimy weasel."

"Margaret," the Director mouthed to his intercom. "We're not to be disturbed."

"Yes, sir." Margaret replied from the little box.

The Director took a stance. "Show our guests out, Nelson. If they resist, sedate them and deposit them on the curb."

Nelson shuffled a step forward and snarled, "What's it gonna be?"

Otis turned to me, hid his mouth with his hand, and whispered, "Shoot him in the knee."

Albert, the guy who taught me to shoot, always said, "When you're facing several guys, shoot first. Especially shoot first if they think you won't."

I pulled my .38 automatic, jacked a round into the chamber, and shot Nelson in his kneecap. A gunshot inside a room is always loud and always feels out of place. The orderly grunted with surprise, shrieked in pain, and dropped to his haunches with his injured leg stuck out before him.

"Who's next?" Otis asked.

I'm not sure anyone heard him because Nelson filled the same space with a pitiful, high-pitched squeal. But the reaction of the group of orderlies was to move toward us—amazing.

I had just shot one of them; I still had the pistol in my hand, and they were advancing. How was this going to play out if they weren't afraid of getting shot?

I kept my pistol ready and stepped back.

Otis on the other hand took a step forward. He kicked Nelson square in the face, knocking him silent and onto his back. He blocked a punch from the stocky guy, grabbed him by his thick, wavy hair and the seat of his pants, and started him toward the windows behind us.

The other two orderlies jumped in and grabbed at Otis. But it was awkward for them. They were trying to get a hold on him as he frog-marched the stocky guy in a circular route toward the windows. It was a free-for-all with everyone jerking about, arms flailing, punches being thrown.

I saw my chance and stunned the dark-skinned guy with the butt of my pistol. Blood went everywhere from the wound I opened on the side of his head. His arms went limp. He staggered and looked confused, but he didn't fall. So I hit him again. That opened a second gash in his crew-cut head and sent him to the floor.

Otis broke away from the redheaded orderly long enough to hurl the stocky guy headfirst and howling through a window. Venetian blinds, broken glass, and sash went with him the foot and a half or so into the ornate wrought iron bars. That had to be an unpleasant experience. The stunned orderly collapsed back into the room, his head and hands bleeding from glass cuts.

The redhead got Otis in a headlock. They tripped over the guy I'd knocked down and crushed a chair as they fell to the floor.

I turned in time to see the weird-looking guy charging me. I sidestepped the direct force of his attack, but we got tangled up, anyway, and stumbled and fell over the remaining straight back chair.

I let out a loud groan and felt like crying when we hit the floor. The numbing pain that shot through my injured shoulder made me see stars—not heavenly stars—jagged stars behind my eyes. But I didn't have time for stargazing with the old guy scrambling about threatening me with his syringe. I pushed him with all my strength, rolled away, and got to my feet.

Before he could get up, I kicked him hard in the chest, knocking him back down. For an instant, I was ahead of the game, but Otis and the redhead, who were grappling near my feet, rolled into me. My legs went out from under me, and I saw those jagged stars again.

A sharp pain shot through my shoulder when I hit the floor. My vision went hazy. I was blacking out. But the fight wasn't over. I had to snap out of it. I managed to struggle up, feeling every move I made in my injured shoulder.

The crazy-looking guy was near me, pawing at his face, trying to get his glasses on straight. I saw his fist an instant too late as he took a blind swing and caught me in the forehead. It was a glancing blow; it hurt, but it wasn't effective. I'd brought my hand up to fend off the punch and realized that I still had my pistol in my fist.

I jammed it into his cheek, just below his eye socket—hell, I pushed it up and under his thick glasses, and jammed it right into his eye.

"Stop that shit," I said as his glasses fell away.

A gun barrel stuck in a man's eye has a calming effect. He froze.

I got to my knees, panting for air, and smacked him hard above his ear with my pistol. A sucker punch has even more of a calming effect. He collapsed to the floor on his face and dropped the syringe. I picked it up.

Otis was red-faced and choking. The orderly still had him in a headlock. They were grunting like farm animals as they twisted about, the orderly riding my partner like a bronco.

I didn't waste a second. I jabbed the hypodermic needle into the orderly's backside and pushed in the plunger. It was like I'd poleaxed him. No messing around. When that hospital-grade sedative hit that man's system, it was like Harry Blackstone had stolen his conscious soul. All that was left for Otis to do was free himself from the weight of the sleeping orderly.

I holstered my pistol and took an account of the situation.

The Director's office was demolished. It looked as if we were in the middle of a Popeye comic strip with all the bodies strewn about. But it was no cartoon, it was a slaughterhouse. Blood everywhere.

The guy that Otis had thrown headlong into the window bars attempted to get to his feet. I picked up a stout piece of broken chair and cracked him on his skull just hard enough to put him to sleep.

Otis pulled himself to his feet and turned his attention to the wide-eyed Director. "Well? What about Miss Miller?"

The little man was too frightened to speak until my partner took a step toward him. "She's not here," he blurted.

"Not good enough." Otis started around the desk.

The Director back-pedaled to the corner of his office. "She's not here. I'm telling you the truth. She's gone. She's gone."

"I'm gonna work you over if you don't tell me who has Sheryl Miller."

"Ooooh, don't work me over," the doctor whimpered like a naughty child. "I'll tell you. I'll tell you."

"Who has Sheryl Miller?" Otis demanded again, and grabbed a fistful of the cringing man's clean white jacket.

"BJ took her," the Director croaked. "A man called BJ."

"Not good enough." He lifted him up until the doctor's feet were dangling somewhere around Otis' knees.

The doctor cried out, "BJ said Hagan Buchanan arranged it."

Otis shot me a look to make sure I'd heard what he'd heard and pulled the Director forward until they were face to face. "You're lying to me, you sniveling little shit."

"I'm not," the Director whined.

"You spoke to Hagan Buchanan?"

"I...I..."

"You spoke to Hagan Buchanan?"

"No, but BJ..."

"Where is she now?"

"I...I don't know. BJ said he'd bring her back."

"She was kidnapped and you're a part of it."

"It wasn't kidnapping," the Director gasped. "BJ said he'd bring her back."

"Bring her back?" Otis glanced at me. "How much do you get for loaning out your patients?"

"BJ said Hagan had the legal right…"

"BJ said. BJ said. Did BJ tell you I was gonna break your leg?"

Otis flipped the little man over on his face, grabbed one of his legs, and holding him by the back of his thigh and his ankle began applying pressure where his knee fit against the edge of the heavy hardwood desk.

The Director's scream was a heartfelt falsetto, his eyes were pinched closed, and he waved his fists in the air.

"How much?" Otis growled. "I ain't asking again."

"Five thousand," he squealed. "Stop. Stop."

Otis spoke to the intercom.

"Did you get that, Margaret? The Director was paid five thousand bucks to assist in the kidnapping of Sherry Beasley aka Sheryl Miller."

Otis applied his ample weight to the task and snapped the man's leg at the knee joint. The Director's scream went full out blood curdling before he fainted.

There was a distinct moment of silence.

"Don't believe I ever met a bigger sissy," Otis said.

"Quiet in, quiet out," I said.

He moved around the desk, reached down, and grabbed the head orderly by his pants cuff. "This Nelson turned out to be all broth and no beans, didn't he?"

I said, "Of course I did shoot him in the kneecap."

Otis dragged the unconscious and bleeding bag of broth behind us as we left the Director's office. Nelson in his left hand and his .45 in his right.

I also held my weapon at ready.

Outside the Director's office we discovered a shocked-faced group of the hospital staff; eight or nine uniformed nurses were gathered there.

Down the hall several others were seen peeking from

rooms. They gawked at Otis and me in our torn and bloody clothing and shrank back as we made our way past them and down the hall, leaving a trail of smeared blood behind us.

Nelson's good looks were going to be worse for wear, after being kicked by Otis and then dragged face down on the old hardwood floor.

"What're you planning on doing with Nelson?" I asked.

"Nothing. I'm just making a point since he was the *perro grande* around here."

When we reached the landing above the stairway, Otis stopped, dropped Nelson's injured leg with a thump, and turned to face the hushed staff.

"You all know these men mistreated Sherry Beasley. That's why they got what was coming to them. If you don't want some of the same, every one of you best get gone pronto. I don't mean from this hospital. I mean from Texas. We're coming back with the FBI, and anybody who's still here is going downtown to explain things."

Silence. My guess was they weren't thrilled to hear what Otis had just said.

"You understand me?"

A timid mutter arose and fell from the frightened group in white. That was enough for us. We turned, strolled down the stairs, and holstered our weapons as we stepped outside into the humid evening air.

If we hadn't looked like a fashion show going in, we certainly didn't look like one coming out. But I don't think we would've attracted much attention in that neighborhood in any event.

We'd gotten the information we'd gone there to get—plus some we hadn't expected. And, I suppose, best of all, Otis had gotten some satisfaction.

18

WHEN WE WERE in the car driving away, Otis said, "Lawyers are loaded guns, Missy. They can put serious hurt on you in a shitload of ways. It's best to never threaten them."

"You're talking about Hagan, I assume."

"I am for a fact. We're already on his bad side, he just don't know it yet. I can't believe how a good deed can turn out so wrong. It's like we been on a whirlin' bronco from the git-go."

"Do you think Hagan was involved in Sherry being taken out of there?"

"Somehow, yeah, I do. Because, you know, he put her there in the first place."

"That's true."

"And there was some kind of plan afoot there, too. Something too smart for Vahaska's nephew. That punk Bobby Jack has his name all over the plan turning to buzzard dump, but the plan itself...I don't think so."

"So they may be at different ends of it, but Hagan and Bobby Jack are both neck deep in this mess."

"Like we ain't, Missy? Like we ain't?"

The mess we were in was what we talked about driving back to the office. What could have justified Hagan taking up with a criminal like Bobby Jack? It was sickening to think he was involved in Sherry's kidnapping.

At the office, I showered and changed clothes—black shirt, black Levi's. How nice it was to be clean. I threw away the torn jacket and put my other bloody things in a tub of cold water to soak.

My shoulder wound was bleeding again, so I applied some alum. But I knew it was best to drive over to Doc McGraw's and have him take a look.

I put my pistol in my purse, since I couldn't wear my shoulder rig. Otis wanted to go with me, but I insisted on going alone.

"You're okay to drive?"

"I'll see you tomorrow, Otis."

"Missy."

"Yeah?"

"Good shooting."

It was well into the evening by the time I'd driven out to Doc McGraw's, listened to another lecture, and gotten my shoulder re-bandaged. The Millett Agency had run up quite a bill there.

Before I left, I planned to stop in and say hi to Sherry, but her lights were out. I was glad she was getting some rest.

Driving to Doc McGraw's and back, I'd had time to rehash the sanitarium experience and came to an obvious conclusion. It didn't make any sense for Hagan to risk Sherry's life when she was so close to her eighteenth birthday. It seemed unlikely that he was involved in something so shortsighted.

What the little Director told us couldn't be correct, even if he believed it. It made more sense that Bobby Jack used Hagan's name plus money to convince the Director—no questions asked.

But even so, it still left a lot up in the air. Not the least of which was how did Bobby Jack know that Sherry was in that wacky hospital?

There was more to talk about, and it wasn't that late. I decided to go back by the office. I pulled around, parked in back, and entered through the restaurant kitchen.

I heard voices as I neared the top of the stairs and had them identified before I got to the open office door. Otis was talking to a detective I knew. My heart rate picked up.

Lee sat on the sofa wearing dark slacks, a fresh, pale yellow cotton shirt, and casual loafers, but who was noticing? He had an open bottle of beer in his hand. So did Otis. Lee got to his feet as I entered.

"Ms. Van Dijk," he said.

"Detective Pierson," I said, and then to Otis, "Was he in here waiting for you, or did he knock like a civilized person?"

"Ouch," Lee said.

Otis laughed. "She's a pisser, ain't she?"

"She is challenging," he said.

"Enough of the third person, gentleman. Okay if I join you?"

Lee settled back on the sofa, and I sat in one of our straight back chairs. Lee took note when I crossed my legs. That was a good sign—I mean I wasn't even wearing a skirt—I was in Levi's.

"Will you have a beer, Missy? Our buddy here brought them."

"Sure. Thanks. What's the occasion?"

"No occasion," Lee said.

"We been talking old times," Otis said, getting to his feet.

Lee and I had a chance to give each other the once over while Otis lumbered over to the icebox for my beer. I wasn't all that dressed up, but at least I was clean. I was glad he'd come to visit, though I had to wonder why.

"Ready for another, Lee?"

"No, one'll do it, Otis. I'm still on duty."

"Well, I ain't, and there's something about you being here that seems special."

Lee and I exchanged a smile.

"Now, where's that church key?" Otis asked the room. "There it is. Right where I left it." He got the cap off the bottle. "Want a glass?"

"Bottle's fine."

Otis handed me my beer, moved back around, and sat down at his desk.

Lee raised his beer in a toast. "To friends," he said, and we all had a pull.

"Nothing like a cold beer on a warm evening," Otis informed us, and then said, "Lee's got a team of officers digging out at the old Vahaska place."

"Found anything?" I asked.

"We saw evidence of some recent activity. I figure we'll have something by the time I get back out there. We're trying to get ahead of the rain that's coming."

"But you're taking a break?"

"Not exactly. I wanted to come by, thank you for the tip, and see if you had a little time to spare to talk some more."

"You forgot to say how nice it was to see me again," Otis said, wagging his head like a schoolboy.

Lee smiled. "That, too, Otis. It's been too long."

"I'm not sure what else I can tell you," I said.

"You've been around Virginia more than I have. Maybe you can add something."

"Maybe," I said.

"Ride out to Bobby Jack's with me. I'll bring you back before it gets too late. We can talk in the car."

Otis chuckled. "Go with him, Missy. You can see he's desperate...can't work his case without you."

"Lord help me. Between the two of you," Lee said, tossing a hand up in defeat.

"You poor thing. Let's finish our beers and get going, then," I said.

The glance that Otis gave me said that he knew Lee Pierson and I were attracted to each other. It also said to be careful.

In the car, Lee suggested a late bite. "The best Mexican you've ever tasted and good music."

"You have the time?"

"It's on the way."

"Are we going out to Bobby Jack's, or was that just talk?"

"Otis didn't tell you I'm an honest guy?"

"Yes or no, mister," I said.

"You...you'll stay as long as you want, and I'll see that you get safely home. Me...I'm gonna be out at that ranch the rest of the night. But even hard-working detectives have to eat. Okay?"

"Well, I am hungry. My lunch was brief and hurried today."

He rolled his eyes and used the car radio to let the dispatcher know he'd be stopping for supper.

We crossed a spacious courtyard with an ornate, penny-littered fountain bubbling in the middle, to arrive at a low-slung, tile-roofed *hacienda* that was Puerto Perdido. The place was large enough to be busy without being crowded and had as many candlelit tables outside as inside.

It was dark for a restaurant. The jukebox music was from south of the border, soft and romantic. I understood enough Spanish to know the songs were about deceit, heartache, and loss. And, of course, death. Mexicans took betrayal seriously.

We chose to sit outside on the covered patio where it wasn't so warm, and there was a faint scent of night blooming jasmine. We ordered beers and dinner.

"Feel like dancing?" he asked.

Did I feel like being in his arms?

"I do," I said, and he took me by my hand.

I tensed up as we walked on to the dance floor together. It was crazy. I could look down a gun barrel without disturbing my nerves, but couldn't get up to dance without butterflies.

I'd been trying to relax with men—and I could feel how much I wanted things to work out with Lee. I mean, high school wasn't that long ago. I remembered necking with boys. It had only been kissing and petting, but it had been easy—not something to make me anxious. It was strange that after what had happened to me, I still felt like a virgin.

That night at Henry Chin's Poolroom had changed so much in me. After that night, just being touched by anyone— in the most innocent way—triggered a pullback reaction that I had not been able to shake. I wanted to be normal again. I wanted to be able to have a physical relationship with a man without jitters and cold sweat.

My friend Wilma said I had to get started somewhere. "Jump in," she said.

It was when I was over in San Angelo, her café was closed, and we were sitting in a back booth where people walking by couldn't see us.

I had tried to jump in—there had been Mac. I'd lost him even before he was killed—a hurtful and complicated memory. I was a long time getting over him. Since then, I'd done some dating. There was one fella in particular that I'd actually gone home with. I'd thought I was ready, but it didn't turn out well. I couldn't follow through. His hands on me—it was like reliving the night at Henry's. He was a gentleman and had tried to understand, even when it was clear that there was no way he could. One moment I wanted him, the next I didn't.

Hell, I'd never really told Wilma what happened the night my father was murdered and I was raped. But even without the details, she guessed that what had happened to me was about sex—if rape can be called sex—and she understood it had been bad. She'd seen my battered ear and the faded scars and ached for me to discuss that night with her.

"I can't talk about it," I told her.

"Well, I'll swan," she said, and popped her gum. "You

sweet thing." She took my hands and looked at me—big brown eyes peeking through shaggy auburn bangs. "Well, I'll talk and you just listen, then. Let me tell you about men, honey. They mostly don't know what they really want. That's the first thing you gotta know about 'em. And, bless their hearts, they can't help it if their dinguses do their thinkin' for 'em till they're old enough to grow some common sense. That's just Mother Nature."

"I know all that," I said.

"Don't we all," she said and laughed. "But you know, them thinkin' that way's not a bad thing, either…when you're young and just havin' fun. But, anywho, as Gracie says, the thing you have to understand is a man'll say anything to get your panties off, and that's the Lord's truth."

I knew that too, but Wilma was on a roll, so I let her tell me about the lies men tell and how to make them behave and about getting used to a man's hands. She was right about those things—it took a special ear when a man was angling for sex, and roaming hands really were going to take some getting used to. But, in truth, the resistance wasn't in my body—it was in my head.

I wanted to be what the magazines called a "modern woman." But I knew for sure I hadn't mastered "the art of abandon" they wrote about—not yet, not by a long shot. I was trying, though. And Detective Lee Pierson seemed to me to be worth the try. He sure knew how to get my face flushed and my heart racing, and he was the smoothest dancer I'd ever met.

Candles lighted the place, so we'd been dancing for a while before I noticed the cactus.

The dance floor was shaped like a donut, with an imposing cactus planted in the large sandy hole in the middle. I found that bizarre.

It was a mature succulent with spines about as long and vicious as I'd ever seen. Once aware of it, I became concerned as we turned about the floor that we might bump into the horrible thing.

"Why a cactus in the middle of the dance floor?" I asked.

"The owner of this restaurant is a very romantic man," Lee said.

"I'm not sure I follow that."

"Well, he says when you're dancing with a lovely *señorita*, such as yourself, and you move her toward the cactus—she'll get veeery close to you."

He was right, and I was glad that he was such a good dancer—for two reasons.

I sat close to Lee for the trip out to Bobby Jack's ranch, some of the time resting my head on his shoulder, allowing my heart to slow down at its own pace.

After leaving the restaurant and standing by the car, he had taken me in his arms and kissed me. I'd liked that and had kissed him back. We'd stood for a while, holding each other close and kissing before getting into the car. I was excited by his passion, but I liked his patience, too.

I was glad that we didn't speak during the drive. Perhaps neither of us wanted to spoil the moment and all that it promised. The warm night air flowing in the open windows was rife with the ozone scent of approaching rain.

The robust and earthy aroma of cattle was a part of that night air, too, and as natural as the country we were in—as natural as the countryside where I'd grown up in a small town in Oklahoma. I remembered gentle evenings on a blanket in the yard looking at stars with my parents before my dad went off to war—like now, a radio in the background, soft and low.

It was easy to drift back when I felt secure.

The moon had been late to rise and was still just an orange smudge low in the murky sky, leaving the surrounding fields shadowy and mysterious. I could feel the loneliness of all the empty space that surrounded the Vahaska property. We were miles from the closest neighbor.

Lightening sprang from the horizon and spread across the dark clouds in jagged shafts of twisting brilliance—not a sound for a long moment, and then the deafening crash and crackle of thunder rolled over us like the heavens had split apart. There was no weather anywhere like in Texas.

The rain began as a light drizzle just as the dispatcher hissed on and advised Lee that his men were looking for him. They had discovered gold, she said.

"Well, it's back to work," he said.

I scooted over and rolled up my window as he picked up speed, keeping to the center of the narrow gravel road, because that long, straight stretch was bordered with deep, weed-choked drainage ditches that swept past on both sides of the car.

He let the sprinkling rain build up on the windshield before turning on the wipers, waiting for enough moisture to clear away the insect mess.

I gazed up ahead through the first smeary swipes of the wipers, my attention out in advance of our headlights, watching for the tall wooden archway that announced the last section of the road into the ranch house. So maybe I saw the headlights an instant before him.

"You see the car?"

"I see him," he said and took his foot off the accelerator. "I'll bet it's one of my guys."

The lights coming toward us were a long way off, but they were coming fast—and, of course, we were moving toward them. We watched as the lights drew closer. The rain began falling harder, and the raindrops were splashing against the windshield and pounding on the roof of the car.

"He's not slowing down," I shouted above the noise of the rainstorm and the flailing wipers.

"Jesus," Lee said, and squeezed us as far to the right as he could, to make room for the oversized, road-hogging pickup truck that hurtled toward us through the blinding rain.

The truck was almost to us when I saw the Texas Longhorns on the hood. An arm came out of the driver's window. There was something in his hand.

"Shotgun!" I shouted.

I grabbed Lee by the neck of his shirt and slid to the floor, jerking him toward me as hard as I could.

The noise was a sustained explosion, a strange, slow motion of ear-splitting sound. The oncoming truck had hit us, or we'd swerved into the side of it—I didn't know which. But the impact caused the hardest blow I'd ever suffered to my spine. The shock was sharp and loud and teeth jarring.

Our car spun and jerked about. Broken glass flew. I was launched up hard against the underside of the dashboard, and pounded back down to the floor more than once, as the car bounced and pinballed around. I gripped Lee by his shirt collar and felt him pitch about. He slammed against the dash and roof, trying to dislodge my shoulder from its socket. But I held on.

The car crashed to a stop. My focus was swimming—my heart galloped, my head throbbed, and my neck felt swollen and stiff. My injured shoulder had suffered another setback.

What was going on?

The engine was running at high speed; the car vibrated. The rear wheels were whining—free of traction. The odor of gasoline—hot engine smells. There was smoke and a choking dust settling over everything. The dash lights were on. I could see around me. The radio was playing Rosemary Clooney, low volume. The rain thundered against the roof of the car.

I tried to move, but the weight of Lee's body was holding me down. I hurt, though nothing seemed broken.

The car had tipped up as it was spinning, but hadn't rolled over. It had jolted to a stop nose down. We must be in the rain ditch. I was in a kind of fetal position on the floor under the dash on the passenger side. Lee was on top of me. My face was wet. Rain? No—it was liquid, but sticky. Blood. I didn't know whose blood. Maybe my head was cut.

"Lee. Are you okay? Can you move? Can you get off of me?"

I could see his face, hear him breathing. He was unconscious, but I couldn't tell if he was badly hurt. I shifted around, got some leverage, and pushed hard enough to move him back onto the seat. I reached up, jerked the handle, and gravity pulled the passenger side door open fast and hard. The engine noise was instantly louder. To pull myself up from beneath the dash, over the seat, and out the door was an effort that proved how bruised I was.

My God, I hurt everywhere.

"Damn it!" I scraped my shin getting out of the car. I was at an odd angle, and higher above the ground than I'd anticipated. I fell against the open door, lost my balance, slipped to my knees, and toppled face first into the coarse, wet weeds. The rain pounded me, soaked through my clothes.

I struggled to my feet, my face stinging from the fresh abrasions. I climbed back into the car, banging my shin again, reached across Lee, and turned off the ignition.

Sounds diminished at once as the engine and radio died— rain pelting the roof and the low, steady whir of rotating tires—that's what was left. The front window was broken out and water came in, but the forty-five degree angle of the car kept it away from the front seat where Lee was stretched out. The front of the car was jammed into the far side of the ditch. Light from the headlights leaked out through the mud and weeds. Steam rose from the hood.

I looked at Lee. He had blood on his head, his shoulder, and arm. He'd been shot.

The shotgun.

The dashboard had been torn open. The steering wheel had a chunk missing, and the driver's seat had been blown apart. He'd be dead if I hadn't pulled him with me—but still.

Even though he was breathing at that moment, I didn't know how badly he was hurt.

I gave him a shake. "Lee. Wake up. Talk to me."

He was out of it. I was damned concerned about him, but first things first. Where was Bobby Jack? I'd recognized his big Chevy just in time—or, at least I hoped I'd reacted in time.

I looked for my purse, but I couldn't find it. It had been on the seat beside me.

Shit!

I snatched Lee's revolver out of his belt holster. This time he carried a Rossi .357 Magnum. It was heavy compared to the pistol in my purse—wherever that was. Or the one in my sock. I still had the .32 in my ankle holster.

A .357 would stop a man big time. I kept a tight grip on the weapon as I slithered back out of the car and found my footing in the ditch. My clothes were soaked. I'd known it was going to rain. Why hadn't I brought a rain jacket, for crying out loud?

I got my bearings. We'd ended up on the other side of the road. When I faced Lee's car, the ranch was a half-mile or so behind me. I moved with caution through the waist-deep weeds. The rain had already made the ground slick. Holding onto the car, I pulled myself up and out of the ditch. I got my footing in the gravel at the edge of the road-way.

The back of the Chevy was stuck in the air with the close taillight broken and the far one gleaming. The rear tires were a foot off the ground and still rotating. I kept low, eased my head around, and peered past the rear of the car—back up the road, the way we'd come. It was difficult trying to peer through the rain that drummed my head and streamed down over my face.

Bobby Jack's truck was stopped fifty or sixty yards from us. What was he doing? Maybe he'd been shaken up, too. As I watched, the truck began moving. He was coming back, but moving much slower than before.

"Damn it," I spat out. "Why would he come back?"

Lee's car was all the cover I'd need if Bobby Jack didn't back up too far. I would have to slip down into the ditch if he planned to back past me.

I tried to imagine why he would be coming back. The thing I came up with was he wanted to see if the combination of his shotgun and the accident had done the job. If it was Bobby Jack in that truck, I was certain he would be willing to finish what he'd started.

He couldn't have known who we were. My guess was he assumed we were police. He'd come home, found the house crawling with cops, made a run for it, and discovered us on the road coming toward him. Since our destination had to be his place, that made us the law.

The truck stopped about three truck lengths away and sat idling in the middle of the road. The rain fell hard and steady, and even when the interior light came on momentarily, I couldn't see clearly inside the big vehicle.

But I knew the driver had gotten out. I could tell that much. I could see his dark blue Levi's jacket as he moved along the far side of the truck bed. He was coming my way, the wide brim of his cowboy hat protecting his eyes from the rain. He rounded the tailgate.

Bobby Jack.

He carried the same short-barreled, pump action, pistol grip 12-gauge that he'd used to kill Chuck and Cecil.

I lifted my head as I cocked the revolver and brought it up to fire at him, and he reacted like a bird hunter. The tiny movement I'd made was all he needed. He brought his shotgun to bear on me, fast and sure. I ducked just in time, slipping straight down into the ditch beside the car.

The heavy shotgun slugs tore off the single working taillight, gouged holes in the steel body of the car where I'd been standing, and ripped the trunk lid open. He tracked my downward motion and sent his second barrage into the undercarriage below the trunk. Gasoline began spewing from the ruptured tank.

Specks of hot shrapnel had sprayed me from the damage he'd done to the car. A load of double-ought buck was like firing eight or ten pistol shots each time he cut down on me. I was almost twenty shots behind the bastard. Staying on my knees in the weeds, I brought the .357 up and peeked at him from beneath the car.

He'd moved closer. I couldn't see his head, which meant he couldn't see me. I wiped the rain from my face and used both hands to steady the heavy weapon. I aimed for his upper legs and squeezed off a round. The kick from the revolver was substantial, but so was the impact of the bullet. He went down in a pile, losing his hat. But he held onto his shotgun and flopped his body around to point it at me. I saw his face—he was in pain.

I fired again—and so did he.

I'd aimed for his face, but I had no idea where I'd hit him that second time. I was too busy ducking. His shot exploded a tire, riddled the car's rear undercarriage again, and sparked a fire. Flames burst up around me—rain and fire everywhere at once.

I scrambled to my feet, jammed the revolver under my belt, and jumped back to the open door. I grabbed Lee by his shirt, pulled his full weight into my arms, lost my balance, and fell backwards with him into the flaming gasoline that was cascading into the ditch below the car.

It was insane—the heat from the fire—the torrential rain.

I twisted out from under him, got to my feet, gripped his shirt again, and began backing away, pulling him through the licking flames and thick weeds. I waded away from the blazing car through ankle deep, fiery water, dragging Lee until I had us beyond the burning fuel in the ditch—until we were some thirty yards or so from the flaming car.

That's when the gas tank exploded. The concussion slammed into me. I found myself on my back once again in the watery ditch.

With my ears ringing and my head spinning, I got to my

feet and grabbed Lee. This time I dragged him up against the far wall—as high as I could get him out of the rising water.

"Lee! Lee!" I shouted through the downpour, but there was no waking him.

I wanted to haul him up higher out of the gully, but I couldn't muster the strength.

They came like ghosts; no foreign sounds penetrated the pounding rain. The flickering lights pushed through the deep curtain of falling water, distorting distance, stretching time. The swirling colors became hands and arms…excited voices…the strength of policemen in yellow rain gear. I was light as a feather. I was flying.

19

I OPENED MY eyes and wondered for a moment where the rain had gone. Otis was asleep in a chair beside the bed; stripes of sunlight held him there. I listened. Except for my partner's snoring, it was quiet.

I was in a hospital room. The steep slant of the light streaming through the blinds made it late morning. I wasn't hooked up to anything, but I'd been messed with—I had some recollection of that—lights above a table, the odor of antiseptic.

They'd applied a fresh bandage to my knife wound, put my left arm in a sling, and taped it down against my body. I was a half done-up mummy. And I'm sure they'd given me something to make me sleep; I had that dry aluminum taste in my mouth. Hospitals love to dish out sedatives, since sleep does a lot of their work for them.

I made an effort to sit up and wished I hadn't. My head swam and my body was a single source of pain—everything hurt. Okay. I'd deal with the issue of sitting upright later. There were things to do first, anyway.

I wore one of those immodest hospital gowns—which meant the doctors and nurses knew me a lot better than I knew them.

The bathroom door was open. The other door would be the closet. My clothes were in there.

My boots had sheathes sewn into them, a knife in each boot. I'd been wearing an ankle holster with a .32 revolver in it, and I'd had Lee's .357 in my belt.

Lee.

"Otis," I said in a normal tone of voice.

"Huh?" he said mid-snore, and brought himself up straight in his chair.

"How's Lee? Is he alright?"

Otis stuck his arms out and bent them, showed me his muscles, groaned, and stretched.

"Lee has a concussion...banged his head."

"How serious is that?"

"Well, it ain't good, but it could be worse. He's gonna sleep for a while, have a hell-of-a-headache, and won't recollect shit. That's what I know about concussions."

"He got shot, too," I said.

"Yeah, he did...a couple of double-ought slugs in his upper arm. But what about you? They said you tried to go into shock. What in the b'jesus happened out there?"

"Before I get into that, do something for me."

"Whatever you need, Missy."

"Crank this bed up, will you? I want to be in a sitting position."

"Why, sure," he said, pulling himself out of the chair he'd been in all night. After some fooling around with the mechanism, he brought the bed to the angle I wanted. "Now, what happened out there?"

"Well, we got Bobby Jack."

He looked uncertain. "That was his hat they found?"

"What're you talking about?"

"What're you talking about?"

"I shot him, Otis. Twice."

"Bobby Jack? Where'd he go?"

"The last I saw of him, he was in the middle of the road. I remember his jacket and the hat you're talking about."

"Well, he must've flew off to Heaven, because he weren't there when Lee's crew got to you."

"He couldn't have driven that truck away."

"Nothing was said about a truck."

"Trust me. There was a truck."

"If you shot that shit for brains and he vamoosed before them boys arrived to pull you out of that ditch, there was somebody with him, Missy. Simple as that."

"Tell the police to check doctors, hospitals, and morgues. They'll find that bastard."

"Well, you know, I'm gonna do that. But first, I wanna know what all happened. They said you wasn't no more'n a drowned rat when they brought you in."

"I'll tell you everything, but first I want my clothes. Check that closet over there, will you?"

He shot me one of his looks and went to the closet. My clothes were there, filthy and not yet dry. My water-soaked boots were there, too, with my knives still in them. My ankle rig was hanging on the back of the door, but no pistol.

"How come your purse is dry?" he asked.

"It's there?"

"Yep."

"It was in the car. I thought it went up in flames. Is my .38 in it?"

"Don't feel heavy enough," he said and brought the purse over to the bed.

He was right. The purse didn't weigh enough to have my automatic in it.

"I'm guessing you'll get your arsenal back when you fess up to the Dallas PD about what happened last night. That's why I'm trying to get you to talk to me before they put a foot on your neck."

"Tell you what…are those extra gowns there?"

"In the closet, you mean? Yep. A stack of them."

"Get me one. Two of these stupid things worn opposite will get me presentable enough. And grab some of those flimsy slippers, too."

"You're walking out of here. Is that it?"

"The rain stopped, didn't it?"

"Hours ago. It was just passing through."

"Well, yeah, then. I'm walking out of here in cotton slippers."

"And at the right time, too. They'll be serving up one of their awful lunches next thing you know." He shook out a fresh gown. "Need some help getting into this thing?"

"Absolutely," I said and began the painful one-arm maneuvering to extricate myself from the sheets.

Otis helped me off the high bed, to the floor, and onto my feet. He said, "I admire your grit, you little maverick."

Once I knew that Lee would recover without any major problems, I didn't see a reason to stay in that hospital room and wait for the Dallas PD to show up. Having to explain how I was able to identify Bobby Jack was not something I felt like getting into just then.

When we had driven down the street a ways, Otis stopped at a pay phone to put a call into his friend at the Dallas PD. When he got back in the car, he told me the search had started for Bobby Jack.

"Glad to hear it," I said.

The balance of the drive to my apartment was spent telling Otis what had happened on the road to the Vahaska ranch last night, the intentional accident, the shootout, the fire, dragging Lee to safety, and the explosion.

"So nobody but you even saw Bobby Jack out there on that road," Otis said.

"That appears to be the case," I said.

"I hope you didn't kill him," he said. "I want him on death row choking down prison chow for a while before they finish him off."

Otis and I heard the phone ringing as we started up the back stairs to my place above the pool hall. It must have rung two dozen times by the time I picked it up. It was a collect call from my ex-houseguest.

Instead of hello, she said, "You've been on a safari somewhere, right? I've been calling you for hours."

"I'm sorry, Virginia. I try to always be at your beck and call, but things happen."

I was a little winded from climbing the stairs and sat down at the kitchen table. Otis walked over, picked up my coffee pot, and gave it a shake.

"I'll bet you wanna know where I am and how we got away," she said.

"I guess I do, yeah."

Virginia launched into a much too detailed explanation of how she and Leon used back roads to slip out of Fort Worth, and how they'd made it out of the state without being spotted by the police. She wasn't saying anything that seemed worthy of long-term memory, but I listened, anyway, and watched as Otis found a pan for the leftover coffee. He turned up a fire under it and winked at me before walking off to explore my apartment.

"You know, Virginia, as interesting as all this is, I'm in the middle of something here. I'm glad you got away, and I'm glad you're safe. Let me hear from you now and again."

"You are sooo sincere. Look, I need your help."

"Oh? In what way?"

"You know my stuff at your place?"

"You want me to send your things to you?"

"Sure, in a day or so when I get away from here. But right now, Leon's piece of crap car broke down. I need money."

Here we go.

"How much money would that be?"

"Relax, Christian. I have some bucks of my own."

"Yeah?"

"Yeah. My stash is under the wax in my kettle candle."

Of course. She called that candle her dowry.

"Can you dig my kitty outta there and wire some to Chickasha?"

"You're in Oklahoma?"

"A town called Chickasha? Of course I'm in Okla-homa."

"That's where the car stopped?"

"Well, down the road a spell. That old Studebaker just gave up the ghost. We're hanging out at a café across the street from the Western Union office."

"What name should I use? They'll ask for I.D."

She paused. "Better use Trudy...Trudy Blanchard."

"You said some of it. How much do you want?"

"Enough to drag Bozo's jalopy into the mechanic to get fixed. And enough for a bus ticket for me outta here."

"You're splitting up?"

"He's an idiot. I'll pay to get his jalopy running because he did sneak me out of town. Then I'm catching the next bus. He can wait for his car to roll out of the shop and go wherever he wants after that. Me? I plan to be two states away before he knows what hit him."

"How much should I wire to you?"

She paused, so I figured she was calculating her needs. It turned out to be a moment of introspection.

"You know, Christian, I always wanted to stand out from the crowd."

"Yeah?"

"Yeah. I always thought some day I'd do something special. You know, something that people would notice."

"What exactly?" I asked.

"I don't know for sure, but that's not the important part. The point is I would be doing something special."

"Uh huh."

"I never wanted to be like everybody else," she said.

"I see."

"But here I am finding myself in an excellent position to become a missing person. It's hard to figure, know what I mean?"

"Don't give up, Virginia. You can take my word for it. You're not like anyone else."

It took her about fifteen minutes more to wrap up her

soul searching, and it took Otis a half-hour after that to help me get into fresh Levi's, boots, and a clean blouse. Then we sat at the kitchen table while I caught my breath, and he drank the sludge he'd boiled up and dug Virginia's six hundred and forty dollars out of the candle wax with a paring knife. I stuck two hundred in my pocket to take to Western Union.

Over an hour had passed before we were in his car and on our way to Doc McGraw's.

"I'm buying Virginia a gift," I told Otis. "I'm going to get her a decent suitcase. And when she settles someplace, I'll send her things to her in that."

"You're gonna end up your life somewhere taking in stray varmints. I can see it now," he said. "You in a rocking chair surrounded by God's little misunderstood rodents and such."

"Hell, nursing your shoulder is like a career unto itself," Doc McGraw announced when he learned why we'd shown up at his place for the umpteenth time that week.

He said the hospital didn't want me hurting myself in my sleep was why they'd wrapped me up the way they did. "Can't think of any other reason," he said, and got out of the way so Loretta could put some cold, stainless steel scissors against my bare skin and cut away the bandages. "What are those little burn marks on your face?" he asked me.

"Shrapnel," I said.

He sighed, shook his head, and spoke to Otis. "I tried to get you on the phone last night."

"I was looking into a matter," Otis told him. "It took all night."

"Your heiress flew the coop. I thought you'd wanna know."

I must have reacted. Loretta made a face to show me she was concerned, too.

"How'd she manage that?" Otis asked.

"A young guy came by, and they drove off together. I called you."

"No one's blaming you, Doc. She was free to go. We'd just hoped for her sake that she would've stayed a tad longer."

"She was sufficiently recovered, and I think she knew that," Doc said.

"Have any idea where she went?" Otis asked.

"She didn't say, but maybe Mexico."

"Why do you think that?"

"The fellow who picked her up drove a car with Mexican plates."

"A tan '48 Chrysler," Otis said.

"Rico Hernandez," I said.

"So you know the guy," Doc said.

"He's a friend of hers," I told him.

Once Loretta got me cut out of the body wrap, Doc didn't see any need to take off the bandage that was over the wound proper. "That looks professional enough." He told me again about taking the painkillers and antibiotics that he'd prescribed, said to come see him next week, and then shrugged. "What am I thinking? You'll be back sooner than that. You'll have hand grenade wounds next."

Loretta and my partner thought that was amusing.

20

IT WAS PLEASANT not to be the chauffeur for a change, having Otis do the driving. And it was nice not having my left arm plastered to my body—to have some mobility in that half of my body again. The painkillers were working. The shoulder was stiff, but it didn't hurt, and the all-over ache from the car accident was being held at bay. If I could shed the slight fatigue that I felt, I would be back to normal—or as close to normal as I'd been recently.

"I think we oughta get one of them reel-to-reel machines that answer calls when we ain't there," Otis said. "I'll bet we're missing some business."

"I heard they don't work all that well," I said, and that's how it went for most of the trip back to the office. Shoptalk. Neither of us was anxious to discuss Sherry taking a hike.

Although, Otis did state his belief that she would show up at the reading of the will. And that was just a couple of days away. I had to agree with him. The disbursing of the Beasley estate was too big an event for her to miss. The passing out of that kind of money would attract the attention of the worldwide press.

It would mean the end of her family's obsession with her safety, but would her new station in life deter Vahaska and his gang from hunting her down?

"She should have protection," Otis said. "And by rights, we should be the ones providing it."

"Better us than Hagan," I said.

"That's another issue, ain't it? What the hell is his story?"

We'd never had a case that had gotten so messed up. It had started out in such a straightforward manner, too; find Sherry and bring her home. We'd done that before, but this time the job took a turn; it had gotten nasty and dangerous.

That line of thought made me wonder how Lee was doing. I'd call the hospital as soon as we got to the office. Otis said he'd check on how the Dallas PD was doing in its search for Bobby Jack.

However, when Otis and I walked into the office, before we had a chance to do anything, the buzzer sounded. Someone was on the way up, and Madame Li let us know.

"And I was thinking about having something to eat, Goddamn it. We're late for lunch."

"I haven't eaten since last night," I said.

Otis heaved a sigh, got some heat going under his coffee, and stepped over behind his desk. I stayed on my feet and took a position near the sofa.

We heard high heels in the hall and then she appeared—short ash-blonde hair—a stripper's body in a pastel yellow, tailored suit—whisper-thin summer linen—sophisticated. Sex and money was the message, and she made it work. She carried two bags, a large alligator satchel and a designer purse in pale yellow linen. She wore sunglasses that I'd seen advertised in Vogue.

She advanced into the office, trailing a sinfully expensive fragrance.

"Amanda," Otis said. "What brings you by?"

"I need to talk to you." Her voice was just above a whisper—raspy, sensual.

"Would you prefer privacy, Mrs. Buchanan?" I asked her.

She tipped her head, feigning a lack of concern. "You'll hear it sooner or later."

I'd met Mrs. Hagan Buchanan on one other occasion, and that was in passing at her husband's law offices in a glass tower over in Dallas. I've mentioned before that she might've been a bit young for him, and meeting her again that afternoon reaffirmed that opinion. She was a good twenty years younger than Hagan, which placed her in her late thirties, early forties.

Forgetting the math, however, she'd pass for early thirties any day of the week. Ah, the pampered rich.

"I wish to hire your services," she said in a no-nonsense manner.

"We can talk about that," Otis said. "But first, have a seat, and let's get you something cool to drink."

She replied that water would be fine, placed the 'gator satchel in one of our client chairs, and sat in the other with her purse in her lap. It was subtle, but it was still a production when she crossed her legs, removed her sunglasses, and put them in her purse.

What eyes! They were as pure brown as taxidermy glass with tiny flecks of gold and eyelashes that should've been illegal. Even with her eyes a bit red at the rims from crying, she was still one gorgeous package. When she pulled some smokes from her purse, Otis got his Zippo working and slipped around his desk like a running back a step ahead of the tackle.

I delivered a glass of ice water and took a seat as far away from the two of them as I could without being impolite. With both firing up, it took no time at all to create an atmosphere murkier than a beatnik coffeehouse. I was grateful for the high ceilings and our steady old fan.

Amanda Buchanan sipped her water. Otis returned to his place behind the desk, and we waited. My plan was to remain silent unless something was directed to me. After a moment, she emitted a sigh and pushed out her cigarette in the ashtray on the table beside her chair.

"Excuse my voice. I'm afraid I've smoked and cried myself hoarse," she said.

We waited some more.

"Hagan's gotten himself in a jam," she rasped.

"A jam, huh? What does that mean?" Otis asked, politely.

"He needs a large amount of cash, and he needs it right away."

"Uh huh," he said.

"I've arranged the amount, but now it's a matter of getting it to him."

"Here in town?"

"Dallas. A hotel there."

"How much cash, Amanda?"

"A hundred thousand dollars."

Otis gave his head a little shake and mumbled, "That's a chunk of change," as he shot me a look. That particular sum of money had now shown up twice in a matter of days.

"It's what was demanded," she said.

"Mmmm," Otis said. "Hagan has partners. Why didn't he contact them to take care of that? Why you?"

"He wasn't able to talk, but he knew I'd read between the lines."

"I see."

"He's being held hostage."

"He said that?"

"That was what was between the lines."

"Mmmm," Otis said. "Have you spoken to the police?" She shook her head. "Don't you think you should?"

She sighed. "This is not a matter for the police."

"All right then. You know who you're talking to. At the Millett Agency, we don't pass judgment, and we won't repeat what a client tells us. Just start at the beginning and don't leave anything out."

The story that Amanda told was about a man that we'd never met: Hagan Buchanan, the insecure and anxiety-ridden addicted gambler. Just as an alcoholic might, he had fallen off the wagon now and again over the years, risking everything. But with Amanda's support they had been able to avoid scandal, hold onto their wealth, and maintain their position in Dallas society. His partners had their suspicions, of course, but his astute control of the powerful Beasley estate kept the firm mollified.

However, she told us, constant vigilance had been required. "I noticed he'd become uneasy, agitated. I knew the signs and suggested that we take a vacation, get away for a while. That was usually enough to get him back on track. But he said I'd misread him. He said he was just concerned about some surprise issues at work."

She told us she didn't believe him since trusts and estates was the business of his law firm, and there were few surprises in probate court. When she said, "The majority of Hagan's clients are resting in the cemetery," she'd let us in on a little inside joke she shared with her husband.

Otis wanted details. "You say recently, but when exactly did you notice the change in him?"

"After this last trip to Beaumont. I usually travel with him for all the obvious reasons, but I had a commitment at church I couldn't get out of, and he went alone. A week or so after he returned home, I began noticing things weren't right."

Otis mulled that over before summing up. "Okay, he said his nervousness had nothing to do with gambling, but now he needs cash, and you think he's being held against his will until that cash is delivered. Have I got the bit in the horse's mouth here?"

"Yes, you have. And of course it's about gambling, and it happened in Beaumont during the few days he was down there. He got in over his head with some bad people, even if he says he didn't. Only a fool would have missed all the signs, and I'm no fool."

"So, this brings us to Hagan in a hotel room with some palookas who won't let him leave till the money shows up. Anything else to add to that?"

"That's it without decoration," Amanda confirmed.

"Okay. Now we can talk about what it is you want me and my partner to do for you."

Amanda glanced over at me with a face that said maybe she'd forgotten I was there. I proffered an appropriate expression and kept eye contact until she looked back at my partner. "I want him home, Otis. I want him home alive and well," she said, turning her palms up as if in supplication. "His backsliding tears my heart apart. I told him the last…"

Determined not to cry anymore, she tightened her jaw, clasped her hands in her lap, and took a breather. As we waited, I had to wonder how sincere the drama was. Or was PI work making me cynical?

When she'd recaptured her composure, she took a deep breath and said, "I told him the last time that if he did this to me again, I'd cut my losses and file for divorce…look to salvage the balance of my life without him."

Otis gave her a moment before saying, "Uh huh."

"And I may still do it…I may still do that," she said. "But right now some bad men have him, and he needs my help. He's not physical, not big and strong like you. He won't have any staying power for rough stuff. He needs you, Otis. We need you. Whatever he's done wrong, we'll straighten it out. You know we'll make it right."

"Of course," Otis said.

"And day after tomorrow, after the Beasley estate is settled, I'll insist he retire. But first, I want him back…with all his faults, I just want him back."

There was more to it, of course. There was always more to it.

Amanda had last seen Hagan when he left for work that morning. The night before he had confessed everything to her—how he'd played the horses while he was in Beaumont, and how he'd kept losing and kept playing.

"He signed IOU's while he was down there," she said. "So, when he got back, he needed to move funds from the Beasley estate to cover his debts. It was either that or sell the house."

Otis asked, "Hagan took money from the Beasley estate?"

"Yes."

"Anyone else aware of this?"

She shook her head.

"His partners, maybe?"

"No. Only me, and now you. Just enough to cover his losses."

"So we're clear on this," Otis said. "Hagan didn't borrow this money."

"No."

"He just took some to use for his own purpose."

"That's what I'm telling you."

"What you're telling me is Hagan stole money from the Beasleys."

"Not precisely," she said.

"What does that mean?" Otis asked.

"Hagan took the money without breaking any laws," Amanda explained. "It's simple, really. As executor of the estate, he has the authority to take money from a discretionary account set up for emergencies. The urgent situation that he documented for the record was Sherry being kidnapped. It was quite believable, of course, because of her pattern of runaways and other rash and irresponsible escapades."

"So he faked it," Otis said.

Amanda went on, "If Hagan ever has to account for his actions, all he has to say is Sherry's life was in jeopardy, the police couldn't be contacted, and he had to act at once with a ransom. It's a one-time incident, Otis. The estate has no history of unusual withdrawals or peculiar occurrences of any kind, and Hagan's sterling character would never be called into question."

"So, you're telling us all this for what reason?"

Amanda sighed. "It should have worked like a dream."

"But something went wrong," Otis said.

"Very wrong," Amanda said. "Hagan's mistake was to involve the very people to whom he owed the money."

"That would be Vahaska and the Einsteins who work for him?"

She looked confused. "Why, yes. I thought you knew that."

"I suppose I did, but it confirms it for me to hear you say it."

"Yes, we're talking about Vahaska and his people. And it just shows Hagan's state of mind that he would have thought lowlife Beaumont gangsters would do the right thing. Of course they double-crossed him."

"How'd they do that?" Otis asked.

"They removed the girl from a secure, out-of-the-way hospital environment that had been agreed upon, and hid her someplace else. Someplace where even you haven't been able to find her."

Otis shot me a quick glance as he told Amanda, "We're still looking."

"I didn't mean anything by that, Otis. Hagan says there's nobody in the business better than you."

"You were saying they took Sherry Beasley..."

"Yes, and naturally, they took the ransom, as well, and then claimed it had never been paid. Now they have Hagan as well as the girl, and I don't think they're giving up either until they get more money. And, Lord knows, we're willing to give them more, but what if they don't keep their word again? What if they just keep demanding money? Why should I trust these thugs?" Her speech slowed, her words grew more deliberate. "I'm not afraid of them. I know Hagan is, but I'm not. My brothers taught me to shoot when I was just a tadpole. I'm not afraid of them."

"We won't let it come to that, Amanda."

"But you can see, can't you, Otis? It couldn't be a more desperate situation. You're the one person I felt I could turn to."

When Otis returned to the office from walking Amanda Buchanan down to her car, he asked me, "What do you think of Hagan's way of paying his gambling debts?"

"On its face, it sounds like a lawyer's way around the law," I said. "But for an idea that is so simple, how did it get so complicated?"

"Because folks can't leave things alone. You know...I can't help wondering if it was Hagan's idea or Amanda's to take that money from the Beasley estate. Although it don't matter, I guess."

"Did she come up the hard scrabble way?"

"You have a nose, don't you, Missy? Well, she didn't come from much. You can say that."

"It's all in the breeding," my mother used to say.

Otis went on, "Women can marry up. It don't work for men, but gals with her...well, let's say with her attributes...can always find their selves a lawyer or a doctor. She ain't been bad for Hagan. She's kept her end of the deal."

Otis got himself another cup of his awful coffee, snagged a Dr Pepper from the icebox for me, and sat down at his desk. He put fire to a butt and blew a stream of smoke at the ceiling. We sat for a long moment, ignoring Amanda's satchel that sat like a big alligator on the desk where she left it after showing us the contents.

"But, you know, Amanda was right. Their plan would've worked as slick as dog slobber except for one thing."

"Bobby Jack."

"You ain't wrong. Vahaska's nephew was the hitch in the gitty up. When that boy got high, horny, and murderous, he veered away from the plan. He started a stampede that has caused one problem after another right up to this very minute. You should've plugged him through his *cabeza* that first night, Missy."

"I know you don't mean that, Otis."

"Maybe I do and maybe I don't." He picked up the phone and called his buddy at the Dallas PD. He asked if they'd found Bobby Jack. "They ain't found him yet," he said when he hung up. "But they're still looking."

"So, what about this hotel where Vahaska's holding Hagan?" I asked. "Is it as ritzy as I've heard?"

"Well, a few years back when Prince Ali Khan was hound-dogging Rita Hayworth across America, he caught up to her here in our great state, and they stayed for a night in Dallas. I'll bet it was the only time in their sheltered lives either one of them ever stayed over in Texas, and the Hudson Towers was the hotel they stayed at."

"And we're going to ransom Hagan out of a penthouse in that place?"

Otis had the look of a cat with a canary halfway down his gullet when he said, "That's what we've been hired to do."

It took me a moment, but I got there. "You don't plan on giving Vahaska that money, do you?"

"Not a red cent, missy. Not one red cent."

I thought about the hand grenade wounds that Doc had predicted.

While my partner put the contents of Amanda's expensive shoulder bag in the safe, I gave the hospital a call and checked on Lee.

"How's he doing?" Otis asked when he came back into the office.

"He can have visitors tomorrow."

"So he's okay?"

"They said he'd be fine."

We exchanged a smile. We didn't have to say anything else.

21

MADAME LI, A striking woman in her middle years, stood near our table and listened as a waiter took our order. Before he left for the kitchen, she added instructions in Chinese to be given to the cook. Otis was respected in her establishment, and the meals they served him were always special. She and her staff would never forget how one evening he'd taken a shotgun away from two robbers, dragged them out to the street, and beaten them silly with it.

That event marked the start of his business relationship with the local Chinese. They were, of course, impressed with his boldness and daring, but what they appreciated was his reluctance to involve the police in his dealings. His natural tendency to handle things himself worked well in their clannish community.

"Enjoy your meal, Otis...Miss Van Dijk," Madame Li said in her crisp, unaccented English.

She returned to perch upon a high, black-lacquered stool that was placed between an ancient cash register and the front glass window. With her glowing complexion, small, slim frame, and penchant for French fashion, she seemed very much the confident empress ruling her Mandarin Palace Restaurant from that high stool.

"Okay, we know our timetable," Otis said when we were alone.

"Amanda said Hagan expected the money today," I said.

"And we should stick to that schedule," he said. "But we show up when we're ready...at least give ourselves some time to look things over, work things out. It's not like we ain't pulled clients out of hot spots before, but this one's gonna have to be like stealing eggs without waking the hens."

"How familiar are you with the hotel?"

"So-so. I know they have a back hall system. I've done business there in the past."

I thought about the Cambridge Court Sanitarium and said, "I'm sure the Hudson Towers is too snooty for rough stuff. They'll call the police at the first sign of a disturbance."

"Well, maybe not the police, but they've got a few men they call Security...which they won't need. There won't be no rough stuff."

"No?"

"I don't think so."

"So, we're going to con Hagan away from Vahaska."

"That's the smart way, don't you think? And if Wilson Swift is still the Bell Captain, we should be able to swing something."

"You know the head bellboy over there?"

"I ain't seen him for a while, but yeah, I suppose I do. Spiffy little guy. Let's put it this way...if he's still there, he owes me a favor. He'll give us the lay of the land, and we'll figure something out."

Having a contact at a hotel where we needed one was not a coincidence. Otis had been around town chasing cheaters for a while.

I smiled.

"What?"

"Something Lee said."

"Yeah?"

"He said infidelity was how PI's pay the rent."

He arched his brows. "Oh, he did, did he? What would

that young detective know about paying rent? He draws a city salary…when he's not breaking and entering or having his life saved by a PI." He huffed. "Like he'd know about paying rent."

I smiled again. That should give them something to talk about the next time they see each other.

Otis poured us hot tea.

It was nearing ten thirty that night when I drove up and stopped beside one of Otis' big old dull-colored Buicks. We were down the block from the Hudson Towers in a parking lot that had closed at the end of the business day. Even with the wind that had come up, it was still warm enough that all his windows were rolled down. The heat spell's back wasn't broken yet.

I joined Otis in his car. He was listening to the radio.

"Who's that?" I asked. "Glenn Miller?"

"Sounds like 'im , don't it? It's Tex Beneke."

We listened for a moment more before he switched it off.

"Your hair looks good," he said.

"Thanks." I wore the ebony pageboy wig that I'd gotten back a year or so ago from Ivy, my beautician. She'd told me when I bought it that when I got naked I'd look like Bettie Page. I blushed, of course, and she guffawed.

Everything I wore was black: my boots, Levi's, light cotton turtleneck, and a lightweight black leather jacket. I would disappear in a dark room. Otis wore one of his gray three-piece suits and a dark fedora.

"You get everything?" he asked. I nodded that I had, and he went on. "Does Doc understand what's happening?"

"Pretty much, but I think he would've liked it better if you'd become a lawyer instead of a policeman. The work we do keeps him on edge."

"I know. Who would've pictured him getting so…"

"Conventional?"

"Yeah. Maybe that's it. We used to run wild, the two of us. Now, to hear him tell it, you'd think being a PI is like tightrope walking on razor blades." He sighed. "Okay. You got everything you was supposed to, and I've made all my arrangements. Let's go see if our plan works."

We entered the alley at the end of the block, each of us carrying a small canvas gym bag, and walked to the hotel employee entrance. A guy stood out there with his blue hotel jacket folded over his arm.

"I told you he was reliable," Otis said.

Captain of Bellboys, Wilson Swift, was thirty something, a clean-shaven five-nine middleweight with the muscular shoulders, arms, scarred brow, and pushed-in nose that said he'd been a boxer.

Otis started to introduce me, but Wilson lifted his hand and put a stop to it. "I don't need to know your name, miss." His voice was breathy and high pitched. "The men you're looking for are on fifteen, Otis. Fifteen twelve, to be exact. Come on."

He opened the door, and we followed him down a hall to another door. This one had a chicken wire and glass porthole window. He looked before opening that door. We followed him down an air-conditioned hall, where he paused before rounding a corner and going a short distance more to the freight elevator. Voices from employees, not so far away, rang hollow against the shiny painted cement walls of the wide and empty, spotless hallway.

Wilson lifted the elevator door and indicated a large wheeled laundry hamper that set in there by itself. "I think that's what you asked for," he said, not allowing his voice to carry.

"Perfect," Otis said.

Wilson handed Otis a key. "Lock the door as you leave and make the key disappear." He pointed to one of the several hallways that emptied into the area where we were standing. "When you come down, go that way with your laundry."

"Everything up there like it was earlier?" Otis asked.

"Far as I know," the Bell Captain said. "They had supper sent up about eight. Good luck, Otis." Wilson spun on his heel and put on his jacket as he walked away.

I stepped into the freight elevator after my partner. He closed the door, gave me one of his looks, winked, and started us up into the tall, hushed building. We put silencers on our pistols and had them back in our unzipped gym bags by the time we jerked to a stop at our floor.

The dim back hall on the fifteenth floor was as silent as a cat ready to pounce.

"Should it be this quiet?" I whispered.

Otis answered me in a normal tone of voice as he dragged the laundry hamper out of the elevator. "Sound proofing. The folks who plop down the pesos for these suites don't wanna hear the sounds the hired help make. Get the door."

I shut the elevator door, and joined Otis where he'd rolled the hamper a short distance, pushed it up tight against the wall, and stepped over to the door marked 1512. His preamble to me was a glance and a nod before inserting the key that Wilson had given him. He turned the key, opened the door, and we stepped in.

Once inside, with the door closed behind us, I became aware of the temperature. My God—the air inside the suite was frigid.

There were two nightlights on that provided all the light we needed to make our way around the big room. There were four doors leading from the kitchen: the one through which we'd entered, the open double doors that led to the spacious dining room, a narrow door that was either a pantry or a bathroom, and a door off to the side at the end of a short hall.

Otis placed his gym bag on the counter, took out a cherry red bandanna, tied it around his neck, and pulled it up to cover the lower half of his face. I put on a pair of black horn-rimmed clear eyeglasses. With my black wig, I thought that was enough.

Otis used his thumb and first two fingers to indicate the action of a hypodermic needle. When I had a syringe ready, we went down the short hall and paused there as he opened the door a crack and peered into the next space. I could feel the tension at my temples that was always a part of being close to danger.

He pushed the door open, and we entered the foyer, a white marble-floored space twice the size of most hotel rooms. The entrance to the suite was to the right a dozen feet, and a dozen feet to the left was an open archway that led into a living room area. The voices of several gruff-talking men could be heard. I smelled cigar smoke and cheap perfume.

Midway between where we entered the foyer and the entrance to the living room, there was a heavyset man sleeping in an overstuffed, comfortable chair. His gaping mouth exposed some shiny dental work; his gaping jacket exposed a pistol in a shoulder holster. The newspaper on his lap was open to the sports page.

My partner pulled a sap from his hip pocket, thumped the watchman behind his ear, and relieved him of his pistol. I inserted the syringe into his thigh like a thumbtack into a corkboard and pushed in the plunger. Doc said the animal tranquilizer we were using would keep a grown man out of our hair for six to eight hours. He said the hangover was like being run down by a freight train.

As I put the used syringe in a special pocket inside my bag, Otis whispered in my ear, "Remember, if this goes bad, get nasty fast."

We knew from Wilson Swift that earlier there had been more bodyguards in the suite, but presently he thought there were only two. Otis referred to them as goons.

There was a poker game going on, and no one noticed us until we were well into the huge room. We carried our pistols behind our legs. Two youngish working girls were balanced on stools at the bar showing a lot of leg. They saw us but didn't make a peep.

There were four gray-haired old guys in shirtsleeves and suspenders at a poker table. A goon in shirtsleeves with a pistol under each arm was slouched on one of the silk sofas. He looked under thirty—sort of simian, sloping forehead, low hairline.

I veered away from Otis and went toward that guy. He saw the bandanna that Otis sported and then glanced at the foyer entrance. He got the picture. It was a stick up, and he was the last line of defense. His gaze came back to me, and he tossed aside the girly magazine he'd been reading.

I saw in his little piggy eyes that he knew I had a weapon in my hand. I liked nothing about the guy.

Pay attention.

I heard Otis from across the room telling the poker players that this was a robbery and that nobody would get hurt if they did as they were told. The old men began grousing in unison. You would have thought he'd raised the price on the early bird special, the way they complained one over the other.

"I'm winning, you dumb fuck," one old man said to Otis. "You're not stopping this game."

"Do you know who you're fucking with?" another man demanded of Otis.

"Where're your men, Vahaska?" an arrogant voice asked. "I thought this wasn't supposed to happen."

I stopped ten feet or so from the greaseball and brought my pistol up—the one he already knew I had. He showed no response when I leveled it at his face.

I said, "Get on the floor on your hands and knees."

He laughed.

I shot his left ear.

"Fuck!" he said, and stopped laughing.

It was hard to tell, but it looked as if I'd taken off the upper third of the appendage. I may have taken a chunk out of his head, as well. Blood splattered the side of his face, his neck, and shoulder. He brought his hand up to hold what ear he had left there.

My pistol had made a piiiish sound. Not very loud at all, but I noticed the room had gone quiet behind me.

I said, "Maybe it was the way I phrased it. Get on your hands and knees, please."

"I'm not gonna…" Piiiish. I shot him again, hitting the hand that held the ear. Blood and body matter burst out over the sofa and sprayed the wall behind him. One of the girls at the bar muffled a cry, and the goon, unwilling to stretch his vocabulary, again said, "Fuck!"

"How do I get through to you? Get on the floor," I said.

He was a moment absorbing the shock, staring at his hand that now had droopy fingers and lacked knuckles. He leaned forward and, using his good hand, pushed up from the deep sofa cushions. "You crazy bitch," he growled.

He was coming to get me. He could have drawn a pistol, but he was more accustomed to slapping his women around.

I shot him in the kneecap—or thereabouts. I didn't know exactly where I hit him because of the loose slacks he wore, but I drew blood. He grunted and pitched forward, collapsing to the carpeted floor.

I allowed him a moment to appreciate his situation before I tapped the back of his head with my pistol barrel. "I'm going to tell you one more thing to do. If you don't do it, I'm putting the next one through your skull."

From across the room, a voice I didn't recognize said, "Do as you're told, Carlo. Live to fight another day."

I said, "Put your hands on the back of your head, Carlo."

He didn't hurry, but he did it. The hand that I'd shot looked like fresh hamburger and trailed blood. With my back to the others in the room, I injected a syringe full of tranquilizer into his butt. We now had another sleeping goon, except this one had bled on the wallpaper, a pale yellow silk davenport, and was bleeding still on the ecru wool carpeting.

So much for stealing eggs without the hens finding out.

By the time I got over to where Otis was dealing with the cantankerous old gamblers, he was almost finished with the task of getting them to put their wallets, cash, watches, and rings on the table. They looked to be retired business-men in their sixties and seventies, spoiled by success, and unaccustomed to being told what to do. There was a constant stream of comments and threats coming from them.

"This ain't the end of this, Vahaska," the fat guy bellowed across the table, the turkey skin under his chin flapping. "I'm holding you responsible."

The man with the hearing aid and a half dozen strands of hair that looked like gray wires plastered against his liver-spotted pate, nodded that he agreed—Vahaska was responsible.

Vahaska was dressed like a wealthy cattleman. His boots cost more than my car. I guessed his age at late sixties. He had a slim frame, but he wasn't fragile—maybe five-ten or eleven. Vahaska, as well as the other men, wore a tie loosened at the neck. He was pasty-faced, had dark, deep-set eyes, thick eyebrows, and a mouth that was a thin-lipped horizontal line below a longish, straight nose that showed no character.

The baldheaded man with the fogged glasses who looked as if he'd been dipped in pink ink, said, "You'll have to shoot me to get this watch fob. It was a gift from my wife."

Otis said, "Shoot him."

I leveled my pistol, and the man tossed the watch fob on the table.

And that's how it went.

When the men were divested of their valuables, I indicated Vahaska and asked Otis, "This one?"

"That one," Otis said and flicked his fingers out, slapping Vahaska in the head.

"What the hell do you think you're doing?" Vahaska growled.

"Quiet down, grandpa," Otis said. "You're going with her."

"Going with her..." he repeated, not understanding.

Otis said, "If he doesn't do what you tell him, shoot him."

Just to press home the point that we were messing with the *queso grande*, the men at the table stopped breathing, and the working girls at the bar went slack-jawed.

"Do you know who he is?" the pink man with the thick glasses asked me.

I said, "Everyone who reads the obituaries will know who he is if he doesn't do as he's told." I tapped Vahaska's forehead with the extended barrel of my pistol. "On your feet."

He sighed and stood up. I touched him with my pistol, and we headed off in a direction that I assumed would take us to a bedroom.

I was right. I directed him down a hall and through an open door into a bedchamber that was larger than my entire *hacienda* out at Henry's. Sometimes it's not easy to get a handle on how the rich live.

"Get in the center of the bed," I told him. "On your back."

He stopped by the edge of the bed and faced me. "Does the name Vahaska mean anything to you?"

I cocked my pistol.

Without further conversation, Beaumont's top dog of drugs, prostitution, auto theft, gambling, and other nefarious interests took a seat on the edge of the bed, scooted back until he was in the center, and stretched out on his back. It didn't take long to tie him to the bedposts and tape shut his eyes and mouth, using the cord and tape I'd brought with me in my gym bag.

Before leaving the bedroom, I cut the telephone cord.

My next job was to check the rest of the suite, find Hagan, and get him ready to go—and I did that. I looked in the other two bedrooms, all the bathrooms, all the closets, the kitchen, the pantry, the dining room, the servant's quarters, every-where—everywhere—and there was no sign of him.

I felt like searching again through the same rooms, but I knew that would be a waste of time. I'd looked and I hadn't found him. My heart rate picked up, and my stomach gave birth to butterflies—not finding Hagan Buchanan was a bad surprise. We'd spent time we didn't have and taken a lot of chances for nothing.

22

IN THE LIVING room, Otis had coerced the remaining three poker players to drink glasses of watered-down vodka that contained an animal laxative. My partner wanted to render our elderly captives passive without having to physically restrain them.

Doc had said that the laxative was fast acting, long lasting, and relentless. He promised that the persons ingesting the concoction would mark it as the most electrifying event in their lives. The phrase 'inside out' kept entering his description.

I helped Otis herd the curmudgeons into an interior bathroom—no windows—and, of course, they noted that the room was too small.

"You'll soon have more pressing complaints," I told them and closed the door.

Otis removed his bandanna mask, took a hammer and nails from his gym bag, and nailed shut the bathroom door. That event had the men shouting, but not for long. Their tone changed when the laxative started kicking in.

Otis and I went back to the living room.

"How about your mask," I said.

"Not a problem," he said. "Where's Hagan?"

"I looked everywhere, but I couldn't find him."

"He's not here?"

"There were no signs that anyone had even been in any of the other rooms. If Hagan was ever here, I'm thinking it was for a short time. Maybe just long enough to make a phone call."

"Wouldn't you goddamn know it?" he said and took a deep breath. "Let's get this over with."

He walked ahead of me back into the living room. The working girls had minded their manners and were still sitting at the bar.

"Okay, Bunny," Otis said.

"Holy shit, Otis. My leg was going to sleep," Bunny said and stepped to the floor and held the stool until she had feeling back in her leg. "I need a drink. Do you mind?"

"Of course not. Help yourself."

"Who's your friend?" Otis asked.

"My name's Darlene," the other hooker said.

Darlene was younger than Bunny, but Bunny had the looks—bottle blonde, good skin, could have been Homecoming Queen. Darlene had a cute figure, but her features were pinched, and she didn't help things by frowning all the time. Both girls fixed drinks. Both fired up cigarettes.

"You know this ain't no real robbery, Bunny. You know I don't do this sort of thing," Otis said.

"I know, Otis. You do cop work," she said. "You just tricked these guys, right?"

"That's right. I'm working on a kidnapping case…a young girl. So help us out here for a minute or two and then you gals can be on your way."

"Sure, Otis," Bunny said.

"Sure," Darlene said.

"Was there another man here this evening?" Otis asked.

The girls looked at each and shrugged. "You mean playing poker or Vahaska's jerks?" Bunny asked.

"More like a poker player. A middle-aged guy, younger than the others and better dressed. He might not have stayed too long."

The girls shook their heads no, and Otis shot a glance my way. Hagan was a missing person. Otis lit a cigarette.

"Did Porkpie put your deal together with Vahaska?" he asked, blowing smoke at the high ceiling.

"Yeah," Bunny said.

"Has the old man been good to you?"

"Well, yeah, but he's cheap," she said.

"And they all could use some deodorant," Darlene kicked in.

"Cheap and stinky, huh?" Otis said. "Tell you what. Get the wallets, cash, watches, and rings off the goon on the floor there and the one in the entrance, and put it all on the table with the other stuff. Will you do that for me?"

While Bunny and Darlene were doing that, Otis took me aside and said, "We'll finish up here and then I've got a plan. Go get a pillowcase, will you?"

"Will do," I said and went off to one of the bedrooms.

I got back in time to hear Otis tell the girls they could have all the cash.

"That's a lot of money," Bunny said, interested, but cautious, too. "What do you want for it?"

"I want you gals to get out of town for a couple of weeks. Go to Galveston. Get some sun; do some shopping. What I don't want is you telling Porkpie about what happened here."

Bunny looked offended and said, "Just because I sell out of my pants don't mean I'm dumb enough to tell Porkpie about this."

"That's good," Otis said. "Because if you stick around and he finds out you've got money, he's gonna take it away from you, and then, after he knocks you around, you'll end up telling him what happened here. That's right, ain't it?"

Bunny and Darlene stalled for a moment, and then nodded yes.

"So you have to ask yourself...you wanna be getting some sun and shopping down on the coast, or do you wanna get punched around by Porkpie and end up on my bad side?"

"I wanna go to Galveston for a couple of weeks," Bunny said.

"Me, too," Darlene said.

"I'm saying now, Bunny. Not after you go home and pack. I'm saying the next train. Do we have an understanding here?"

"Sure, Otis," Bunny said. "I get it."

"I got a cousin lives in Port Bolivar," Darlene kicked in. "She could be sick, maybe."

"There you go," Otis said. "That'll be something to tell Porkpie when you show up again. Now take the cash, but leave the wallets and all the other stuff. It's gonna be evidence in my case."

The ladies of the night landed on the table like buzzards on a fresh cadaver. In no time flat, they had all the cash stuffed in their purses, and they were ready to leave.

Bunny looked over at me and said, "I don't know who you are, miss, but I'm never gonna get in your shit."

I made them wait an uncomfortable moment before I said, "Then I guess you'll have a suntan when I see you next, right?"

Neither hooker liked my answer, and both nodded yes fast and hard.

Bunny and Darlene clutched their handbags and hustled across the room, their high heels making the backs of their thighs and their vibrating buttocks taut against their tight skirts.

Otis waited until they'd clattered through the marble foyer and the suite door closed before he said, "Goddamn it! If he ain't here, they've stuck him somewhere."

"Somewhere in the hotel here?"

"No, Wilson would've known about that. They've got him someplace else."

"What if they let him go? What if he just walked out of here on his own before we showed up?"

"Mmmm. I doubt that, but it's worth a try. Telephone Amanda. Let's see if she's heard from him."

I got on the phone and called Amanda. Hagan wasn't with her, and she didn't know where he was. I spent the next fifteen minutes calming her down.

"You ready to tell me your plan?" I asked when I hung up.

"Vahaska is gonna take us to him."

I waited a moment to see if there was more before I said, "Take you long to put that together?"

The guys in the bathroom had grown desperate by that time. They were all reacting to the laxative and, as any sensitive human would, they wanted out of the close quarters. They were calling out and pounding the door.

As we walked by, Otis shouted at them. "Shut up or I'll come in there and shoot you."

The shouting and pounding quieted down, but the moaning could still be heard.

Vahaska didn't want to cooperate, but he had no tolerance for pain. Otis convinced him to take us to where Hagan was being held hostage.

"My men will be happy to see you," the snarling old gangster told us.

We tied him up again, taped his mouth, hid him under a pile of sheets, and moved him out the back door of the suite in the big laundry basket. I went ahead of Otis, brought my car around to the back of the hotel, and when my partner came out, I helped him get the laundry into the back seat.

Once we were on the road, Otis reached back and

ripped the tape from Vahaska's mouth so he could give us directions.

"You've lost your edge, Old Man," Otis said. "You have all these goons on your payroll, and when they're not around to wipe your butt, you're screwed."

"You're the one who's gonna be screwed, Otis Millett... can't even be a proper bagman. I remember you and your pip-squeak partner, Butch something or other, when you were pounding a beat. You were a do-gooder then, and you're a do-gooder now, which means you'll never know the score."

"What score would that be, you bag of wind?"

"You've made some big mistakes tonight. Mistakes that are gonna come back to bite you. You think people just disappear? Maybe they get their faces ripped off first. Remember, all those years ago, how your little partner went bye-bye..."

Otis used an open hand and slapped Vahaska so hard it knocked him half unconscious. I heard him bounce off the door and go to the floor behind my seat. He was quiet for so long it worried me.

"Check on him, Otis. He's an old man. We don't want to lose him before he takes us to Hagan."

"You're right. You're right." Otis struggled around, reached down and dragged Vahaska into the back seat. He gave him a shake. "Snap out of it, you old criminal. Snap out of it."

The old man moaned for a long moment and then began mumbling.

"What's he saying?" I asked.

"Nothing. He's just been knocked silly, that's all."

Vahaska made sounds and muttered for a while until he got his head clear, and then he grumbled to Otis, "You're gonna pay for the way you're treating me."

"Keep your threats to yourself unless you want some more," Otis said.

"You're not going out here to save a kidnapped man...if that's what you think you're doing."

"Oh, yeah?" Otis said.

"Hagan's a cheat and a liar," Vahaska said. "He backed out of a deal. He owes me money, and I'm doing what he understands to make him pay up."

"He already paid up, but your stupid nephew lost it. That's what you meant to say, wasn't it?"

"You don't know what you're talking about."

"Sure I do. You just don't want to admit it. Bobby Jack had a nose full of speed when he murdered your men out at your ranch and lost your money."

"Who told you those lies?" Vahaska asked.

"And that ain't all your nitwit nephew fucked up. He let that girl walk away, too, didn't he? He can't do nothing right."

"You're full of shit," he said, but without conviction. I could see his face in the rearview mirror, and he didn't look happy.

"Your game is almost over, old man. You should've stayed in Beaumont, a big ugly fish in a small pond. The police have already dug up Chuck and Cecil. It'll be interesting to see who else they find in your garden out there, thanks to your stupid nephew."

Vahaska growled, "You haven't changed a bit. You still don't know shit from Shinola, who to trust, who's on your side and who's not. You're being played, muscle man. You're like one of those wind-up toys. You don't have a clue."

I knew Otis wanted to hit him again, but I was glad he held back. Things stayed quiet in the car for the next few miles while my partner and I thought over what had been said.

Vahaska gave me a final direction. "Turn there and follow that road till you come to the house," he said.

I made the turn and brought the car to a crawl as we entered a rutted dirt road with trees hugging each side of the car. It was as if trees surrounded us. We were way the hell and gone, out in a section of rural Texas where ribbons of woods flowed like wide green rivers through flat grazing lands. It was the middle of the night; we didn't know where we were, or what we might be coming up against.

We were moving through a forest of hickory and blackjack oak, watching for a house that the criminal in the backseat had told us was out there. Well—maybe it was, maybe it wasn't. It was time to pay attention, and Otis and I both knew it.

And then I saw something and stopped the car. "Do you see that light?"

Otis stared out the front window and said, "Oh, yeah; way back in there. Is that it, Vahaska?"

"I don't know why you'd want to stop so far away. Drive on in. My boys won't hurt you when they find out I'm with you. This is just business, after all."

"Where's that tape we put over his mouth?" Otis asked me.

While Otis taped Vahaska's mouth and made sure he was trussed up, I drove on using my parking lights. When we were closer, but still a good walking distance from the cabin lights, I stopped, backed off the road, and hid the car in the thick brush and trees.

Otis manhandled Vahaska onto the backseat floor and said, "I better find you right there when I come back or I'll kick your ass to Thursday and back." He covered him with a pile of sheets, and got out of the car. "Lock your doors. We don't want nobody finding this crap for brains and turning him loose. I want him here in case this is a wild goose chase."

We locked up and pushed our way through the underbrush around to the trunk where I kept some weapons.

"A cut-down twelve-gauge for this kind of work," Otis said, mumbling to himself. He pumped a round into the chamber, then slipped a replacement into the magazine.

I chambered rounds, eased down the hammers, and stuffed the loaded .38's in my hip pockets. I got the pistol in my shoulder holster ready, as well. I grabbed some extra magazines, and I was set to go.

I closed the trunk and Otis sniffed the breeze. "The night seems balmy for so late in the year, don't it? I don't know what's happening with the weather. People say them atomic bombs going off over in Nevada have changed the weather. That sound right to you?"

"Haven't given it much thought," I said.

"Well...could be," he said. "Okay, now listen, Missy. There ain't no plumbing and electricity out this far. They'll have lanterns and flashlights, too, most likely. If they have dogs, the mutts already know we're out here. No dogs, I'll bet we can get pretty close."

"And if shooting starts?"

"Nail anything that moves. We didn't come out here to do no dying."

The tar black night was filled with the drone of locusts, the whine of mosquitoes, the scampering of night creatures, and now and again the low hoot of a hunting owl. The breeze fluffed the treetops as we moved along the rutted road toward the pale yellow light that we could see through the dense underbrush.

When we'd rounded a bend and gotten close enough to see a couple of cars parked in front of a rustic shack that was out in the middle of a large clearing, we paused, and Otis put his mouth to my ear.

"There ain't no dogs, or they'd be making fools of us right now. Get out a little ahead of me. Because of them black things you wear, they'll see my big ass without ever seeing you. That way you'll be in a closer position to take 'em out, if they do see me and start to shoot."

That made sense. I took the lead, crossed the clearing, and got to the parked cars ahead of my partner. From behind one of the cars, it was easy to hear two men arguing inside the little unpainted house. Something about cigars—and one of the men wanted to catch some sleep. They sounded as if they'd been drinking.

There were tall narrow windows to each side of the front door, and three steps up to a porch as wide as the house. One window was dark. Bugs were fluttering at the rusty window screen of the other window trying to get to the kerosene lantern that burned on a table in that room. I could see the kitchen stove in the background. The dark front room and the room behind it were bedrooms. If Hagan was there, he was in one of those rooms.

Just as Otis huffed up and stopped beside me, a man moved between the lantern and the window. He came stomping out of the house, cursing, and slammed the screen door closed behind him. He looked to be in his forties; he wore suspenders and shirtsleeves. He stood motionless for a moment, then put all his weight on one leg and broke wind.

We remained still and kept our eyes on him as he chewed the end off a cigar and spit it aside. When he snapped a match off his thumbnail, put the fire to his stogie, and began drawing at it, Otis made some signs at me.

He was staying there with his shotgun, and I should go around the house and find Hagan. Before I could move, he made one more sign. Be careful.

The way the cars were parked, I was able to stay hidden from the cigar man until I was around the corner and out of his line of sight. The guy inside near the lantern couldn't see out of a lighted room into pitch darkness, no matter how hard he tried. Besides that, he was stretched out on a daybed with his eyes closed. All I had to do was keep quiet as I went past the windows on that side of the house. I just had to make less noise than the insects, and I'd be all right.

I skirted out a bit from the back porch and the lidded rain barrel that was at the corner of the kitchen side of the house and aimed for the back bedroom window on the opposite side. The bedroom wasn't as dark as I'd expected. I found out why when I stood on my tiptoes and looked through the filthy, rusted screen. The door was open a few inches, letting in light from the lantern in the other room. That gave me all I needed to see Hagan tied up and on the bed.

The sash window was open wide for ventilation. All that stood between me and being in the room with Hagan was the screen. I guessed the door was open to allow

Vahaska's men to hear anything that happened in Hagan's room. I kept that in mind as I used a knife to cut the filthy screen. I stretched up and sliced it top and sides and lastly across the bottom.

I tossed aside the stiff piece of screen and took a deep breath. I knew the next thing I had to do would hurt my shoulder. I clinched my teeth as I muscled up onto the sill and wiggled forward until my weight tipped me into the room. I placed my hands on the bedroom floor and, as slowly as I could, somersaulted onto my back. I landed more quietly than I expected, but I'd been right. My shoulder hurt like hell. I hoped it wasn't bad enough to go back to see Doc McGraw. I didn't think I could take another lecture.

I checked to make sure my pistols were secure before crawling on my hands and knees over to the bed. The rough wood floor squeaked, but not enough to alert Hagan's captors.

Hagan knew I was there, of course, and watched every move I made. I put my finger to my lips because the adage, Better safe than sorry, made too much sense to ignore. I cut the ropes from his ankles and then his arms. Because he had been tied to the iron bedstead, I helped him sit up. The bedsprings squeaked, but I know they seemed louder to me than they actually were.

When I removed the tape from his mouth, I cautioned him again to remain silent. I knew he would be stiff from having been tied up, so I helped him to his feet and walked him to the window. I assisted him in getting his legs over the sill, and used all my strength to help him ease out the narrow window.

The lawyer slipped over the sill, and his feet had almost touched the ground when I heard the outhouse door slam. The man emerging from back in the trees carried a lantern and followed a path of long wooden planks that led from the outhouse to the back door of the cabin.

Hagan couldn't hold on much longer, and I couldn't handle his weight.

23

VAHASKA'S MAN, ON his way back from the outhouse, noticed when Hagan fell the last foot or so and collapsed to the ground below the bedroom window.

"Hey!" he called out, and ran toward us.

"Run, hide," I told Hagan, and shot the man who had come from the outhouse. I hit him twice and saw his body jerk both times. He wasn't tall, maybe five six or so, but looked like he weighed over two hundred pounds. He was a stump of a man—an easy target. I knew for sure I'd put two into his ample midsection. But he kept coming and, with a shout, heaved his lantern at Hagan who remained unmoving beneath the window.

I heard two shotgun blasts from the front of the house. Otis had entered the game, and my guess was the man on the front porch was dead.

The kerosene lantern broke against the house above Hagan and just below the window. Flames were everywhere, inside and outside the house. Unless I wanted to go through fire, the window was no longer an exit. I turned back into the bedroom as I heard small arms fire begin snapping from the other room.

There was another window, but the iron bed frame was pushed up against it. As I pulled the bedstead away from the wall, I heard stomping footsteps, and the bedroom door opened. I dropped to the floor and began firing at the tree trunk of a man who appeared in the doorway. I hit him several times.

The man cursed and slammed the door. I kept firing through the wooden door and heard him yelp a time or two as if I'd hit him some more. I kept firing until I'd emptied the magazine, feeling certain that some of those shots had to have done more than just let streams of light into the room.

A load of buckshot burst through the door, pulverizing a section of the old wood the size of a supper plate. The blast also blew out the window on the other side of the bed and scared the holy crap out of me. I scuttled backwards on my knees and elbows, staying low, going for more of an off angle to the door.

Another load of buckshot followed the first, taking out most of the middle of the door and punching into the wall near the window. I opened up again with my .38, shooting fast through the door and wall, aiming where I thought the shooter stood in the other room. Again, I heard some yelps and curses as if I were hitting the big man. I emptied another magazine and changed pistols.

The light in the bedroom came from the fire behind me that raged around the window. The lamp that had been burning in the other room was now out. I heard occasional pistol shots coming from the front of the house, but otherwise it was quiet. It was the quiet before the storm.

The door was kicked so hard it shattered; splintered wood was left hanging from the hinges. It was beyond understanding that the big man I'd been shooting could still be alive, but he was. My God! He came charging into the bedroom, kicking his way past the demolished door, sending wood debris everywhere. He held a pick ax out in front of him, gripped in both hands. He scanned the room trying to find me.

When he discovered me on the floor between the

shattered door and the burning window, he let out a maniacal growl, swung the pick ax in a sweeping arc up over his head, and brought it down with savage force to pierce the floor too damned close to my head for comfort.

I had begun shooting him, point blank, while he wound up with the pick ax—shot after shot, at least another five or six hits to the stout man's chest, the area around the heart that brings down normal men.

Finally—finally—he straightened up, his hands slipped away from the farm tool, and he staggered back a heavy step or two. He groaned as he collapsed and fell against the edge of the bed and then to the floor. With my heart slamming against my ribs, I kept an eye on him and an eye on the open door as I reloaded.

I let a long moment pass, wanting to determine what was happening elsewhere in the house before I moved. It was quiet except for the hiss and crackle of the fire. So I almost screamed when the big man spoke to me.

"Hold my hand," he said.

Jesus! He must have taken a couple of dozen bullet hits. His clothing was riddled with bloody spots where I'd shot him. I was amazed that he was alive, much less talking. I stared at his earnest face, his fifty-cent haircut, his massive neck and shoulders, and gave him my left. I kept my pistol ready in my right. The next shot would be between his eyes if he made the wrong move.

He gripped my hand as if his life depended on it. "I'm all tuckered out," he said.

"I can imagine."

"Hear them crickets singing?"

"I do," I said.

"God's creatures, my mama told me."

"Uh huh."

"Her name was Esther Gibbons...from Tennessee..." His breathing had become choppy. He cocked his head and looked me in the eye. "I'm gonna die, ain't I?"

"It looks that way."

"Don't that beat all?" He panted for breath. "I didn't start out to be no villain."

"No?"

"It was my cousin Archie. He was the bad one…"

"Worse than you, huh?" But I was talking to a corpse.

Otis came to the door. "What're you doing?" he asked.

"Having a confessional."

"The place is burning down. You aware of that?"

The entire back wall of the house was in flames and the fire was making quick work of the shingle roof.

"I thought I smelled something."

"Where's Hagan?"

"He's around," I said.

"Come on. Let's get out of here."

I placed the big man's hand on his chest and got to my feet.

As we left the house, I discovered that the man who had been sleeping in the other room had died at the front window, his pistol in his hand. The man who died on the porch, his pistol untouched in his shoulder holster, still had his cigar clamped in his teeth. I wondered if those two had had a cousin Archie.

When we were out by the cars, I called out, "Hagan. It's Kristin and Otis. It's safe now."

After a moment, Hagan came crawling out from beneath the house, his expensive slacks ruined. "Thank you. Thank you," he choked out as he got to his feet and staggered toward us.

"Come on, Hagan," Otis said, meeting him halfway, reaching out to take the attorney's arm. "Let's get you home."

"They were going to kill me…throw my body in the well," Hagan whimpered, and began to blubber. "I heard them talking."

Otis threw an arm over his shoulders. "They ain't gonna do no such thing," Otis said, and walked the broken man out away from the burning house. "Get the car, will you, Missy?"

"I'm on my way," I said, and started off down the road.

With the burning house behind me, I made wild and unruly shadows—but not for long. Once I was around the curve in the road, darkness took over. The farther I walked, the darker it got. To add to that, we hadn't left breadcrumbs, so I was struck with the possibility of not being able to find my car at all. I didn't have a flashlight, and the car was hidden back in the underbrush well off the road.

I disliked feeling stupid, but I had to admit that this trick with the car on a dark night was not the brightest move I'd ever made. I wondered if Otis had some solution to this that he'd failed to mention. I was embarrassed by the thought of waiting for sunrise to find where I'd stashed the car. However, that was becoming a consideration as I walked along staring into the inky woods.

Concentrating on the dark woods caused me a nasty surprise when I looked down the road and saw headlights coming. They were distant, but they were coming fast.

With my heart in my throat, I stepped well off the road, dropped to one knee, and brought an arm across my face covering everything but my eyes. I made myself little more than a black bump. There was no reason why I should be noticed.

But that wasn't the issue. The obvious problem was that Otis might think I was behind those headlights and be caught off guard. I had to warn him. As the speeding lights got closer, I made out that it was a pickup truck. I'd pulled my pistol with the intention of firing a few rounds to alert Otis, but when I saw the Texas Longhorns roaring toward me, I decided to do more than tip off my partner.

When the truck flew past, I spun around and fired at the back right tire. I don't know how many slugs I put in that tire, but much of it left the rim when it blew out.

Bobby Jack's truck careened off the road, tore through the underbrush, sideswiped a big tree and spun around, cutting the darkness with its sweeping headlights, illuminating scurrying birds and other frightened forest life. The big three-quarter-ton pickup battered down several small trees, bounced over their stumps, tipped up on two wheels, flopped onto the driver's door with a loud crunch of collapsing metal and breaking glass, and skidded to a stop beside the road facing the opposite direction it had been traveling.

That was all the warning Otis was going to get.

Moving out of the glaring headlights, I crossed the road and approached the wreck from the darkness. I heard the radio—a country band played "San Antonio Rose."

I stopped when I was even with the truck cab roof and stepped back into the underbrush. The engine was running hot, and the rear wheel that could turn spun shredded rubber, making a loud flap-flap-flap. With the driver's door against the ground, the way out of the cab was straight up through the open window on the passenger side.

I had the spookiest feeling. I knew that I'd shot Bobby Jack—twice. I felt certain that I'd hit him in the groin or the upper legs, so it was difficult for me to believe that he could be driving that truck. But I'd just gone through a nightmare with a man who had to be shot over and over again before he took it seriously. I wasn't certain what to believe anymore.

Although I did believe that the truck was being driven by one of Vahaska's men. What I had to question was the "shoot first ask later" habit that I'd developed. I knew it was late for such sentiments, but I was worried about who I might find in the cab of that truck. Hell, it could be any-body. When the ignition was cut and the engine and radio shut down and the sounds of the night took over again, I felt the tightness at my temples. I was about to get some answers.

The flapping tire remnants had almost come to a stop when a hand came up through the open truck window. Then a head poked out. It was a man with a bruised face and a bandage across his nose. Could it be Bobby Jack? But the patch over his eye gave him up—it was Joey Loco. The wheelchair vet had sent his face into the hotel hall floor so hard it had broken his nose. That accounted for the bandage.

Joey was a lefty, and the hand I could see was his right. He seemed in no hurry as he looked around.

"Let's see both hands, Joey."

His head snapped around, and he squinted in my direction. I blended with the darkness. I didn't think he could see me standing there with a pistol in each hand—both pointed at him.

"I know that voice," he said in his high-pitched nasal twang. He moved his head, trying to get a fix on my location. "That's you, ain't it, Blondie?"

"Both hands, One Eye."

"You do get around."

"Your other hand right now, or you're a dead man."

Joey smiled and said, "Did you hear your friend who drives the wheelchair's gone missing?"

I fired both of my pistols, and he flinched from the heat of the lead I sent past his ears.

"You missed," Joey said, no longer smiling. He knew where I was now from the flash of the pistols.

"She misses when she means to," Otis said from the darkness over to my left.

The instant Joey turned his attention toward the new voice, I shifted my position several steps to my right and settled down on one knee. I counted on the insect din to cover the sounds I made moving.

"Now let's see that other hand," Otis said.

"Glad to oblige," Joey said, and shot-gunned a fist-sized hole through the truck cab roof that tore through the underbrush where I had been standing.

I cut loose with both pistols, and Otis began firing, too.

We hit Joey Loco—more than once. He fell away, leaving a lingering mist of blood spray as he dropped back into the cab. Otis and I shot a few more times, following his unseen body as it descended, our lead tearing more holes in the roof of Bobby Jack's truck. We stopped before it looked like the pictures I'd seen of Bonnie and Clyde's car, but there was a similarity.

Otis and I moved toward each other—both of us keeping an eye on the truck, as if anyone could have survived that onslaught—or, more to the point, was there anyone else in there?

"I was pissed off because of the vet," I said. "Were you thinking about your partner from the old days?"

"Don't worry about all that, Missy. He shot first."

"Still...we've killed four men tonight, Otis."

"You pay with blood to learn the ropes of war, Missy. It's made us hard, that's true. But we ain't killed nobody who didn't come out here set on killing us."

Otis the philosopher...but he was right.

While he looked in on Joey's remains, I used the truck headlights to find my car. I checked on Vahaska. He told me he needed to take a whiz.

"The cabin's on fire," he said, staring over his shoulder as he did his business.

"That's none of your affair," I told the kingpin and returned him to the backseat floor of the car, re-taped his mouth, covered him up, and drove down to the burning cabin.

Hagan came over. He was anxious to get away.

"There's someone under the sheets there at your feet," I told him as he got into the car. "He won't bother you if you don't bother him."

The lawyer's face scrunched up with distaste to discover that he was to share the back with someone under a sheet.

Otis pulled the cigar smoker off the front porch and dragged him out away from the burning building. He put the stolen property from the poker game in his arms, adjusting the pillowcase so the embroidered Hudson Towers logo was easy to see.

The sun came up a bright orange in my rearview mirror as we drove back toward Dallas, the sky erupting with pink and scarlet clouds. Hagan had fallen asleep across the back seat; Otis slept against his door, and my guess was Vahaska was asleep, too, under his purloined bedding.

The gas gauge pushed empty, and the windshield was covered with bug juice. So I pulled into the first open filling station we came to.

"Is your ladies room clean?" I asked the sleepy kid in overalls who wandered out of the station house.

"Cleaned it myself," he mumbled.

"Fill the car with ethyl, please."

"Yes, ma'am."

"There're a couple of bucks in it for you, if you pay special attention to the windshield."

That brought him around. "Yes, ma'am," he said.

The kid was still hosing and scrubbing the front glass when I came from the restroom. To give him time to finish, I used the pay phone and called Hagan's wife. She sounded groggy with sleep, but agreed to meet us in downtown Dallas.

On a side street near the Hudson Towers Hotel, Otis waited while Amanda and Hagan reunited before he said, "I know you two are relieved and at the same time more upset'n treed possums. But you have to keep being upset to yourselves."

"Why's that?" Amanda growled, her voice still hoarse.

"Because if you don't keep your lip zipped, you'll end up saying something about Sherry's kidnapping," Otis said straight from the shoulder. "Or something about sticking her in that sanitarium. Unless you wanna be implicated in her disappearance, my advice is don't talk."

"I don't like your tone of voice," Amanda told Otis.

"Mandy…" Hagan murmured.

"Mrs. Buchanan," Otis said, his patience strained. "Sherry Beasley was not treated good. Maybe you didn't mean her no harm when you used her like a pawn in your money game. But it's clear you didn't give her as much thought as you might've. It's okay if you wanna be pissed at me, but you oughta be praying that young woman shows up alive."

"Oh, God," Hagan said.

"And another thing," Otis said. "Say nothing about Hagan's gambling problem or what you did to solve that problem. That's just your business. In other words, nobody needs to know about you consorting with gangsters. And nothing should ever be said about Hagan getting kidnapped. In other words, you don't wanna start talking about stuff that won't end good for the Buchanans. Now do you see?"

"And Vahaska gets away with treating us the way he has?" Amanda snarled.

"That's right. You wanna leave that be."

"What if I don't choose to do that, Mr. Millett?"

"Ask your husband if calling the devil is the same as seeing him walking atcha."

Hagan's haggard expression spoke volumes.

"Listen to me," Otis said to the lawyer. "You have the Beasley will to settle today. Go home. Clean up. Get a little rest and go to work like nothing happened."

"Thank you. Thank you, Otis...Kristin," Hagan murmured.

Amanda, her face burnished with anger, didn't bother with a thank you; she didn't even bother with a kiss-my-elbow. She just tightened her jaw, gathered her husband into their big new car, and drove away.

I raised my eyebrows at Otis.

He said, "That woman can whip her weight in wild-cats."

24

ONCE HAGAN WAS gone, Otis untied Vahaska and pulled the tape from his mouth.

"It's about goddamned time," the old man complained, his tired face sporting a five o'clock shadow.

We drove him over to the Hudson Towers and dropped him off at the front door.

"You and Cleopatra there haven't seen the last of me," Vahaska snapped and walked unsteadily toward the entrance to the hotel, resembling a derelict in his rumpled pants and grubby sweat-stained shirt. He had to talk his way past a skeptical doorman.

As we drove off, Otis said, "I hope his life is a living hell today."

"I want to talk to you about him," I said, as I stashed my horn-rimmed glasses in the glove compartment and pulled off the 'Cleopatra' wig I'd worn all night. I wanted to shampoo my hair in the worst way.

"I can't get used to you as a brunette," Otis said.

"I'm thinking I won't stay this way too long."

"You wanna talk about Vahaska?"

"Yeah. I know we couldn't just shoot him. He doesn't even carry a weapon, does he?"

"I've never known him to. He lets others do his dirty work."

"But like you'd say, he sure needs shooting."

"That's what I'd say, all right."

"Wasn't there something else we could've done with him? Why'd we just drop him off at his hotel?"

"So he'll be easy to find when the police start looking for him."

"You're going to make a few calls…"

"I am at that. There's robbery and destruction of property at one of the city's finest hotels. There's murder and destruction of property out in the woods east of here. And Vahaska's tied to all of the above in one way or another."

"And you want the police to…?"

"I want the police to detain the old scoundrel until they finish digging up bodies out at his ranch."

"You think your partner's out there."

"I'd like to put that to rest. It's worth a shot, ain't it?"

"Makes sense," I said. "But I'll tell you what doesn't make sense."

"What's that?"

"The army that Vahaska's lost since he's been up here from Beaumont."

"How many do you figure?"

"Ten that I know about."

Otis whistled. "I hadn't kept count, but that's a mess of troops. I see what you're getting at."

I pulled up and parked beside his old Buick. It was where we'd left it last night.

I said, "That's a heavy price to pay just to shake down the Buchanans. We're missing something."

"Well, I don't think he started off to lose so many of his men, but he didn't back off when they started dropping, did he? You're right, Missy. There's more here than a gambling debt."

"From what Vahaska said, Hagan is a thorn in his side," I tossed in. "Whatever that means."

Otis sighed. "Yeah…well, whatever that is, it's still about the money."

"And the magic number seems to be one hundred thousand."

"Uh huh," Otis said as he opened the door and got out, "but I think that's just prime-the-pump money. The serious number is a lot bigger." He leaned back into the car and spoke under his breath. "Sort of makes you wonder, don't it? Especially when you think of the timing and then figure in the Beasley fortune."

"And a scheme to get to it," I said.

"Hatched by the fox that's guarding the henhouse," he added.

"Or the vixen married to the fox," I said.

"Uh huh…well, get some shuteye and then let's meet at the office and go together to hear the will read," Otis said. "I'll bet our little Sherry Beasley'll be there, don'cha think?" He winked at me before he closed the door.

I caught some sleep, showered, and dressed up a bit before picking up Otis. We drove together over to the posh, conservative offices of Buchanan, Farnley, Meadows and Meadows.

Members of the fourth estate had already begun to gather in the reception area. They had readers who wanted every juicy detail.

"Good morning, Mr. Millett," the redheaded receptionist in combat-ready makeup said. "Mr. Buchanan told me that you were to go right in. You'll be meeting in the conference room. And you're…?" she said to me.

"Why, Lucy, I thought you met Kristin the last time we were up," Otis replied. "This is my partner. Kristin Van Dijk."

"I'm sorry, Miss Van Dijk," she said, looking confused. "Please go right in."

"Thank you," he said and we both gave her a smile. After all, this firm was getting ready to pay us a hefty fee for services rendered. We could afford a smile, even if my name had slipped her memory—and then I remembered that Ivy had made me a brunette. The last time I was up here, I was a platinum blonde.

We walked past Lucy's polished walnut counter through some double doors that led to another set of double doors. Those doors led to a wide-open area carpeted in gray and paneled in dark wood where there were seating arrangements of leather chairs separated by small trees in large pots.

All eyes swung our direction as we entered the conference room, but, since we were nobodies, the curiosity was swiftly sated—except for Nadine Beasley's warm interest in Otis. Her gaze lingered as my partner and I moved to the back of the room.

My God, the woman was seventy, or close to it, looked the part of a Cecil B. DeMille discovery, and had fluttering lashes that were advertising an active libido. Well, I had to admit, from across the conference room table, she was a stunner. Perhaps that explained why no one was seated near her. Otis gave her a polite nod and he and I sat down in chairs that were placed against the back wall.

A quick count gave me a dozen alert Beasleys scattered around the long table, five men and seven women. Within easy reach of Hiram's descendents and in-laws were pads and pencils and thick glass tumblers and pitchers of water—a conservative law firm's stab at providing creature comforts as well as the necessities.

Around the state, there were a dozen more family members at mansions and ranches, all with one thing in common: an interest in the fine print and dollar amounts in Hiram Beasley's much-publicized last will and testament. And, of course, there was the public, to whom the press felt obligated to report every scrap of information concerning the content of the will, as well as the reactions of the Beasley kin.

"No Sherry," Otis whispered.

I glanced at the clock on the wall. "There's still time," I

said, but it worried me that she wasn't already there.

Time passed, and a couple of minutes before the designated start time, and several minutes after the Beasleys had become annoyed and then agitated, two secretaries entered. All watched them take seats off to the side and open their stenographer pads.

After a moment Hagan appeared, wearing a poker face and carrying an important-looking leather folder. I could tell that he was still tired and anxious, but he was dressed to the nines and looked every bit the man in charge.

He moved to the head of the table and stood for a long moment glancing about. It appeared to me that he made eye contact with most in the room before speaking to Nadine.

"Have you heard from Miss Beasley?" he asked her.

"Not a word," Nadine responded, and the Beasleys grimaced and grumbled.

"We can't start without her," one of the men at the table said.

"Ladies and Gentlemen," Hagan said, "there is no contingency for starting these proceedings late. The instructions are clear. So, even though Miss Sherry Louise Beasley is not present, we must begin."

The gathering emitted a low murmur, and the secretaries scribbled away, recording in shorthand every word that was being said.

Hagan took a seat, put on his reading glasses, opened the leather folder, and began to read from the paper document within: "Know all men by these presents, that I, Hiram Monroe Beasley, now of Dallas, Texas, being over the age of twenty-one years and being of sound and disposing mind and memory, and not laboring under any duress, fraud or undue influence of any person whomsoever, and realizing the uncertainty of this mortal life, and wishing to make proper disposition of my earthly possessions, do hereby make, publish, and declare this my Last Will and Testament..." and on he went until the patriarch's wishes were made clear in reference to the settlement of his fortune. It was a wordy document, but not lengthy.

Sherry had already told Otis and me how old man Beasley had dictated the terms by which she was to be treated—or rather how she was to be protected—if the surviving Beasleys expected to inherit a share of his fortune.

Protected or not, Sherry was not in that room for the reading of the will. Though they were not privy to the details, those present knew that her absence would create consequences—and it didn't take long to find out what those were.

Hiram Beasley's family, his ex-wife, his sons, and grandchildren, were remembered with the same amount of money that they had received fourteen years ago upon his death. Which meant that they each were given a figure generous enough to satisfy any normal person. Handled properly, their inheritances would support a lifetime of comfort for them and their offspring.

However, the Beasleys weren't satisfied, especially when they learned that the real fortune, the kind of money that could purchase a small to medium-sized country most places on the globe, had been left to the old radio evangelist, Joshua Lee Scurver. In fact, they were shocked. Color drained from healthy faces, and several voices rose as one to shout out their displeasure.

The response was so heated, so resentful that Otis whispered to me, "There'll be a heart attack here today. Mark my words."

Many of the Beasleys were too young to know of Brother Joshua and his Good Works Radio Ministry from Del Rio. However, those who did know were quick to explain that he was a charlatan. "His specialty was bamboozling old women into leaving their estates to his Good Works Crusade," an older son announced to the room.

"Apparently," a younger Beasley noted, "he knew how to bilk old men, as well."

One of the sons blamed Nadine for not doing her job of

keeping track of Sherry. Nadine ignored him. Another of the sons shouted that the will was not legal.

Hagan brought the group to order. "I must assure you that the will is ironclad. If you had been left nothing, perhaps you might have had some grounds to contest, but Hiram Beasley has been quite generous to everyone—and, after all, it was his decision to make. Please understand, once and for all, that not one cent of the core Beasley inheritance will go to any member of the Beasley family."

Again, verbal abuse and finger pointing broke out, interrupting Hagan. He waited for a natural pause and said, "Take heart in the knowledge that the Beasley fortune will go to someone who does God's work."

That observation was met with cynical guffaws and more unpleasant shouting. When Hagan pushed back his chair, rose to his feet, and closed the leather folder, the room grew silent.

"The transfers of funds will be completed this week and documentation hand-delivered to the addresses we have on file. Please advise us if you want notices delivered elsewhere. Thank you for allowing Buchanan, Farnley, Meadows and Meadows to serve you. Our firm has long had deeply founded respect for the Beasley family—many of you have been our clients for years. But, let me say that we will be pleased to meet with you privately to discuss your questions and concerns—and, of course, to assist you in matters of estate planning. Feel free to contact me. Good day."

Otis and I were concerned about Sherry missing the reading of the will.

"I ain't worried about her bank account," Otis said. "The real questions are: where's she at, and is she safe?"

We left the yammering millionaires behind us in the conference room and caught up with Hagan.

"You ain't heard from Sherry Beasley at all?" Otis asked.

"Nothing," Hagan said. "I've prayed that you would have located her by now."

"Not yet, but I figure we're still on the clock until we find her."

"Of course. Of course," Hagan muttered.

We said our goodbyes, and departed ahead of the rush.

When we were alone and on our way down in the elevator, Otis said, "We gotta find Miss Sherry. I reckon she's with Rico Hernandez somewhere, high as a peregrine caught in a thermal."

"Probably," I said.

"We'll have to check out all their haunts."

"Uh huh," I said. "But, you know, I was thinking—I'm not sure money has ever meant that much to her."

"Maybe, but I didn't like all that blabber from Vahaska about me not knowing who to trust. It's sure he knows something we don't know."

"I think that's more about Hagan than Sherry."

"You're probably right, but it made me think back on some things. You recollect telling me when you was getting Sherry out of Bobby Jack's bedroom how she said something about it being all wrong?"

It took me a moment, but I got there. "Yeah…'It's all wrong' is what she said."

"Did you ever think, Missy, how did she expect it to be?"

"You mean what made it all wrong?"

"That's what I'm wondering."

"She'd been on Bobby Jack's diet of speed, sex, and more speed," I said. "I think that was just crazy talk."

"Uh huh, and out of the mouths of babes sometimes, too. If you see what I mean."

"So you're saying she expected something to happen, just not actually what did."

"I wish I knew what I was saying. All I do know is, when I think back, I don't have an answer to that one."

As the elevator doors opened on the main floor, I said,

"Okay. Tonight we start looking for Rico's old Chrysler. We'll find her."

"Yes, ma'am...and now, drop me off at the office and go see your detective friend at the hospital. Because I know that's what you wanna do."

As we crossed the lobby, he gave me a gentle pat on the shoulder, something he seldom did.

"Now don't go all mushy on me," I warned him.

He laughed and dug out a Lucky.

A nurse told me Lee's room number. The door was open, and I saw him in bed. His head was bandaged. There were flowers on the side table—family, maybe. He smiled when he saw me.

"I've missed you," he said as I went over and sat near him, our faces close.

"I've missed you, too," I said.

There was no one there with us. We could have spoken in a normal tone of voice and not been heard outside of the room. But we used hushed tones, as if we were keeping secrets—as lovers might.

"I had a dream." He took my hand. "We were in a *cantina*... an old-timey Mexican cantina; it was smoky and crowded. You were wearing black, like you always do. There was a guitar...a woman was singing from back in the room...she had a voice made from smoking too much, drinking too much. *'Besame, besame mucho.'*"

He spaced the words as if he were singing. And then he hummed softly, almost to himself—confident and in perfect pitch—the first few lines of the song.

Then he looked into my eyes and said, *"Temo que me estoy enamorando."*

"Your Spanish is beautiful," I told him, my heart turning over.

"You're beautiful," he said.

I smiled. "Slow down. You'll give yourself a relapse."

He smiled, too, and stared at me for a long moment before saying, "Eschew obfuscation, be polite to women, and always sip your claret."

"Who are you quoting?" I asked, recognizing the old saws he'd slung together.

"My uncle who went to Princeton; my dad's younger brother. I've been thinking about him."

"What's he doing these days?"

"He was lost at sea during the war."

"I'm sorry," I said.

"Yeah, me, too. I liked him a lot...eschew obfuscation. He would've approved of you."

I liked it when we looked into each other's eyes.

"Princeton, huh?" I said.

"He was the smart one. School was never one of my successes. Mom wanted me to be a lawyer, but I liked police work best. I sailed through those exams."

"Then you chose the right thing."

"Kristin..."

"Yeah?"

"I don't remember the other night...most of it, anyway... you know, the truck coming at us..."

That night seemed like ages ago.

"It doesn't matter."

"My buddies on the force don't know what happened out there in the rain. But you do, don't you?"

"I'll tell you about it someday."

"Your eyes are the color of cornflowers," he said.

I blushed and looked away.

"Cornflower blue...the color of the most valuable sapphires."

"Lee..." I said, facing him, my heart turning over again.

"I can't believe that," he whispered, leaning closer until his sweet breath was warm against my cheek. "It seems impossible that I should be the first to learn that sapphires get their color from your eyes."

I took his face in my hands and brought his lips to mine. It was the passionate kiss that we had both wanted from the moment I entered the room. I felt in my heart that Lee Pierson, the romantic detective, was someone I could fall in love with.

"I'd say you're due for discharge, Detective Pierson."

Lee and I looked up to discover a doctor standing at the foot of the bed, peering over eyeglasses that perched halfway down his long thin nose. A smiling nurse with sparkling eyes stood beside him.

Without ill will, Lee said, "I thought this was a private room."

"And so it is," the doctor said. "I only need a few minutes…if you'll excuse us, miss."

"Don't go far," Lee said.

And I wouldn't have gone far if I hadn't gotten a phone call.

I was standing down the hall near the nurses' station. That was why I was so easy to find.

"Meet me at Hagan's house as soon as you can get there," Otis said. "Amanda killed Vahaska."

25

TWENTY-FIVE MINUTES later I was on a wide, tree-shaded street where big houses sat back behind freshly tended lawns. I located Hagan's number at the curb, followed the long drive past perfectly placed weeping willows up to a split-level ranch.

I parked behind Otis' car.

He hadn't been there long; I felt the heat of his engine as I walked past. There were three other cars parked in the spacious area to the side of the drive. One was Amanda's. I didn't recognize the other two, but I assumed one was Hagan's and the other the property of Vahaska's heirs.

The coronation of a queen rang out when I pushed the doorbell.

Otis came to the door.

"What's the deal?" I asked him.

"She called Hagan, and he called me when he got here," he said, keeping his voice down. I entered and he added, "I called you and the police."

"I beat the police here?"

He closed the door. "I gave you a head start."

"She's okay?" I asked, as he led the way back into the hushed and spacious light-filled house.

"She's not flustered like most housewives I've seen after they've killed someone."

"How'd she do it?"

".38 Smith & Wesson."

"That's heavy for a lady."

"She says it weren't hers, but we ain't never gonna get a straight story. I wanna hear what you make of it," he whispered just before we entered the sitting room where the Buchanans were waiting.

Amanda stared at me with the cold eyes of a bird of prey. Her hair was wet and flattened back, and she was immaculate in shades of copper and russet—slacks, blouse, and a light sweater. She appeared collected, but her posture was too erect. She seemed frozen, as if she were part of a tableau.

Also, she seemed small—seated, as she was, on the front edge of a deep Italian sofa, one of a matched pair in white silk facing each other at right angles to the fireplace. On the glass coffee table between the sofas, a thin column of smoke rose from a cut crystal ashtray where a forgotten cigarette smoldered.

Hagan glided toward us across the thick carpeting, a hand in the pocket of his slacks, his lips curled up in a Glenn Ford grin.

"Mr. Buchanan," I said.

"Kristin," he said, projecting a false insouciance. "It seems you're coming to our rescue quite regularly these days."

Now that Hagan was close, I could tell he'd been drinking.

"Mrs. Buchanan," I said past Hagan. Her eyes had been fixed on me since I'd entered the room. But once I spoke, she looked away without comment.

Otis said, "Come on," and I followed him to the adjoining sun porch, a southwest-facing room with many windows that looked out across an expanse of lawn to a wooded slope crowded with trees that would soon give up their autumn displays.

It was a colorful and cheery space that would hold

its warmth on frosty days. The furniture was simple in comparison to the rest of the house. This was their game room—canasta parties and laughing guests. Spilled drinks wouldn't matter on the tile floor—but what about dead bodies?

Vahaska, the Beaumont mob boss, lay on his back on top of a coffee-colored throw rug, his legs twisted back under him. His face, neck, shoulder, and chest showed five entry wounds, but the first shot hadn't brought him down. He'd traversed the room, knocking furniture aside, upsetting chairs, pulling down a section of wooden blinds and distributing unsightly blood smears and splatters to map his final journey. He'd faced the slugs coming at him and then staggered about as he died. There was a place on his cheek, too—he'd been hit with something.

Near him were shards of a ceramic vase, spilled water mixing with pooled blood, and crushed flowers, trampled in the commotion. A .38 Chiefs Special was placed near the edge of the round table in the center of the room, the odor of gunpowder still clinging to it. I leaned over and noted that all six rounds had been fired.

"And Vahaska was supposed to have brought this with him?"

"That's what the lady says," Otis replied.

"She looks freshly dressed."

"She had blood on her. She washed up and changed clothes."

"No," I exhaled in disbelief.

"I'm afraid so."

"The law is going to be pissed off about that."

"Hell, I wouldn't be surprised to hear she threw her bloody clothes in the washer."

"Didn't Hagan advise her about obstructing an investigation?"

"I'm convinced she did what she wanted before she called him. There's gonna be a lot of blanks to fill in on this one."

"I'll give you a blank," I said.

"What's that?"

"Vahaska without his goons."

Otis sent his eyebrows up. "You're so right. Where was his muscle?"

"Hard to believe he'd come here alone," I said.

"Maybe he's clean out of cucarachas."

"We left him two at the hotel...we messed with them, but they're alive."

"That's more'n we can say about Vahaska," Otis said.

We reacted as one and looked over when Amanda appeared in the doorway. Hagan was behind her, hanging back just beyond her shadow, so to speak.

"You're judged by the company you keep," my mother used to say.

Amanda's voice was still a bit raspy, and she kept the volume at just above a whisper. "This man said his name was Vahaska," she said.

"That's how you're playing this?" Otis asked.

Amanda ignored him and continued talking. "He seemed to know a lot about Beasley matters, the reading of the will and all," she said. "I guess everyone knows about that, but he thought Hagan had some way of accessing the Beasley fortune. He thought Hagan could be persuaded into stealing from the Beasley estate if he threatened my life."

She had reprised some of the facial expressions and gestures that she'd used at our office yesterday. I got a chill up my back. She was practicing for the police.

"He pulled that gun out and threatened me with it," she said, indicating the murder weapon. "He ordered me to phone Hagan and tell him to come home, or he would hurt me. He sort of rambled, like he was on drugs or something...he'd suffered some losses...he was desperate. He said that he wasn't to be messed with...or something like that."

"Did he say why he wanted Hagan to come home?" Otis asked, like an investigator might.

"He said that Hagan knew how to get what he wanted.

I called Hagan and told him that this man was here, in our home, and that he had threatened me. The man said if Hagan called the police, it would guarantee my death."

"He said he'd kill you?" Otis asked.

"That's right," she said. "That was when I realized I had to do something. I wasn't going to let him kill me. I saw my chance and hit him with the vase. And then I grabbed the gun."

She paused and we waited as she cocked her head and appeared to listen to an inner voice. It was a long moment before she spoke again in that low, raspy whisper. "When I pulled at the gun, he shot the table over there."

We looked at where the alleged wild bullet had gouged a piece from the corner of a table.

"But I got the gun away from him. Then he came at me to take it back, and I shot him. He kept coming, and I kept shooting him."

The doorbell rang. The Buchanans looked at each other, but neither moved.

"I'll get it," Otis said and walked away.

Hagan trailed after him.

I stepped over to Amanda and said, "Hold still," as I raised my hand to her face. She had missed a tiny spot of blood near her eye. I wet the tip of my finger and wiped it away. We were very close at that point—eye to eye, you might say, and I was reminded of the fearsome stare and unpredictable nature of a wild beast. I was glad that I was armed.

She turned away, without changing her facial expression, returned to her seat on the white sofa, and picked up her cigarettes and lighter from the glass table. I started to follow her but stopped in the doorway and looked again at Vahaska's corpse.

Otis told me once that the big dark secret to detective work was to get somebody to tell you plainly what happened. Amanda, I feared, was not going to be that person.

The law didn't like being the last called. Otis explained to the detective in charge that he was unaware that the police had not been notified until he arrived on the scene.

Knowing how it happened didn't keep the detective from complaining about it. It turned out he had a lot to complain about concerning how the crime scene had been compromised. And he was justified in his criticism of Mrs. Buchanan's actions after the event—the bathing and changing of clothes. But when he came to believe that she was in mild shock, he treated her more gently.

Of course, he was also aware that her attorney was present.

The afternoon ground by, police specialists came and went, and evening arrived before the Dallas PD wrapped up their investigation, and their men began to disperse. Vahaska's body was eventually toted out and driven away, and Otis and I were told we could go.

As we went out the front door, one of the detectives took my partner aside to talk privately. I walked on and waited by our cars. It was getting dark, but the parking area was well lighted.

Otis didn't say much. He just listened, then shook hands with the detective and came over to me.

"They found Bobby Jack," he said.

My heart jumped. "Where was he?"

"Out near his ranch."

"Where do you mean?"

"Near Lee's burnt-out Chevy. Some of the boys noticed buzzards messing around and discovered his body down the road a spell in the rain ditch."

"I'll bet he crawled over there and died the night I shot him. That coward Joey Loco must've driven off and left him."

"They said coyotes and other animals had found him, so there wasn't a whole lot left. But he carried a driver's license, so they knew whose chawed-up remains they had."

"Bobby Jack eaten by coyotes and buzzards. There's justice after all," I said. There was more. I could see it in Otis' face. "What is it?"

"The boys who were digging out there found the remains of six bodies all together."

"Your partner?"

"Yeah. Little Butch Stovall was one of them. The Department is gonna give him a proper burial with honors, and they want me to attend."

"I want to go, too, Otis. If I may."

"I want you there, Missy."

He looked around as the last of the policemen were getting in their cars and pulling away. I didn't say anything. I gave him the time he needed to think about things. It wasn't long before everyone was gone and we were alone. We hadn't had a chance to talk all day.

"They'll have a formal inquiry now," Otis said. "And, in the end, they'll buy self-defense, since Hagan is an officer of the court and an upstanding member of Dallas society…"

"And Vahaska was a known gangster," I finished for him.

"Uh huh," he said, "a known gangster and the last link in a botched scam to take the Beasley estate for a chunk of its fortune."

"It seems obvious now," I said. "Everything was timed to the reading of the will and the transfer of all that money to the family."

"Little Sherry Beasley was supposed to be held in that hospital until she was needed to show up on her birthday. Poor gal wasn't nothing more'n a plaything in their game."

"But how quickly all that changed," I said.

Otis chuckled. "It did turn to dog poop, didn't it?"

I had to smile. "Without Bobby Jack…and then us…the Buchanans would be somewhere in the south of France right now using assumed names and trying on villas for size."

"And here we thought Vahaska and his boys had some plot going. It was the Buchanans all along. Do you think there was any truth to that story about a gambling debt?"

"Hell, I don't know," I said. "But let's say for argument's

sake we got that mess figured out. Do you think we could ever prove anything?"

"I don't think we should even mention it, Missy. Much less try to prove it. Vahaska took the biggest hit when the caper went south, and he ain't no longer at the rodeo. Why should anyone else say or do anything?"

I had to agree. "Who's left to say or do anything, anyway?" I asked.

Otis dusted his hands and said, "Let's meet at the office. We can talk about supper."

We turned to get in our cars, but stopped when we saw Amanda open the front door. When she saw us, she marched forward with purpose. Hagan wasn't far behind her as she came up.

My partner would say later that they looked like they'd been ridden hard and put away wet. Hagan was tired and anxious, Amanda distracted and agitated.

Otis said, "Well...that took a while, but it didn't turn out too bad, did it?"

"This is not a social call," Amanda growled. "I'm just glad I caught you before you left."

"Yeah? What can I do for you?"

"I want you to give our money back to us," she said and planted her feet.

The size difference between Amanda and Otis would have made her aggressive stance amusing, had she not earlier that day taken a similar stance and shot a man five times point blank with a .38 Smith & Wesson.

I moved a step to the side and kept my eyes on her hands.

Otis looked past Amanda and said, "Excuse my French, but goldarn it, Hagan, I ain't even made out your invoice yet. How can you be asking for your money back?"

"Well..." Hagan began, but Amanda cut in.

"I'm not in the mood for your folksy humor," she said. "I'm referring to the money I gave you to ransom my husband." Otis shook his head, and she went on, "The money I brought into your office in an alligator bag. You do remember that, don't you, Mr. Millett?"

"I don't take kindly to sarcasm, Mrs. Buchanan. The money you're all lathered up about was used to ransom your husband."

"That's hogwash, and you know it."

"Mandy…" Hagan said.

"Vahaska told me himself that you never gave him that money," she said.

"He told you that, did he?"

"He most certainly did," she said.

"This was when you was having tea before you shot him?"

"Are you trying to provoke me?"

"Did you pay the first ransom that Vahaska demanded?" Otis asked her.

"The first…?"

"Yes, ma'am…the fifty thousand dollars that was supposed to ransom Sherry Beasley. Did you pay that?"

"You know we did," Amanda growled.

"And did Vahaska deny later that you'd paid him that?"

Amanda's voice had become more hoarse. "I see where you're going with this, mister, and it will not cut the mustard."

"You paid him, and he demanded more. Ain't that the way it happened?"

"You listen to me, Otis Millett…" Amanda began.

"No, you listen. You yourself said that he was a liar, and his intention was to bleed you dry. So, who're you gonna believe…a two-timing gangster or me?"

There was a pause. For a long moment we all just listened to the quiet that money buys in a neighborhood like that.

Hagan broke the silence. "My dealings with you have always been quite honorable," he said. "And I'll never forget that you and your partner saved my life."

"We was just doing our job," Otis said.

"No, you risked your lives to save mine. That far exceeds just doing your jobs."

Amanda grimaced during that exchange and didn't try to hide it. "Get to the point, Hagan. What are you saying?"

"I'm saying that if Otis Millett says he paid the money, he paid the money," he said.

Otis followed up. "Handing over that ransom to Vahaska was why he told us where you was at. Without that, you would've ended up at the bottom of the well out there."

"That's what they had in mind. I heard them discussing it," Hagan confirmed.

Otis said, "That money turned the trick, all right. I congratulate you, Amanda, for knowing how to negotiate with criminals. It was you that saved Hagan's life."

Butter wouldn't melt in his mouth.

Amanda gritted her teeth. She glared at Otis and said under her breath, "I wonder what he did with that money?"

"It was money that was…well, borrowed from the Beasleys anyway, wasn't it? I'm sure you just wanna put it back where you got it." Without them seeing, Otis winked at me. "So we'll keep our eye out for it. Won't we, Missy?"

"We certainly will," I said, which earned me a frosty glance from Amanda.

"By the by," Otis said, "when you was sipping tea with Vahaska, he didn't happen to mention where Sherry Beasley might be holed up, did he?" Amanda clamped her mouth shut and stared off into the distance. "I'm afraid she might be dead," Otis went on.

Hagan cleared his throat. "You're still searching for her, are you not?"

"You bet we are," Otis said.

Amanda pulled at her husband's arm and said, "Let's go. We're keeping Mr. Millett from leaving."

Hagan said, "You'll let me hear as soon as you know something about Sherry."

"I'll do that," Otis said, and then added, "I'm glad we had this talk. It's good to clear the air now and again."

Amanda had already turned away, but Hagan smiled, and nodded his agreement before following her. I continued to watch until Mrs. Buchanan's high heels had tapped out their retreat to the front door and into the house.

"Allow me to state the obvious," I said. "That woman may need analysis."

Otis said, "After a few run-ins with somebody, you start thinking you know them. But, you know what? Turns out all you ever really know about them is what they're willing to let you see...not a cow pie more."

My partner mentioned supper a second time before we got in our cars to leave the Buchanans'. That was always a sign I could relax. At the conclusion of something, a case, a long conversation, whatever—Otis was always hungry. So, I was pleased to realize, all we had on our agenda that evening was eating and discussing how to find our heiress.

I gave some thought to Sherry Beasley, but truthfully, I mostly thought about Lee, my romantic detective, as I followed Otis across town. And, because I'd daydreamed, I'd let a half dozen cars get between his car and mine by the time we reached our office in Fort Worth.

That's why I was in a perfect spot to see the dark-colored Cadillac that was parked in front of our building pull away from the curb and fall in behind Otis.

It followed him when he turned into the drive that went between the brick buildings to the parking lot in back of the Mandarin Palace.

Next, two detectives in an unmarked police car pulled out and caused me to steer away and hit my brakes as they burned rubber getting started.

What the hell—I didn't need an invitation.

I ground into low, hit the accelerator, popped the clutch, and had my tires shrieking and smoking before the plain-clothes men had bounced over the curb and whipped into the drive after the Cadillac.

I stomped the brakes, steered opposite my turn, and drifted into the right angle it took to get into that narrow space between the buildings. I left stripes of tread on the street and ground some sparks off a rear fender as I fishtailed back to where I heard gunshots.

My headlights caught the action as I wheeled around the back corner of the Mandarin Palace. A burst of shots snapped through my windshield. They heated the air, dusted me with powdered glass, and jump-started my heart. I didn't know where they'd come from, but they were all I needed. I slammed on the parking brake and went out my door.

The cars that I'd followed were haphazardly stopped—lined up the way they'd come into the lot with their head-lights illuminating the area, making strange shadows. The Caddy and the cops had their doors open. Shots were being exchanged between them—a lot of shots. Magazines were being emptied.

From the ground, looking from below my open door, I could see little more than my own front tire. I didn't know if Otis needed help, but I wasn't going to stay where I was and wonder about it. I pulled my .38, got into a crouch, and took off like a bat out of hell for the cover of a nearby pickup truck.

Jesus! My heart was doing the fandango as I peeked past the back of the truck. I had a better view. Gun smoke was heavy around the Cadillac where two guys with automatic weapons were laying down heavy fire at the cops. The driver stood outside his open door and shot at them over the roof. The guy who rode shotgun was spitting bullets from the side windows—it was like a firing range. Together they had forced the detectives to take cover behind their car.

The back window was blown out of Otis' car, and there were scars from bullet hits across the trunk lid. No sign of my partner.

I didn't have a clear field of fire on either guy. I ducked as

ROBERT FATE

I ran along the backside of the pickup truck. I looked again, this time from over the hood. Not much better, but I used the cars that were in the way as my cover as I ducked again and ran some more, moving closer to the Caddy. My heart was trying to break a rib. I was grabbing breath.

When I quit moving and popped my head up from behind a new Plymouth, I found myself a car length or so from the driver of the Cadillac. He was facing me, but his head was down as he slammed a fresh magazine into his rifle. Glass broke near him from the detectives' incoming.

It was now or never. As I brought my pistol up to shoot him, he saw me.

I got off two shots before the loud rattle of automatic fire slammed into the far side of the Plymouth and raked upward. I threw myself to the ground and crawled like a crazy person for the front of the car. I had my nose in the dirt and wished I were underground as the shower of slugs broke windows and burst through the car doors.

I could hear the detectives still firing, and then my heart got a lift when I heard the distinctive sound of Otis' .45 snapping off shots from the other direction. I peered toward the driver from beneath the car. He was standing again, and I could tell from the motion of his feet that he was firing back and forth between the detectives and Otis.

I had a clear line of fire at his ankles. I aimed, squeezed off six quick rounds, and brought the man down, screaming in pain. My luck could've been better. He had his finger on the trigger as he fell to the ground. I twisted as fast as I could to line up behind the rear wheels of the Plymouth.

Bullets tore past me and through the tires. Slugs pounded the wheels, axle, and undercarriage of the new car as I prayed I was skinny enough to stay protected where I was. And then the staccato chatter of the automatic weapon stopped. I was an instant realizing that the driver's screaming had stopped, too. There were several final reports from a .45, and then the pistol fire from the detectives ended as well.

My ears were ringing and my eyes stung from dirt, sweat,

and smoke as I peered around the blown-out tires that had saved my life. I saw that the driver was dead. Sirens wailed not far away coming from different directions.

Both detectives began shouting.

"Throw your gun out the window! Throw that gun out!"

"Let me see your hands! Stick your hands out where I can see 'em!"

I heard someone else's voice—a man. But I couldn't make out what he was saying. I got to my knees, holstered my pistol out of sight, and stuck my arms straight up in the air as I came to my feet. My shoulder hurt, of course. I was getting tired of that.

The taller of the two detectives noticed and pointed at me. "Stay where you are," he shouted. "Stay right there!"

"I'm a civilian," I told him.

"Stay there!" he shouted again.

I looked around and saw some kitchen help gathering outside the back door of Madame Li's restaurant. Finally, I saw Otis as he came around the open door of the Cadillac. He was lighting a Lucky as he joined the policemen, looking very much the survivor.

"Otis," I called out.

He looked over, spoke to the detectives, and tossed his head for me to join them.

I recognized Carlo as I walked up. He was bandaged everywhere I'd shot him—his head, his hand, his leg. He'd stayed in the Caddy during the gunfight and fired with his right hand out the side windows. He was alive, but he'd been wounded and was bleeding. The police had pulled him out of the Cadillac, pushed him up against the fender, and handcuffed him.

The other man, the driver, was on the ground. He was the heavyset guy that we'd found snoozing in the chair. He was as dead as losers get.

"The nitwits from the hotel," Otis said to me under his breath. "They was gonna ambush me."

"Vahaska's final orders," I said, remembering the old man saying that we hadn't seen the last of him.

"They put a hole through my hat...my best hat...the bastards. But that's as close as they got. You okay? I knew you wouldn't stay out of it."

"I'm okay. We can talk about it later."

Otis winked at me and said to the detectives, "I'm glad you guys was tailing them scumbuckets."

"This asshole here'll do a long stretch for his part in this...if he lives," the tall detective said, and gave Carlo a shove that made him howl. He was hurt and needed attention, but his complaint fell on deaf ears.

"We figured they were up to something," the other detective chimed in. "Especially when they parked outside your place." Otis threw me a look. The Dallas police knew where our office was. Interesting. "We owe you, Otis, for taking the other fuck down."

"My partner took his legs out. I just finished him off," he told the detectives, who finally took a real look at me.

"Thanks to you, too, then," the tall one said. But I could see that saying that to a woman was hard for him.

"We'll need you to come downtown on this one," the other detective put in. "You, too, I mean," he said to me.

They were trying. I had to give them that.

"We'll be happy to, boys. Just let us know when you need us." My partner gave them a big smile and began moving away because the sirens were arriving, throwing colored lights everywhere, and the curious were starting to gather. It was time to make ourselves scarce.

When Otis saw me glance at the man I'd helped kill, he threw his arm over my shoulders, and turned me away.

"Forget 'im, Missy. He asked for what he got."

My partner had misread my expression. I had no trouble plugging a criminal who was trying to kill him and officers of the law. Mind you, I didn't think it was right to kill him, just necessary.

Albert Sun Man Ramirez, the man that taught me to

shoot, said it was essential to know how to handle a gun, since everyone in Texas carried one—and most were ready to use it. He was right about that.

Otis went on like I was his precious little daisy. He said it was a good thing that my feelings didn't get in my way when I had a job to do. I didn't try to iron out his confusion. But what he said reminded me of the Harry Truman comment: "If it's too hot for you in the kitchen, get out."

He was right, too—and I wasn't looking for another job, was I?

My car was blocking the arriving sirens, so I hustled over and moved it to the other side of the lot. The bullets that had come through my windshield had also taken out my back window. I didn't know if my policy covered windows broken in that manner. My guess was the insurance company would laugh at me and all the other folks unlucky enough to have parked in that lot that evening.

Maybe we could all bill the city. They'd take care of it. Uh huh, when pigs learn to fly.

As we entered our office, Otis said, "My stomach's rumbling. Let's spring Lee out of that sick ward and go have steaks."

"I was just starting to lose some weight," I said.

"This ain't about you. Think about your friend. A porterhouse smothered in onions'll help get him back on his *zapatos*."

He meant feet not shoes, but the buzzer sounded before I could correct him. Madame Li was telling us someone was on the way up.

"Goddamn it," Otis said. "Now what?"

"Probably another policeman," I said.

"I thought they was finished with us." He sat down behind his desk where he was close to the .45 he hung on his chair. It was never cut and dried in our line of work. "How come folks think PI's have office hours all over the place? You wouldn't drop by a dentist's office at any old hour."

"It's not so late," I said, and glanced at my watch. "Eight-ten."

"Still," he grumbled, and fired up a Lucky.

I remained on my feet, stayed where I was beside the sofa, and brushed myself off. I was filthy from crawling all over the parking lot.

A moment later Sherry Beasley and Rico Hernandez walked up to our open door. They were dressed like ranch hands in boots, Levi's, and work shirts. They stopped there and looked in.

"Speak of the devil," Otis said and waved his hand for them to come in.

Rico removed his cowboy hat and kept his eyes on Otis. Sherry glanced about as they walked across the room. "So this is your office, huh?"

Otis stood up and extended his hand to Rico, who shook it. Sherry looked over at me and smiled. "How you doing?" she asked.

"A lot better now that I know you're safe," I said.

Rico gave me a shy smile.

"May I take your hat?" I asked him. He gave his head a shake. He wanted to hold it.

"Sit down. Sit down," Otis said. "You're a sight for sore eyes. Can we offer you something to drink? We have Dr Pepper, coffee, and water. Your choice."

"Nothing to drink, but I'll bum a cigarette," Sherry said.

"I'll have a Dr Pepper," Rico said.

Otis shook out a Lucky for Sherry while I got Rico a bottle of pop. After we were all settled and Sherry and Otis had lit up, my partner said, "I can't tell you how proud I am to see you." It was smiles all around. "Where did you go after you left Doc McGraw's?"

Sherry looked at Rico as if he might tell the story, but he deferred to her. "Well," she began, "we had some things to do around town, and then we drove to Mexico."

"That's where you live, Rico?"

Rico spoke English well, but with an accent. "My family has a cattle ranch in Chihuahua. There are many homes on the property. One of them is mine."

"And one of them is mine," Sherry said, pinching away a tobacco fragment from the tip of her tongue.

"Really? All them homes…big ranch, is it?" Otis asked.

"In acres…" Rico paused. "Let's see, it would be…" He looked at Sherry.

"A hundred twenty thousand acres," Sherry said.

Otis whistled, his eyebrows at full arch. "That ain't no small spread."

"No, it's not small," she confirmed with a pleasant smile.

"So you drove there," Otis encouraged her.

"So, we drove there, had the wedding, and then waited until after the reading of the will to come back."

"Uh huh," Otis said. "And who was it got married?"

"I did," she said.

Otis tried to contain his surprise. He glanced at me and then back to Sherry.

She laughed. "You don't believe me, Mr. Millett?" She showed him her bright gold wedding band.

I wasn't as surprised as Otis, since I'd noticed her ring already, but there was more to come.

"Well, Rico, I guess congratulations are in order," Otis said.

Rico shook his head.

Sherry laughed. "No, no. Rico's my lover," she said. "I married Joshua Scurver."

26

OTIS SPILLED HIS coffee and had to spring to his feet to keep the mess off his lap.

Joshua Scurver?

I couldn't have heard that right.

"You don't say," my partner said, stepping back and mopping the spilled coffee onto the floor with the rag he kept handy for such emergencies.

"Yes, I do say," Sherry said, enjoying her surprise.

"The radio evangelist," Otis confirmed, under his breath.

"Yes. I'm Mrs. Joshua Scurver. I think your next question is going to be about his age...so I'll tell you. He's eighty-nine, a widower of many years, and not in good health." Sherry gave me a broad smile before adding, "The apple, as they say, doesn't fall far from the tree."

It was obvious she was pleased with herself as she added, "The Hernandez family invited Brother Joshua to their ranch over six months ago to oversee some religious matters, and the poor old thing's never been well enough to return to the United States. He became fond of me, so I granted his wish and married him."

"I'll be hornswoggled," Otis said, which made Sherry laugh and confused Rico.

Sherry must have gotten the radio charlatan moved to Mexico right after Hagan informed her of Hiram Beasley's intentions in his will. And that piece of information was all she needed.

"Does Hagan Buchanan or any of your relatives know about your marriage yet?" Otis asked.

"Not yet," she said. "But I'm sure they'll be happy for me."

That absurdity even made Rico grin.

"Well, we have some news for you, too," Otis told her.

"You do?" Sherry was interested.

Otis said, "It might not matter too much to a woman of your means, but we've been holding some funds here that belong to you."

"To me?"

"Yes, ma'am."

"How do you come to have money of mine?"

"It was ransom that Hagan took from your estate to get you free of Vahaska and his boys. We came about it that night when we got you away from Bobby Jack."

"And you held it for me instead of keeping it for yourselves?"

Otis responded with a look that made our ethical position clear.

"Okay," she laughed. "You have to understand who I've been dealing with all these years."

"No offense taken," Otis said.

"Is it a lot of money?" Sherry asked.

"Two hundred thousand or thereabouts."

"That's all they figured I was worth?"

"There's no accounting for the mind of a thief," Otis told her.

Sherry pondered that for a moment before she said, "Here's what to do with that money, Mr. Millett. First, settle my bill at Doc McGraw's. Then split what's left right down the middle...half to you and your partner for all your hard work...and half for the Cimo Home for Wayward Girls over in Abilene. You tell them the money is from an anonymous donor who wants to acknowledge their good work. I spent a night there once before I met you, and they were nice to me."

She stood up and Rico did the same. "Could you do that?" she asked Otis.

"I reckon we could, ma'am," Otis said, and moved around his desk to shake the hand of the Mexican cattle rancher, Rico Hernandez.

Then little Sherry Beasley, aka Mrs. Joshua Scurver, perhaps the richest woman in Texas, uttered a squeak of happiness, and gave Otis a big hug.

I shook Rico's hand and acquiesced to Sherry giving me a hug and a kiss on my cheek.

"You know where to find us," Sherry said. "Don't be strangers."

"*Adios, señor...señorita,*" Rico said and put on his hat.

After the lovers left the office, I went to the window and watched them cross the sidewalk and go to their car.

"They're still driving Rico's old Chrysler," I said. "It's like I thought. Money doesn't mean that much to her."

Otis nodded his agreement. "She didn't hogtie that old man out of greed, it was to keep Hiram's fortune away from her kin. They picked on the wrong gal."

Live well. It's the best revenge.

"Otis..."

"Yeah, Missy?"

"I want you to buy a car with air conditioning. Okay?"

"I've been looking at that new Buick..."

"Good choice."

My partner and I gave each other a long look before he said, "Well, in the end, we didn't come out so bad, did we?"

"And we haven't billed Hagan's firm yet," I said, thinking about putting my broken windows on our expense report.

"Billing them guys'll be a pleasure, won't it?"

We exchanged a smile, and then Otis heaved a big sigh and shook his head. "But you know, Missy, the truth is, the whole kit and caboodle of us got played like a two-bit banjo by a snippet of a gal not yet ready to vote."

I shrugged. He was right, but so what. "I'm just glad to see an end to the whole twisted matter. You still wanna go to supper?"

"Does the Pope speak Latin? Let's round up that detective friend of yours and head for Sylvia's."

I smiled. "Just give me a minute to wash my face," I said, and started for the other room humming, *"Besame, besame mucho."*

Capital Crime Press
offers you an excerpt from Robert Fate's
next crime adventure

Baby Shark's

Panhandle Caravan

May 1957

It was dark by the time I got to Oklahoma City. And darker still by the time I'd driven out to the northwest edge of town where my partner had checked into a dump called Sleepy Haven.

I snooped around the motel grounds before going to the office—just the quick look-around in case I had to exit fast with or without a car. It was always better to know where you were going.

The manager, a balding grandpa in thick glasses and wrinkled pajamas, smelled like cigarettes and had a hacking cough. The drone of TV voices and canned laughter came from the other room.

"Kristin Van...how do you say that? Is that Dike?" I nodded yes. "Funny spelling." He turned the guest register toward me. "You were supposed to be here earlier."

As I signed in, he coughed and stared at me, his glasses enlarging his rheumy eyes. When he was able, he said, "You come up from Texas?" I didn't answer. "That tornado must've cut across your path. It's all over the TV."

I turned the register back toward him as he hacked and spit into a wastebasket he picked up from below the counter.

When he was finished, he said, "I don't usually stay up this late, but I told Mister Millett I would."

People often did things for Otis they normally didn't do. He had a way of asking—reinforced by his broken nose and tough, no-nonsense face that said he was ex-cop or ex-Marine, or just someone dangerous. And even if he was fifty, no one in his right mind wanted to mess with a guy his size.

Grandpa handed me my room key and a sealed envelope. "Number nine." He threw his thumb the direction I was supposed to go.

He was hacking as I walked out.

In my car, I read the note.

I couldn't wait. I'll be at Benny's Tavern out on West 10th—not open for business. You'll find it if you keep driving. If I'm not there meet me back at the motel later.

I backed into the space outside number nine and carried in my things. In the bathroom, I opened and closed the window to make sure it wasn't painted shut. That was the only other exit besides the front door. It would be tight, but I could squeeze out that way if I had to.

I cleaned up some, put on and tucked in a fresh but wrinkled dark gray cotton blouse, strapped a holster under my arm, filled it with a .38 Colt automatic, and covered it with a short black jacket. Boots and Levi's were okay for what I was going to do.

Down the road from the motel, I took a side street, found a secluded place under some trees, and made it fast removing my Texas license plates and putting on the Oklahoma plates Otis had left in my room.

While I was doing that I thought about what he had

told me on the phone yesterday, and got another .38 Colt automatic out of the trunk***and a couple of extra magazines. I dropped all that in my shoulder bag and paused a moment before closing the lid.

Hell…why not?

I covered my short platinum blonde hair with a curly brunette wig that Ivy, my beautician, said made me look like Gloria DeHaven. Uh huh…not on my best day, but at least I wouldn't look like me if things went south.

"It could get rough," Otis had said. "There ain't a choirboy among 'em."

And even as windy as my partner was, I recognized a warning when I heard one.

It wasn't hard finding 10th, though the drive west was farther than I expected. I'd started thinking I'd passed the place until my headlights caught a weather-beaten sign.

'Benny's Tavern' it said above an arrow that pointed to what had once been the driveway, but was now little more than a rutted trail that escaped from the highway between a break in a sagging barbwire fence.

The tavern was set far back on a piece of property that folks in that part of the country called an acreage. The building had probably once been a farmhouse. The present-day landscaping was waist-high weeds.

I pulled over into the wild growth on the shoulder of the road, stopped, and turned off my headlights. I left the engine running and took a look at the place.

The tavern windows were blacked out. Like most joints, it was nighttime inside, no matter what time of day it really was. The dim light coming from the open front door barely got across the wraparound porch, so I knew it didn't reach out to the road where I was. I could see them, but they couldn't see me on that dark night.

There were binoculars in the glove box, but I could

nail the bottom line on an eye chart without squinting. I only needed help for real distance. There were two cars parked near the tavern—could be more behind the house. The new Buick off to the side belonged to Otis.

I didn't have all the details, but I did know we were doing a *quid pro quo* that was requested by a Texas liquor salesman named Travis Horne.

"We don't need the money," I'd said to Otis. "Why are we taking this job?"

"I owe the bastard a favor," he'd said. "This'll clean the slate. Just a quick switch and we're back home."

Uh huh.

There were two things I didn't like about the deal. Hell, there were more than two, but first off, I hated trading. No one respected a bagman. And second, I didn't like doing business with a two-faced bootlegger who wore a suit and tie and had lunch with politicians.

I'd never met the man, but I knew his name and reputation. It was an open secret that his syndicate sold booze in Oklahoma, a dry state—and we were in Oklahoma, weren't we? So I didn't really need the details. Whatever we were doing, it had to do with booze. Illegal booze.

Anyway, we took the job, and I was supposed to be watching my partner's back.

And, I was late.

A man came out of the tavern. Athletic. Pale-colored short sleeve shirt tucked into dark slacks. He carried a small suitcase, which he put in the trunk of the Packard that was parked near the front steps. If there was money involved, that was it.

After he closed the trunk lid, he lit a cigarette and stood around smoking it. Until he showed up, I had considered leaving my car where it was and hiking up the stretch of road to the tavern—less intrusive than driving in. However, time was passing, and Otis was probably wondering where the hell I was.

I swung my Olds 88 across the road and was bouncing my way up the rutted pathway before I threw on my headlights. A cloud of panicked insects led my advance up the long drive.

The man reacted with a quick turn of his head and started my direction. His fast pace through the weeds made me think he wanted to meet me as far away from the tavern as possible.

As I drew up to him, I switched on my brights. Babyface. Twenties. Shock of sandy hair. Light blue shirt. He frowned and shaded his eyes with one hand; with the other, he waved at me to stop. I drove by him, mowing down tall, tough weeds that flapped and scratched along the bottom of my car. He yelled something that I didn't hear clearly.

I pulled up to the side of the house, circled around, and stopped near Otis' car so that I was pointed toward the highway. That again put my brights in the eyes of Baby Face. I cut the engine but kept my lights on. I stuck the .38 from my purse into my belt, dropped the extra magazines in my jacket pocket, and pushed my purse under the seat. I rummaged in the glove box and came out with a blackjack. Then I stepped out of the car and stood behind the open door.

Baby Face was frowning. He used one hand to shade his eyes, in the other—his left—he now gripped a pistol—looked like a revolver. He'd taken it from a holster he wore on his belt.

Quick temper, quick draw.

He couldn't see crap as he marched toward my headlights, and did a jerky little sidestep when he flushed two jackrabbits. They ran a zigzag path off into the open field that lay adjacent to the tavern property—long, hard shadows cavorted after the hares as if they had crazy lives of their own.

The way he moved said he was embarrassed by his reaction to the rabbits. "What's the matter with you?" he shouted.

He was still far enough away that shouting made sense, but his pace was closing the gap fast. I thought I heard music coming from the tavern, but given my flawed hearing from a beating that I'd taken a few years back, I could've been wrong.

"Are you fucking blind? I told you to stop!"

By that time, he was too close for that volume, but he was on a roll. He was five six or seven, so I was a shade taller in my boots, though he was muscled up—probably weighed in at one fifty—he had twenty pounds on me. His upper body strength was bound to be superior to mine, and he had a pistol in his hand. But I had a plan.

I reached in, turned out the lights, and closed the door as he approached the car. He blinked, trying to adjust to the sudden darkness.

"Are you mad at me?" I asked in a girly voice, and took a couple of steps to the side, away from the car.

He was breathing heavily as he tore through the weeds, coming straight at me. "I'm gonna slap you shitless," he growled, squinting hard.

Baby Face didn't see my boot toe as I snapped it up and into his crotch. But he felt it.

"Haaaaaaaaaa," he exhaled as he came to a wide-eyed dead stop, knees bent, and hands up like a mime, fingertips against imaginary glass. "You kicked my ball sac," he gasped.

That's all the time he had to complain before I roundhoused him above his ear with my palm sap. He grunted and fell into the weeds, down for the count. I picked up the revolver he'd dropped and flung it after the jackrabbits.

Ball sac?

I had to laugh.

As I rounded the corner of the house, through the rough weeds and thick humidity, I *did* hear music—good music—a *pianissimo* version of *Autumn in New York*. Someone in that dark old house had talent though the instrument needed tuning.

It was a woman sitting at an upright. As I started up the porch stairs I saw her in the soft yellow glow from a lantern, the sole light in the room.

When our eyes met, it didn't change her playing, and she didn't let on in any way that I was crossing the porch. She just watched me and played—and there was something not right about that.

I felt a pressure begin at my temples, got my Colt in my hand, and stopped.

What was happening?

Jazz-flavored cocktail piano—odor of burning kerosene—

I turned my good ear toward the room and heard a male voice—not loud enough to make out what was being said over the raspy static of the insect chorus behind me.

As I moved up to the door, I got a better look at the woman and wondered what she was wearing. There was so little light in the room she appeared naked at first glance—just skin and a full mane of red hair. But she was in fact wearing a red bra and matching panties.

Okay.

I put an eye around the edge of the doorjamb and was a moment sorting things out. The lantern light threw shadows that softened edges and distorted what I saw. In among some tables and chairs, my partner was seated facing me. A heavyset man in a short sleeve shirt stood in front of him, his back to me. Just as I looked, the man punched Otis in the face, a beaten face that said that wasn't the first punch my partner had suffered that evening.

My heart rate picked up.

There was a tall man with thinning hair and dark-framed glasses standing on the other side of and mostly hidden by Otis. He had a .38 Smith & Wesson in his fist and was the solitary reason my partner was taking a beating. Where the tall man stood and the fact that his weapon was pointed at Otis was why I hadn't already killed him.

I didn't see anybody else besides the exhibitionist at the upright, so I pulled my other Colt, cocked both, and entered the dimly lit room.

"Pay attention," I said loudly as I walked toward the three of them, my hands up with arms extended, my pistols aimed at Specks.

The big man, who was dishing out the punishment, whipped his head around and said, "Wha...?" He gave me a hard look and then glanced past me, curious about what happened to Baby Face was my guess. Or, wondering if I was alone.

Specks had brought his .38 to bear on me as soon as I spoke up. I covered the two men and shifted my direction to an angle that kept the redheaded piano player in my peripheral vision.

"Who dies first?" I asked, and stopped about a dozen feet away from them. Even a bad shot could kill at that distance, and they both knew it. My hands were steady. They could see that, too.

They looked like thirty-year-old insurance salesmen—or maybe cops. Similar brown shoes, brown slacks, pistol holsters on their belts, short sleeve shirts open at the collars, cigarette packs in their pockets.

Big Man's bad skin must've cost him girlfriends in high school. The broken capillaries in his swollen nose were costing him girlfriends now. "Wait a minute..." he began.

"Shut up," I said. "Move back and keep your hand away from your gun."

"You took your time," Otis said to me, then hawked up

a mouthful of blood and spit it on Specks' white shirt.

"Damn it," Specks said, making a face and stepping back but keeping his weapon on me.

Otis pushed his chair over as he got to his feet. The thugs shifted their positions slightly to accommodate the new arrangement, but basically it was Specks' and my game. As long as we did the Mexican standoff, what Otis did was secondary.

The bounce and clatter of the chair made me realize that the music hadn't stopped—still soft, still pleasing to the ear, still odd that it was happening at all.

"Now, hold on, little girl…" Big Man started again.

He stopped talking as I shifted the aim of both my weapons to his face. I took a lazy step to the side, lined up the two men, and brought one of my pistols back to Specks. They got it. This wasn't my first stand off.

Otis turned away and shuffled toward the back of the room.

"Where do you think you're going?" Specks growled.

"Fuck you," Otis replied under his breath, blocking the light for a moment as he approached the bar where the lantern was placed.

"You're making a mistake," Big Man said to me.

Just as I shifted both pistols back to Big Man's face, the redhead stopped playing and looked out the door.

I turned.

It was Baby Face coming across the porch with a pistol in his hand. I should've hit him harder.

I dropped to one knee as he fired at me. My sense of it was the slug went over me—where I would've been if I hadn't ducked down. What I knew for sure was he missed me.

The shot I put in his left shoulder made him drop his pistol, but it didn't stop him. He stumbled forward a couple of steps—finally collapsing to the floor and sliding toward me on his face, fulfilling the heroic momentum he'd brought with him through the door.

I turned around to find that Big Man and Specks had hunkered back some, fearful of Baby Face's indiscriminate aim, but neither had moved to take advantage of the confusion. I came to my feet with both men still covered.

Big Man said, "You didn't have to shoot him."

Otis rose from behind the bar and said, "*He* shot at *her*, you simple shit. He's lucky she didn't plug his eye out."

The sound of Otis cocking the .38 he'd taken from his ankle holster was like a tiny lightning snap in that quiet space. When he leveled the pistol at Specks, I shifted both my pistols to him, as well, and backed over to the man on the floor.

"You're outgunned now, ain't you?" Otis said.

Big man sucked his breath in so loudly even I heard it. "Shit. Shit," he said.

"Come here," Otis said to Specks. "Come over here and put that pistol on the bar or faster'n a hog farts you ain't gonna be nothing but Swiss cheese."

"Do what he says, Herbert. Do what he says," Big Man growled.

Herbert didn't like the position he was in. The frozen grimace on his face proved it. But before he had to make up his mind, Baby Face groaned and stirred.

I flicked his pistol away with the toe of my boot.

He looked up at me and said, "I fouled myself."

He had, too. The odor that rose from him was disgusting. He tried to sit up. "My shoulder…" He was confused. His face sagged and his head dropped to the floor with a thunk. He was out.

"I ain't telling you again," Otis said to Herbert.

"Well…uh, Herbert. Ya see, don'cha?" Big Man said. He sounded sincere.

Herbert blinked a few times behind his glasses,

lowered his Smith & Wesson, walked over, and put it on the bar. Otis motioned with his .38, and Herbert took a .45 out of his belt and put that on the bar, too. Otis changed weapons, ending up with his own .45 in his hand.

Otis told Herbert, "Get over there," and when he turned away, Otis slugged him in the head with the butt of his heavy weapon. That sent the tall man's specks flying as he fell to the floor with a nasty gash behind his ear.

Otis then stepped around the end of the bar, and put his heel down hard on the fingers of Herbert's right hand. The crushing of bones was easy to hear in the quiet room. Herbert didn't make a sound, but he'd make some when he woke up.

"Oh, my God," Big Man whispered. "I don't believe this."

"It turned to shit, didn't it?" Otis said and pushed his pistol into his shoulder holster.

"Why'd you have to do that?" Big Man asked.

"He won't point a rod at me again," Otis said. "In fact, I want him to cross the street if he sees me coming."

"Okay…I mean, we was punching you around some, but we didn't do nothing like break your fingers."

"Don't go all righteous on me," Otis said. "I come here to trade. Pure and simple. It was you that started the rough stuff."

"We was following orders," Big Man said.

"Since you're so good at following orders, sit down," Otis said.

The man glanced at me, picked up the chair my partner had knocked over, and sat down on it.

Otis doubled up his fist as he started toward him.

Another eye-shift to me, and then his lids closed. "Mmmmmm," he moaned, in anticipation of my partner slugging him.

Otis only hit him once, but the punch had enough

heat in it to knock Big Man unconscious and probably break some bone. It was a downward chopping right jab that caught him high on his jaw. His whole body jerked to the side and then wilted to the floor, his glazed eyes and misshapen face leading the way.

The chair spun away on one leg, fell over with a bang, and slid to a stop.

Otis sighed.

That was that—the filthy floor was littered with three passive thugs.

I stashed my pistols and Otis took out his handkerchief to blot his bloody gums, the cuts on his cheekbone, and the one at the corner of this mouth.

I lifted the .38 Special from Big Man's holster and tossed it over to clunk into a corner. And then it was quiet. Only the hiss of the lantern wick cut the dead air.

The pianist stood up.

Timing's everything.

She owned the stage, and she was content there in her own melancholy way. Otis and I watched as she tiptoed over to the bar on bare feet, pinching a highball glass by its lip in one hand and gripping the neck of a half-full fifth of vodka in the other. She wore her skimpy attire with indifference—not in the least self-conscious.

Late twenties, probably. A full-grown girl, as Otis would've said—firm, if a bit thin. She had a wan beauty with sad eyes, a narrow nose, and a redhead's translucent skin—cheeks and shoulders dusted with pale freckles. Dangling filigreed gold earrings, pampered hands and feet, shaved legs, glistening hair—she was someone's girly pet.

What was she doing in this dump, damn near naked?

I saw the angry tip of an appendectomy scar peeking out from her underwear—Otis probably noticed that, too. I also saw a folded red dress on a stool at the other end of the bar from where Otis stood. That he may have missed, and the red sandals on the floor close by.

She put her glass on the bar, splashed a couple of fingers of vodka into it, turned to Otis, and in a voice as dreamy as her piano technique, said, "We'll have to share the glass, but…you look like you could use a drink."

Before he could answer, a man's voice from behind us said, "You can forget the drink. Get your hands in the air."

Robert Fate is a Marine Corps veteran who studied at the Sorbonne in France, and has worked as an oilfield roughneck and a TV cameraman in OK, a fashion model in NYC, a sales exec in Las Vegas, a chef at a chi-chi LA eatery, and has held his own in the motion picture industry. He lives in Los Angeles with his wife Fern, a ceramic artist. Their daughter, Jenny, is off being a freshman at USC. A dog, four cats, and a turtle help with the empty nest thing.

www.robertfate.com

6|07